T Singer

Dag Solstad

T Singer

TRANSLATED

FROM THE NORWEGIAN

BY

Tiina Nunnally

Harvill *Secker*

LONDON

1 3 5 7 9 10 8 6 4 2

Harvill Secker, an imprint of Vintage,
20 Vauxhall Bridge Road,
London SW1V 2SA

Harvill Secker is part of the Penguin Random House group of companies
whose addresses can be found at global.penguinrandomhouse.com

Penguin
Random House
UK

First published by Harvill Secker in 2018
First published with the title *T. Singer* in Norway by Forlaget Oktober in 2011

A CIP catalogue record for this book is available from the British Library

penguin.co.uk/vintage

ISBN 9781910701553

This translation has been published with the financial support of
NORLA, Norwegian Literature Abroad.

Typeset in 11.5/15 pt Bell MT
by Integra Software Services Pvt. Ltd, Pondicherry

Printed and bound in Great Britain by Clays Ltd, St Ives plc

Penguin Random House is committed to a sustainable future for our
business, our readers and our planet. This book is made
from Forest Stewardship Council® certified paper.

MIX
Paper from
responsible sources
FSC
www.fsc.org   FSC® C018179

T Singer

S inger suffered from a peculiar sense of shame that didn't bother him on a daily basis but did pop up occasionally; he would remember some sort of painful misunderstanding that made him stop short, rigid as a post, with a look of despair on his face, which he immediately hid by holding up both hands as he loudly exclaimed: 'No, no!' This might happen anywhere at all, on the street, in a closed room, on the platform at the train station, and he was always alone whenever it occurred, although he could be in places where other people were gathered, passing him in both directions, for instance on the street or in a park, or in an exhibition hall, and these people would see him stop, rigid as a post, holding his hands in front of his face, and they would hear him exclaim those despairing words: 'No, no.' Or he might be suddenly overcome with shame over something that had happened long ago, a specific scene from his past, most often from way back in his childhood, a memory that would pop up without warning, and again he would raise both hands in front of his face as if to hide as those despairing words burst out: 'No, no.' One such specific childhood memory that filled him with this sort of intense shame happened to pop up when he was in the process of moving to Notodden, he was thirty-four years old back then; but it also popped up now, more than fifteen years later, at the time this is being written, and right now it was as raw and unexpected as when he was thirty-four or even twenty-five, for that matter.

So this childhood memory must have had great significance for him, and it offers an insight into the underlying pattern of his life, although it distinguishes itself as something that has been rejected or expelled from this underlying pattern, as something he does not want to acknowledge. It is, in all its 'insignificance', a burden he cannot bear to carry, and yet – Singer must admit this – it is undeniably an important part of himself, its very presence, despite his palpable rejection, something to which he cannot respond without being paralysed by an agonising feeling of personal shame.

In brief, the incident goes like this: Singer and A (who is his best friend) are in a shop that sells toys. A has picked up a supposedly amusing wind-up toy, which he winds up to show Singer how it works. The women sales assistants are not happy, and sooner or later they step in to tell A to stop doing that; Singer doesn't think the wind-up toy is especially amusing, but he pretends he does in order to please A, and he does so in a strident voice with forced laughter that no doubt gets on the nerves of the sales assistants. Suddenly Singer notices that his uncle is in the shop and has probably been there for a while. His uncle is watching him. Singer sees that his uncle is looking at him as he loudly tries to please A with his forced voice and feigned laughter. Singer sees that his uncle looks astonished. Singer is embarrassed.

His uncle greets him and offers a few mundane comments. Singer greets him in return, and then he and A slip out of the shop. They head down the street, scurrying along, looking in shop windows at random, stepping into a doorway, stepping back out, roaming here and there; an ordinary afternoon in a small town for anyone growing up who's still a child, near the coast in the Vestfold county of Norway. But something has happened that has stuck with Singer and will make him remember this incident decades later, something that embarrassed him and will continue to embarrass him whenever he thinks about it.

It's not the fact that his uncle saw them acting in such an uncouth manner. It's not because he was being a naughty boy that Singer felt embarrassed, even though that was exactly what he was. He and A had gone into the toy shop and proceeded to do whatever they liked. They had boldly started playing with the toys on display. It's true that when his uncle showed up, they left at once, but neither Singer nor A felt embarrassed because Singer's uncle had seen them doing whatever they liked in the toy shop. Singer wasn't even afraid that his uncle might tell his father; if he did, it really didn't matter, and Singer knew that. He could calmly set off after leaving the shop to roam the streets, going in and out of a doorway, with his cap askew and mischief radiating from his boyish figure.

It was something else that his uncle had caught him doing, something that brought a look of astonishment to the man's face when he caught Singer at it. The loud, forced voice, the feigned laughter. That was what his uncle had observed, and with a sense of astonishment that made Singer feel embarrassed, even ashamed, decades later. Not because of the laughter itself, but because his uncle had observed him laughing in that strident and phoney manner. In terms of A, to whom the laughter was directed in an attempt to please him, it made no difference that Singer had carried on in such a duplicitous fashion, even if A might have noticed this. If he had, and if he'd asked his friend, once they were out on the street, why he'd acted in such a phoney manner, Singer could have simply denied it. Or he could have confirmed it and said that A had bored him with his childish behaviour, but he didn't want to offend him and so he'd tried to laugh along with him, though he couldn't quite pull it off. In other words, Singer wasn't embarrassed by his own forced, childish laughter when it came to the person the laughter was intended for, even if that person had noticed and pointed it out.

It's possible to imagine Singer being able to laugh like that in other contexts, for instance at home, which would have annoyed his father, prompting him to tell his son to stop that fake laughing. Then Singer would have been a little embarrassed, but mostly offended. And if his father had mentioned it to others, such as his uncle, saying that he was displeased by his son's strident, false laughter, and if he said this in front of his son so that he heard him, then Singer would have felt insulted, even betrayed, and he would have never forgiven his father. But he wouldn't have been embarrassed.

It was his uncle's presence that had evoked the feeling of shame. It wasn't the laughter itself, but the fact that he'd been seen. And by someone who knew him and who was astonished. Astonished by Singer's affected voice, by the way he was laughing. Astonished that Singer, whom he knew so well, would suddenly, when thinking he was unseen, utter such a horribly phoney laugh. So loudly. So fake. Caught in the act, and possessed of such a false laughter. A child. Caught and exposed. Singer hoped that his uncle wouldn't mention it at home. Even if he would have only felt insulted and not embarrassed if his father had caught him laughing in that way, he still fervently hoped that his uncle wouldn't mention it at home. Because he knew what his uncle would say if he did. He'd known all his life what his uncle would say. That Singer had such a 'strange' laugh. He was convinced – even today as this is being written – that his uncle wouldn't have said that Singer had such a phoney laugh, or a forced voice, but that he'd had such a 'strange' laugh.

That's actually the extent of it. A minor, inconsequential incident in Singer's life, remembered from his childhood. The fact that he once felt embarrassed at being observed by his uncle is not all that difficult to understand. What is less understandable is why this incident should settle so permanently in his subconscious, occasionally popping up as an image in his conscious mind, so that he not only recalled feeling embarrassed at the time but continued to feel embarrassed whenever the incident popped up, even experiencing a profound sense of shame at the memory.

When this book begins, Singer is thirty-four years old and in the process of moving to Notodden to start a new phase in his life. Looking back, he sees that his life has been marked primarily by restlessness, brooding, spinelessness, and abruptly abandoned plans. To other people, he might appear as a distinct and clear personality, but in his own mind he is vague, even anonymous, which is what he prefers. Should he feel shame for that reason? No, and normally he was not tormented by such feelings. So why couldn't he deal with the embarrassment of his childhood – when he was observed by his uncle as he uttered such unnatural and forced laughter – without being overwhelmed by an unbearable feeling of shame on his own behalf? This was both quite annoying and a mystery to him.

There were also other incidents of an 'erased persona' that popped up in his mind and overwhelmed him in a similar fashion, incidents that weren't linked to his childhood but might be things that happened to him as a grown man, in some cases even quite recently. Incidents that had to do with awkward mistakes, or misunderstandings, if you will.

Singer enters a dark room, a room where a film is going to be shown, or the setting of a jazz concert. Singer is running a little late, and he sits down at a table, joining others whom he knows. This might be right before the film starts or the jazz concert begins, and the light is dim, so that he catches only glimpses of faces in the dark, if at a jazz concert, faintly illuminated by the candles on the tables. He says something to the man next to him, who is B. But B looks astonished and replies in a somewhat disorientated manner, as if he doesn't quite understand why Singer said what he just said, even though what Singer said isn't the least bit remarkable. Then Singer understands that it's not B sitting next to him, but K. The instant he realises that he is guilty of a misunderstanding, he feels totally disconcerted and doesn't know what he should do. He feels like disappearing, sinking through the floor in the classic sense, but unfortunately that's not possible, no matter how dark it is, nor can he make use of the dark to simply run away, because the damage has been done, and K knows full well that Singer is the one who has sat down in the vacant chair next to him and then addressed him in that odd fashion. Odd for K, because Singer doesn't usually talk to K in that way; B is the one he usually addresses in that manner, which would seem natural in that case, while with K it seems unnatural, and that is why K was taken aback. And Singer is sitting next to him, feeling mortified.

Singer is mortified because he has mistaken K for B. K is taken aback but he doesn't know that Singer is guilty of making an embarrassing mistake. At least he doesn't know that he has been mistaken for B. What he heard was Singer speaking to him in an unnatural voice, which means that Singer now needs to be wary of him, and so he continues talking feverishly, in such a way that he won't further draw K's attention to what just occurred, because the thought that K might discover that Singer had actually mistaken him for B is unbearable. Then Singer would feel exposed, and he would sit there feeling so ashamed at addressing K in such a manner.

This incident exists in many different versions in Singer's consciousness. Common to all of them is the fact that the configuration of B, K and Singer is such that it's impossible for Singer to confess to K that he has mistaken him for B. This is true whether B and K are both acquaintances but not close friends of Singer's; or whether B is a close friend and K merely an acquaintance; or whether they are both perceived as close friends by Singer. Under no circumstances could Singer have clarified his gaffe to K, because it was not just a gaffe, it was an irreparable and embarrassing mistake. He can't say to K, when he notices that K is taken aback, 'dammit, I mistook you for B,' because if he did that, K would really have good reason to be astonished and think: Is this how he talks to B? I'm amazed. Because even if B is merely an acquaintance, on par with K, the ordinary remark that Singer uttered to K, whom he has mistaken for B, belied a familiarity that he possesses only when he talks to B, yet this remark was delivered to K, to whom he also talks when speaking directly to him with a certain familiarity, but that familiarity is different and wouldn't have been regarded by K as familiarity but as confidentiality. And B similarly would not consider Singer's remarks as familiar but as a spontaneous and natural confidentiality.

What was it he said to K, whom he thought was B? Something quite ordinary. Perhaps something about how dark the room was. Perhaps something about the film (or the jazz concert) they were about to see (or hear). Perhaps some slightly joking remark about the weather, the chairs, the table, the candlelight. Perhaps a comment about a third mutual acquaintance, Y, whom K also knows, spoken in a somewhat different tone than he would have used if talking to K about Y. Perhaps Singer even spoke of Y in a manner that K didn't think was accurate, either because there were things about Y that K didn't know, or because the remark about him was overly demeaning or overly positive. Or what if Singer said something about the darkness, expressed in a 'dark' manner, a bit gloomily, with a hint of irony, which he would never use when talking about dark rooms with K; because with K he usually talked about things like dark rooms in a more direct manner, referring to, say, light switches: dark room = light switch off; bright room = light switch on. And so K was taken aback by the gloomy, metaphorical way in which Singer now spoke to him about the dark. And Singer couldn't bear the thought that he, unintentionally, had initiated K into this confidentiality regarding his way of speaking of the dark that held true for him and B, who, by the way, may have been no more than an acquaintance, precisely as K may have been; in fact, this thought filled him with shame.

We should actually pause here to state that it may be difficult to understand why this should be so mortifying for Singer. He has, after all, only obeyed the basic rules of conversation, or of addressing someone with whom he's well acquainted, in this case B. He speaks differently to B than he does to K because he knows B and K in different ways, and the contact that has been established between Singer and B is based on different experiences from the contact between Singer and K, even though all three of them know each other and have enough shared interests that they happen to show up at the same time in this dark room, gripped by the same interest in indie films or experimental jazz. But Singer shares something with B that he doesn't share with K, something in his tone of voice, for example, a certain confidentiality, something about which he *wants* to be confidential, precisely because it's B he is speaking to (and he is Singer). With K, he speaks differently, the tone between them is different, and that's something everyone recognises – that's how we, in fact, speak with our friends and acquaintances, with a difference in words and tone from one friend to another, one acquaintance to another; and the only mistake Singer has made in this instance is that he thinks he's talking to B when he's actually talking to K, and surely that is forgivable! But that was not how he experienced it. He experienced this mistake as unforgivable.

Was it because he gave himself away? By what he said? For example, about the dark? By the veiled tone in which he spoke, which took K aback, which seemed so odd to him? The fact that K thought he spoke of the dark in a 'profound' way, which literally shoved him out of here (away from K), precisely because it was a confidential gesture towards someone else, who wouldn't have regarded the remark as 'profound,' but as a confidence based on a mutual recognition of the relentlessness of the dark (which, when speaking to K, Singer would have linked to something positive, say, the turning a light switch on or off; that was their shared confidence about the same darkness, basically equally gloomy)? Don't know, don't know, Singer doesn't know.

The only thing he did know was how he'd experienced the incident, both when it happened and when it popped up in his consciousness a short time later or long afterwards. There was the fact that he'd revealed to K his ordinary, and yet naked, familiarity with B, a familiarity that had nothing to do with K. And the fact that he then had to resort to hiding, in shame. But why this incident, for example – about a different, more 'profound', and possibly more pretentious way of talking about the dark – should provoke in him such a pervasive embarrassment, and so long after the fact, was something he could not explain.

But perhaps it would be easier to understand if the conversation had dealt with a third person, meaning Y. Singer talks about Y, whom K also knows, though not very well. Singer talks about Y in a somewhat demeaning way, a little sarcastically – no, that's not right. It would probably be easier to understand if he spoke of Y in a complimentary, almost admiring way, which takes K aback, and Singer, to his horror, realises that he's guilty of an embarrassing error, mistaking K for B, and it's particularly mortifying because he has spoken of Y in an almost admiring way, which gives the remark he addresses to K, whom he thought was B, a familiarity that not only takes K aback, but also undoubtedly makes him feel a little self-conscious, because he isn't prepared to receive this confiding, and admiring, remark about Y who is largely a peripheral figure for him, yet Singer speaks of Y in such a warm and familiar manner. When talking to B, it would have been natural to speak this way about Y, and it's this confidentiality that K is allowed to hear; but for him it seems odd, even unnatural in all its familiarity; it's as if he hasn't heard Singer but instead the voice of some entirely different person, which takes him aback and might even make him feel a little self-conscious, embarrassed on Singer's behalf. Because in this way K, unintentionally, receives insight into Singer's 'nakedness' when he brings up another person without meaning to; something he registers with a certain astonishment that he doesn't understand and, possibly, with a vague sense of self-consciousness, and he wonders at Singer's unnatural way of speaking. He has no idea that Singer has been caught in the act, in all his 'nakedness'. He has merely heard something that takes him aback, an unnatural voice, an ingratiating way of speaking that he doesn't recognise in Singer. He doesn't know that it is Singer's 'nakedness' he has captured, and observed. But Singer knows it, and he has to hide his 'nakedness', his shame, in that moment. And while Singer behaves with a similar 'nakedness' towards K, based on the confidentiality and familiarity that *the two of them* share, K does not experience this confidentiality as Singer's 'nakedness', but as Singer himself, in the sense that it's Singer, after all – this is Singer speaking about this and that, here in the dark, in the way that Singer usually speaks, and in a way that he, K, has not only grown accustomed to but has even learned to value (it must be assumed). When someone who has your confidence happens unintentionally to observe you as you are displaying a confidentiality towards someone else, that's when this 'nakedness' occurs in you, the person being observed. K sees an unfamiliar and different, more ingratiating, Singer, filled with affectation when he shows this other person his confidence; it's a Singer who has been revealed in his 'nakedness'. Singer completely stripped of all clothing, behind which he might hide before K, as he usually does in all his confidentiality. Singer is disrobed right before the eyes of K, who might well feel a little self-conscious, but fortunately he doesn't know that he's seeing Singer unclothed; yet Singer knows, and he can't hide his shame from himself, or from anyone else who might know. Singer has to hide in some other way, he has to find somewhere to crawl into hiding, taking along his shame. No one must see him like this, wrapped only in his obscenely white, soft, and shapeless existence. Oh, all these mistakes made in the dark, throughout the years, in dark rooms, offering some sort of confidential information to the wrong man; Singer couldn't bear to think about them. In countless variations these sorts of mistakes would pop up, not only in the dark, but also in broad daylight, in rain and wind, in sunshine and clear skies, he might mistake K for B; even though he saw that it was K he was speaking to, he might accidentally talk to him as if he were B, it was to B he could say such things about Y, and not to K. Too late, he would realise, on that deserted, brightly lit street corner, that it was to B he could and should say such things, and not to K, and he sees that K is taken aback. But K doesn't know – not at this time either, on this deserted, sunny street corner – that Singer has mistaken him for B, even though Singer, of course, knows, and he sees that K is the one he's talking to. If K had known, he would have realised that he was now seeing Singer the way he was in reality, as he put on airs for B by uttering such praise, even admiration, for Y. But K doesn't know this, he is merely taken aback; and for a brief moment he levels a puzzled, almost searching look at Singer, who has now realised that he is guilty of a new, embarrassing mistake, in broad daylight, on this deserted, sunny street corner, where the detritus of existence is scattered around in the form of empty cigarette packs that have been smashed underfoot, greasy hot dog wrappers, wet clots of spittle, dried-out dog excrement, withered leaves that have shrivelled after falling, even a banana peel, looking fresh and yellow with the pattern of the fruit still evident inside; and Singer tries feverishly to divert the conversation from the topic of Y, and eventually he succeeds, and he says goodbye to K and continues on, until one day, three months later, a year later, maybe five years later, he crosses a street and then this embarrassing mistake once again pops into his mind, and he goes rigid, as rigid as a post, as he raises both hands to his face, in broad daylight, to hide his expression, in full view of everyone, and he exclaims in despair: 'No, no!' For Singer this was both quite annoying and a mystery.

Not all the versions referred to here – both in the dark room and in broad daylight – occurred in Singer's life as actual events, and thus they didn't necessarily pop up in his consciousness afterwards in the way described. Truth be told, it was all based on a single actual event, a single version, and that was what popped into Singer's mind, over and over again. But all of these versions, and countless others, existed as possibilities.

This did not torment him on a daily basis. Ordinarily, Singer, as seen from the outside, was an affable person, well liked by those around him, though a bit reserved; he tried not to stand out in any way, but those who knew him liked him because he was both open and had a quiet sense of humour, which at times could seem astonishingly pithy, at times downright biting, though that was rare, and afterwards he had a peculiar habit of taking off his glasses to polish the lenses. Perhaps he did this, because it was his way of trying to take the sting out of his biting remark, which – if you looked closely at him as he took off his glasses and polished the lenses – he personally seemed to enjoy; it was visible in his pleased expression, if you happened to look at his face instead of his hands polishing his glasses, or directly into his eyes, which now squinted short-sightedly without the wall of glass in front of them. He also seemed open, in the sense that he appeared to be without illusions, especially on his own behalf. He accepted his own weaknesses, calmly and without making a fuss about them, meaning without sentimentalising his own nature. He accepted, as a fact, that he was not particularly brave, not particularly elegant, not particularly good at sports or other youthful exploits, and that he was not an eloquent speaker if he had to make a speech before a large audience, which for the most part he was able to avoid. Nor did he participate in group singing because he claimed, in a casual way, that he didn't have a good singing voice and so he didn't want to ruin the joy other people had when they sang ballads together in the late hours of the night. He managed to make both himself and others understand that his place was to be found in total anonymity; that was where he thrived, and that was also where he could meet others on an equal footing. He wasn't afraid to admit that he was no dance fiend; in fact, he wasn't any kind of fiend at all. And for this he was well liked. So we might say that Singer, based on these conditions he had chosen for his life, was a sociable person. And for that reason these shame-infested images that popped into his consciousness tormented him, both because of their mysterious nature and because he actually couldn't deny that he felt rigid with embarrassment at having to relive them.

At the time when this book opens, he had seriously begun to brood over what this meant for his life. When this book starts, Singer is in the process of moving permanently to Notodden. He is thirty-four years old and about to take a job at the Notodden library. His youth is over, and he has survived it. But these shame-infested images are now threatening to tear apart the whole mythology of his life. If they are true – which they are in the sense that they keep popping up in his consciousness, a fact that makes them seem sharply accurate – they must have a certain meaning for his life; he realises this now, at the age of thirty-four, having embarked on remarkably late training as a librarian.

Before he turned thirty he was able to shrug his shoulders at the peculiar shame he suffered on his own behalf, in brief glimpses, and he didn't need to view these incidents in the context of his life as a whole. So they hadn't tormented him beyond those stubborn moments, or seconds, when they arose. Now they became part of his brooding about life. What did it all mean? That they had significance was something he couldn't deny. He was forced to see that the shame he felt once again reliving it meant that it was real, it was a shame he couldn't get rid of. It was his, in a strange and inexplicable way. But how much had it marked him? He had to assume that, in its incongruous way, the shame must have corresponded to the general pattern of his life, perhaps even determining the pattern. Could the fact that he experienced this as so unpleasant, so unbearably embarrassing, have made him devote so much of his time, in some sort of unconscious twilight landscape, to acting instinctively, almost with an automatic pilot in his blood, in order to avoid landing in new, embarrassing situations, which later, as we have seen, would constantly pop up in his consciousness? The threat of danger is always there, as we have seen. The possibility of being observed, unintentionally laughing too loudly, or making himself guilty of misunderstandings or mortifying mistakes in identity is ever-present, especially because chance acquaintances – whom he was constantly running into because of his sociable nature, even though he is a reserved person – played such an important role in triggering these embarrassing incidents, and that means that at any time and anywhere he might be at a point where the next step he took was linked to the greatest danger of being exposed, stripped bare. Each step carried the germ of an embarrassing moment, infested with a shame that could never be erased from his consciousness. A person like Singer was in danger wherever he went; and he had to be on guard at all times. A glance, an astonished look, a brief, searching stare, a so-called observation, was enough for Singer to collapse completely inside. Wouldn't such a person use all the instincts of his being to defend himself against the occurrence of these types of incidents, and not only against the incidents themselves, but against any *possibility* that such incidents might occur? The loneliness of a person who has to be on guard like this at all times, wary of the demeaning feeling of shame potentially inherent in ordinary incidents, as is the case for Singer, must be elemental. It must be profound. He can't seek solace from others. Not at all. He can't confide in a friend. He cannot subject friends to his own terrible, internal collapse, he can't even subject himself to that. And peripheral acquaintances are directly threatening. Was that the state of things? Was that how his youth had been? The suspicion that it had indeed been like that made Singer inexpressibly sad.

Because what did that signify? That he had mythologised his youth out of fear for his own shame-infested being. What had given his youth value was not the outcome of free choice but a necessary precaution to protect himself from being exposed in embarrassing situations of mysterious origin. He had believed that he'd freely chosen his youthful attitude as an ironic observer of life. That was how he was seen by others and how he saw himself. And that had pleased him because it's expected of young men that they should be anything *but* observers of life. It does seem a jarring denial of life; because if you can't be a participant in life when you're in the full bloom of youth, when can you be? If someone refuses to make use of the gifts that youth grants him, that will provoke distress in someone who has the pleasure of observing the youth of the next generation. The passive young man is and will always be a repellent sight, and it was just such a sight that Singer, with eyes wide open, sought to become. He didn't give a shit. He didn't give a shit about anything. He squandered his life by observing it, and all the while time passed and his youth did too, and Singer didn't lift a finger to hold on to or enjoy youth's enviable state. He was a spineless brooder, a denier of life lacking all identity, a purely negative spirit, who observed everything in an almost self-effacing manner. He allowed himself to be carried along with such tremendous indifference that it might have given him a liberating sense of freedom or independence. He was an anonymous and impractical wanderer on life's highway, walking stooped forward and staring at the ground, in the midst of the springtime of his youth, year after year.

He hadn't managed to decide what he would be, and he'd displayed a certain joy in this indecisiveness of his. Indecisive both in appearance and when it came to creating a future. Not until he turned thirty-one did he feel it was time to make a decision. That was when he enrolled in the Oslo College of Library Science of all things. The time of his youth was irrevocably over, and with each day Singer distanced himself more and more from his own attitude as a young man, and as each day passed he was another day older; he'd even noticed when he looked at his own face in the mirror that a thin streak of grey had shown up in his beard, and so it was time to make some sort of decision, and he applied to library school, where he was admitted based on gender quotas. Before then he'd drifted from one thing to another. Officially he'd been a student. From the time he'd come to Oslo at the age of twenty, after completing his obligatory military service as a NATO soldier in northern Norway, he'd been enrolled at the university as a student. He took his entrance exams that same autumn and then cheerfully began studying social anthropology. That was in the spring of 1971. The reason that he ended up being such a late bloomer was not because he was vehemently and passionately immersed in his own time, the so-called seventies era. He wasn't. He didn't get caught up in the political conflicts; he had friends in all camps and didn't take sides, because he wasn't sufficiently interested. The reason he let things go so late was because he didn't want to bind himself financially, meaning take on student loans. He knew that he, with his peculiar attitude towards life, shouldn't take on that sort of obligation, because then he would lose his independence. Besides, there was no specific goal for his studies, and that's something you need if you are going to enter into a financially binding contract with the nation itself. So he had to take jobs once in a while, to pay for his goal-less studies. He did all sorts of jobs. He worked the night shift at a hotel, then as a daytime desk clerk at the same hotel. He was a proofreader for the newspaper *Dagbladet*. He supported himself for long periods as a translator of Western romances. He was even a sales assistant in a state-run alcohol shop, and on two afternoons each week, from the age of twenty-three until he turned thirty-four, he worked as a totaliser at the Bjerke Racetrack. He found these jobs through other students who introduced him to their employers. All of these side jobs were in high demand among the students, so the fact that Singer got others to recommend him says a lot about the friendly – meaning self-effacing – manner that Singer presented to those around him.

He also had other, less attractive jobs, as a telemarketer and interviewer for marketing research companies. That was how he financed his university studies, though he frequently took long breaks from the classroom. He might be away from the university for an entire term. And occasionally he would interrupt his studies halfway through in order to take a job. Other times he would show up in the classroom long after the term had started, and then leave again before the term was over. Only when he got so far as to prepare to take exams did he follow the term's regimen to the letter, except for one time when he withdrew from the exam altogether. But eventually he passed his exams in both history and comparative literature. When, at the age of thirty-one, he broke off his university studies for good, he was in the process of preparing for another exam in comparative literature. If he had taken that exam in the autumn when he started at the College of Library Science, he would have needed only one more course, for example in social anthropology, before he could call himself a graduate with a university degree and thus be qualified to take a teaching position, after an additional six-month pedagogy course, most likely a whole year before he graduated from the library school.

But Singer abandoned his studies. He regarded himself as an eternal student, which no longer amused him. He wanted to find something permanent; he was no longer a young man who could waste the precious time of his young life. Time had passed, he had squandered his youth on an anonymous pleasure that had no purpose. During all those years he'd had only one constant point in his life, one goal: he wanted to write, he wanted to be an author. But even that cannot actually be described as a point in his life. Maybe the only real point, though a vague point. Yet this vague point in his life was his secret calling, though it was too vague for him to mention it to anyone, even to Ingemann, his best friend. None of Singer's shifting friends and acquaintances, including his childhood friend Ingemann (who has been given the initial *A* to identify him in the first pages of this book), had any idea that this was what preoccupied the reserved and rootless man. Yet that was indeed what preoccupied Singer. Steadily and regularly, making no progress whatsoever. Because he never really got started. The young Singer never got started. And so, approaching his thirty-first birthday, he had to admit there was no secret calling in his life. He had to admit defeat, and so he enrolled in the College of Library Science, where the eternal student was admitted because of gender quotas.

When it came right down to it, all his attempts to become an author consisted in fine-tuning a single sentence: 'One fine day he stood eye to eye with a memorable sight.' That was how the sentence was formulated when he was twenty, and over the next years – at the height of all his years as a young man – he brooded over and revised that single sentence. 'One fine day he stood eye to eye with a memorable sight.' Why one fine day? Did it have to be a fine day? Couldn't it be an awful day, a day with a snowstorm, for example? 'One fine day he stood eye to eye with a memorable sight in a snowstorm.' Yes, a memorable sight in a snowstorm. What kind of snowstorm? What did he see? What was it he stood eye to eye with? 'One awful day, while the snowstorm lashed his face, he stood eye to eye with a memorable sight.' Wasn't that too dramatic? Surely it was possible to stand eye to eye with a memorable sight without having a snowstorm lashing your face. Also, 'lashing *his* face!' No, it could be a fine day, the important thing was the memorable sight; it was completely irrelevant whether there was snow or rain, sunshine or not. So, one fine day … but that was a cliché, a completely bland way of speaking. He couldn't start off his writing career in such an ordinary way. No, it had to be more specific. 'One fine day as the sun blazed yellow in the clear blue sky.' That wasn't it either. It was better than one fine day, but still not something he could use. Yet what was it he saw, a fine day or no fine day? What was he standing 'eye to eye' with? 'Eye to eye'? Could he stand 'eye to eye' with a memorable sight? What did that mean? That the memorable sight was staring back at him? That there was an eye in the memorable sight

[24]

staring back at him, just as he was staring at it? Apparently. But was that right? He didn't know. 'One fine day he stood before a memorable sight.' 'One fine day when the wind was howling, he stood before a memorable sight.' 'One fine day in a snowstorm he fell headlong, and as he fell he was overwhelmed by a memorable sight.'

Maybe that was it. He was overwhelmed by a memorable sight. As he fell. But why did he have to fall? Was the memorable sight linked to his own fall, which was a 'headlong' fall? Why was that? Couldn't he witness a memorable sight from a standing position? He would at least have to try. And he did try. He liked the association of the fall with the memorable sight, but he couldn't vouch for it. It included a snowstorm he couldn't vouch for either. Because he hadn't forgotten the phrase 'one fine day'. 'One fine day he stood before a memorable sight that overwhelmed him.' Here he stood. He would be overwhelmed by a memorable sight from a standing position. 'One fine day he stood before a memorable sight. It knocked him flat.' Here he managed to get in both the fall and the opening with a fine day, that cliché he couldn't let go of.

By then many years had passed, and Singer had turned twenty-eight, and you might well say that with his writing he had both walked a long road and gone far. He had learned from his own interior efforts to rely on a cliché, and he'd done so simply because he liked the wording. He had also managed to unite it with something else he'd come to love, meaning he had linked the memorable sight with a fall. It's true that he still thought 'it knocked him flat' was a temporary solution, but by working more on the phrase, he might be able to find a linguistically viable expression for this. It all depended on what constituted the 'memorable sight'. Oh, if only he knew. From the age of twenty he'd been trying to find out what the memorable sight might be. The first time it occurred, he wrote: 'The sun flowed across Bygland Fjord.' This sentence had simply come to him, and he wondered why, since he'd never been to Bygland Fjord or to the Setesdal region in southern Norway. But that's what he wrote, and he thought it was lovely. 'One fine day he stood eye to eye with a memorable sight. The sun flowed across Bygland Fjord.' As you can see, this was written at an early point in Singer's youthful literary brooding, because he hadn't yet become sceptical about 'eye to eye'. He was surprised by this sentence, because it spoke of something he hadn't personally seen. But was that what made it a memorable sight? He doubted it. The memorable sight had to constitute something beyond the fact that he'd felt surprised by his own sentence. So he gave up. He couldn't ignore the fact that the memorable sight might be a landscape, even a landscape that he hadn't personally seen, but it could not be sunshine flowing over Bygland Fjord, because even though he assumed that would be a beautiful sight, he couldn't call it that, at least not when a memorable sight had to be such that it justified him spending his young life obeying something he regarded as his secret calling.

So he tried to find it in something else. For long periods he tried to describe a leaf on a tree. He tried to describe the way the leaf trembled, that infinitesimal moment when the wind touched the leaf and rushed through it. But he couldn't do it. Autumn came and he kept trying to describe that leaf, which had now turned reddish-brown and was slightly stiff, though in the morning, and even far into the afternoon, it was wet with dew, shining through the stiffness, but he still couldn't do it. If he'd been able to, it would have been a memorable sight, of that he had no doubt during the year in which he tried to describe the leaf, not knowing back then that few people, if any, had ever managed to describe a leaf on a tree.

'One fine day he stood eye to eye with a memorable sight. The sun flowed across Bygland Fjord.' 'One fine day he stood eye to eye with a memorable sight. A leaf. On a tree. The wind moving through it.' Was this his entry into what would become his calling? It wasn't. He rejected both possibilities: 'The sun flowed across Bygland Fjord', because he didn't know how to go on, and because, when it came right down to it, the image – the sunrise over a body of water in Setesdal – didn't engage him enough; his fascination with this phrase was primarily based on his surprise that he'd been able to write about a sunrise in a place he'd never visited, nor did he have any intention of visiting it. And 'A leaf. On a tree. The wind moving through it', because he wasn't able to describe a leaf the way he'd *seen* the leaf.

But he didn't give up. It wasn't that he sat day after day with that sentence in front of him, pondering what the memorable sight could be, when he really should have been studying. It was only sporadically that this matter occupied his time, and even then he didn't go back to this sentence but instead fantasised freely about all sorts of things, depending on what sort of impression he'd had on the previous occasion. But in hindsight it's still accurate to say that at the core of all his writing plans was this sentence, with the idea about a memorable sight. For example, for a period of time he was preoccupied with the notion of a person floating above, of floating above freely, because the very image gave him a strange feeling of freedom, and so it seemed only natural to link the idea of a person floating, a person flying, to the idea of a memorable sight. But memorable for whom? For him, who stood eye to eye with the memorable sight? Sure, but then who was it he saw flying through the air? Another person? But who? The Other? No, not the Other, himself. It was Singer flying. But then who was the 'he' standing eye to eye with this memorable sight, which was Singer flying freely high up in the air? The Other? No, that wouldn't work. Singer couldn't write 'One fine day he stood eye to eye with a memorable sight', and by that mean that it was the Other, this person seeing the one who was writing – Singer – who happened to be flying. That didn't sit well with him, it was arrogant, and he refused to accept such arrogance. And so the feeling of freedom evoked by the freely floating Singer, high up in the air, preferably over the rooftops of the city, had to be dropped. That was not the way he needed to proceed, if it was true that he had a calling to obey. The fact that Singer flew was not a memorable sight for 'him'; it was only a feeling of freedom for Singer himself, while at the same time cutting off Singer from a personal and profound contact with this 'he' that he was describing, the one who saw the memorable sight, and in his most basic stance, meaning 'eye to eye'.

But this young man who was so fixated on a memorable sight and consequently brooded his way to the fact that the sight of himself flying was not memorable, but merely an intoxicating feeling of freedom that made him uneasy the moment he linked it to a memorable sight, this young man was first and foremost a student, even in danger of being considered an eternal student, at the time that the thought of the free-floating Singer above the city's rooftops popped into his consciousness to amuse him. He defined himself as a student, he was enrolled as a student, and he always wrote 'student' in the space allotted for profession on official documents or applications. Proofreader for *Dagbladet*, sales assistant in the state alcohol shop, and desk clerk at the Gyldenløve Hotel – these were all jobs he took to finance his studies and not his dreams of becoming a writer. It's true that writing was potentially his secret calling, but even to himself he had to admit that it was a hobby, or even a daydream. Anything else would have been irresponsible, because he didn't devote all that much time to it. It was mostly daydreaming. Suddenly a literary image might occur to him that possibly corresponded to his promising original sentence, 'One fine day he stood eye to eye with a memorable sight.' Then he would close his eyes and dream about the image, or the scene. For example, the sight of a flying fish. Not a specimen belonging to the genus of flying fish, but a fish that flew, a flying cod or halibut. Like a streak through the air, in the form of a solid fish. A flying cod or halibut, its tail flapping, its mouth shut.

Singer, closing his eyes, pictures this. Then an owl standing on the ground suddenly takes off, ascends, erect and impassive as it rises, until it reaches the same level as the flying cod or halibut, and there it stops. The owl and the flying fish. Singer closes his eyes and smiles blissfully; this is a daydream. He is lying on the couch in his condemned room in Homansbyen, with sounds from the cars on Josefinsgate, cars braking at the stoplight on Bogstadveien, resounding like a violent roar close to his ears as he lies here, soon to be thirty, immersed in his blissful daydream. This is Singer immersed in his secret calling, which is first and foremost a daydream.

It didn't become a hobby until he got up from the couch and picked up the pen and tried to scribble these images on the page, using his ballpoint pen. When he tried to describe how the owl lifted off – how it took off from its owl toes and rose upward, slowly, with its heavy body and its weighty head, until it reached the impassive, horizontally flying cod (or halibut) – he struggled with the words, struggled to describe that elegant movement upward, which halted at the height of the solid fish, in horizontal position, resting in a flying position up in the air, its tail flapping; he struggled to describe both of these movements, the upward motion of the owl and the horizontal motion of the fish, up until the moment when the movement stopped, happily released. He never succeeded, but occasionally he was on the right track; he thought he'd almost pulled it off, at least so much so that he could begin: 'One fine day he stood eye to eye with a memorable sight.' One fine day? Eye to eye? Stood? Yes, stood. Yes, one fine day, it was a fine day. But eye to eye. Eye to eye with the eyes of the owl? Eye to eye with the fish eye of the cod? No, that didn't work. Singer glanced at the clock. It was time to leave for his night shift at the Gyldenløve Hotel.

We see here that an upward-rising owl and a horizontally floating fish have taken over the spot where Singer previously, in an unwarranted moment, had positioned himself, with an intoxicating feeling of freedom. In general, it was striking how often animal figures appeared in Singer's daydreams when he lay stretched out on the couch in his condemned room in Homansbyen, and in other rooms that he rented, and when he closed his eyes. And they were often deformed shapes, such as when he saw a man holding a severed sheep's head in one hand, and in the background a stiff sheep's body, with no head but still covered in wool. This is all the more striking because Singer was never particularly interested in animals, except for the fact that he worked two evenings a week as a totaliser at the Bjerke Racetrack. But these must have been archaic images that appeared inside the head of the eternal student, images conjured partly from his own nocturnal dreams, partly from his meticulous reading of world litera-ture, and from encounters with world-famous art; barking dogs from his own dreams, or cat teeth and severed cat heads, stuffed in a sack, and a man fleeing with this sack flung over his back, which must have appeared as strata in his consciousness, based on the reading, or staring, he'd done. By the way, the severed cat heads were sewn into the sack, and the fleeing man was a naked figure trying to disappear with the sack over his back, when Singer sat down at the table and attempted to write down these imaginings, or daydreams. But the scene tried too hard to be a memorable sight, it was more of a horrible sight, and he thought maybe he ought to change the whole idea to 'One fine day he stood eye to eye with a horrible sight.' But he rejected this notion at once. Only if the horrible sight turned out to be synonymous with the memorable sight would he be able to use it as the goal he was seeking, as his true calling, as he set off, without purpose, as a young man, and merrily squandered what others regarded as his richest years. He was able, in quite a composed manner, to deal with these horrible animal images by meticulously trying to interpret them in the context of his as yet blank conception of a memorable sight. In that connection he was surprised that so many of these images took place on a beach, at the shoreline. Possibly in order to combine fish and animals, especially beasts of prey. But there were also fish and sheep. In one version of the severed sheep's head, a man was holding a sheep's head in one hand and a fish's head in the other. Blood dripped from both the sheep's head and the fish's head, sheep blood, fish blood. This took place on a beach, and naturally Singer was there too, even though sheep and beaches aren't the first things that come to mind as belonging together. But one day he found the answer to this, and joy coursed through his body. It was because of the sky. At the beach the sky is vast and wide. And since the image of the flying Singer had been repudiated and discarded, he was left with a big, empty, wide sky. And he couldn't get enough of it.

He might find himself out in nature, for example on a beach, or on a city street, or occasionally on the balcony of an apartment building on a city street, with the sky overhead, in all its nuances; or he might find himself on the couch in his room in a condemned building in Homansbyen, closing his eyes and picturing the sky; then picturing this expansive sight, he found himself on a beach, and quite frequently the sky would take on a uniform colour in his inner eye, a series of grey nuances, and the act of staring into this sky-wide sea of grey nuances made a captivating impression on him, and he could lie like that and look at it for long periods of time, often instead of getting up and going over to the university to study. He would often allow other tones of colour into the greyness, for example something yellowish that was practically spun from greyishness, a long, woolly yellowishness on his internal sky; or he might see black suddenly appear in the sky, this too excreted from the grey, a steadily darkening grey, an infinity of grey nuances approaching the black, until the black appeared, as black, absolute black, in the sky, portending a thunderstorm inside him. Lightning. Rain. And now rain was pounding against the warm asphalt in the city street while he was inside, in a building, lying on a couch in a draughty room, where all the sounds, including the sound of rain drumming against the warm asphalt, penetrated with such intensity.

Singer would soon turn thirty-one, and he was a student. At this time he focused on the sky, the empty sky, which was such an enchanting sight that he lay on the couch, looking at it with closed eyes instead of going to the university to study for his next exam in comparative literature. And that was how Singer's writing career ended, with this image of the sky on his retina, in that room. A room in Homansbyen. He lay there daydreaming instead of going to the university to study. He was a worthless bum at the age of thirty-one. Things couldn't continue this way. It's true that he was a punctual and conscientious sales assistant in the state alcohol shop, but as a student he was a worthless bum, and his role was as a student, both in his own eyes and in the eyes of others. So he gave it up. He decided to say goodbye to the intoxicating days of his youth and become a librarian instead.

In what has been presented here as Singer's failed dreams of becoming a writer, there may seem to be quite a few inconsistencies. Sometimes Singer's preoccupation with becoming an author is described as his secret calling, something along the lines of his true calling, while in other places it seems more like some sort of hazy idea, a castle in the air that occasionally made him sit down and scribble a few lines on paper, although he never really took it very seriously. Most likely it's right to point out this discrepancy, but then allow it to remain a discrepancy. During certain periods Singer undoubtedly took his calling very seriously, suffering great despair when he didn't succeed; while at other times he viewed writing as a hobby that didn't preoccupy him much, except for providing him with the joys of a daydream. On the whole it might also be said that some development did occur, during his twenties when he took his writing most seriously, but when his twenties were ending, he viewed it as more of a hobby. His writing dreams from the earliest, most intense period were also of a personal nature, a sort of yearning that he tried to link to his basic worldview (which he never gave up, daydream or not). This might involve portrayals of love, which expressed his hunger for love: bride-and-groom portraits, with himself brazenly playing the role of the groom. These were images that might well be enchanting but in no way could be linked to a 'memorable sight' – that was his own opinion, offered without objection. But was he right? Couldn't a bride-and-groom portrayal, with the twenty-four-year-old Singer as the groom, have been a memorable sight, if not for Singer himself, then at least for the 'he' who saw it, and who was writing these lines? It seemed to him, the person writing this, that there might be some exultation to be found, whether or not this was actually a memorable sight, and not merely an enchanting or a noteworthy one.

So Singer tried, with great seriousness, to link the revocation of his fundamental aloneness (which rests over every young man like a curse) with his own incomplete ambitions to 'one fine day stand eye to eye with a memorable sight'. Written in this way, by Singer (age twenty-two): 'One fine day he stood eye to eye with a memorable sight. Why does the child sleep alone, in his own room, closed in? So as to become hardened in his yearning for the Other?' Or when he realised, at the age of twenty-three, in a sudden outburst: 'How we count the seconds and minutes when we are in the splendour of youth! And how slowly time passes then. How we glance at the clock with a start, out of boredom!' Enticing assertions like the following occurred to him: 'He didn't notice that time was passing.' Was this an entry to the memorable sight? 'One fine day he was overwhelmed by a memorable sight. He didn't notice that time was passing.' But Singer's writing career ended when he fantasised about the nuance-filled, yet empty, sky. On a couch, as a thirty-one-year-old worthless bum, although with a blissful smile on his face. In that sense you might easily perceive some sort of development occurring within him, in that Singer's writing career, or secret calling, ended of its own accord. Yet you would then have to add – and it's in this addition that the image of Singer as a young man emerges most clearly – that he also, as a twenty-one-year-old, had periods when he took a lighter view of this hobby of his, and didn't consider it to be a significant part of his life, but rather a way of passing time, on par with all the other pastimes in his life that he enjoyed, especially because they prompted all sorts of delightful daydream images to appear before him in a glow of indolence; on the other hand, even when well past thirty, he had periods when he wept with despair at not being able to make a go of it, and he loudly lamented to himself that he'd taken too lightly that which, in such despairing moments, he didn't hesitate naively to label – even though it might seem pompous – his potential calling. So it was with no small amount of relief that he eventually gave up his purposeless life as a young man and, somewhat belatedly, sought the goal-orientated training to become a librarian. And with that his youthful dream of being an author ended.

After three years he had completed his training as a librarian. He applied for a number of positions, at random, and took the first and best offer he received. It was a job with the Notodden library. And so, on the last day of July in 1983, he was at Vestbane station in Oslo, about to take a train on the Sørlandet Line to Hjuksebø, and then change trains to Notodden. He was thirty-four years old and about to begin a new life. With neither sorrow nor disappointment at the fact that he was who he was, but also with no particular joy. He set off on a new life. Actually, he felt relieved as he got on the train, relieved that, in spite of everything, things had gone well so far. Now he was on his way to Notodden, and there he would go into hiding; even though he'd never been there before, he was looking forward to living an anonymous and routine-driven life in Notodden.

Oslo is located on the sea. Vestbane station is near Oslo Harbour, and if someone stood there to catch a train on the Sørlandet Line, it was possible to smell the sea if that person sniffed at the air and paid attention, even though Oslo and Oslo Harbour are at the head of a primarily narrow fjord a hundred and fifty kilometres long. The Sørlandet Line goes to Kristiansand, which is also located on the sea, approximately three hundred kilometres from Oslo, as the crow flies, and facing the open Skagerrak Strait, with a view of Denmark on the European continent on the other side, like the promised land. But the tracks for the Sørlandet Line do not go along the coast; they follow the coast only as far as Drammen, forty kilometres south of Oslo, and then head inland along the Drammen River to Hokksund before turning abruptly towards the mountainous and forested stretch heading for Kongsberg, and then onward into the rugged Telemark, which many consider a mysterious place. The first station in rugged, or mysterious, Telemark is Hjuksebø, and that was where Singer was supposed to get off. From there the train continues towards Vest-Telemark, towards the communities of Gvarv and Bø. The tracks of the Sørlandet Line then nominally head south again; but in reality you end up going further into the interior delights of Norway, deep into Telemark, the deepest and most Norwegian of all regions, fabled as the birthplace of folk tales, legends, folk ballads, fiddle music, and superstitions. From Bø the train heads south, towards Lunde, which, stripped of all charm, is still Telemark, the dreariest and most penurious part of Telemark, similar to the village of Neslandsvatn, and then continues along many cheerless kilometres inland. From Neslandsvatn the train tracks run more or less parallel with the coast, but still inland, with the constricted and isolated villages of Aust-Ager, such as Gjerstad, Vegårdshei, Nelaug, Helidalsmo, Herefoss, Oggevatn, and Vatnstraum. But from Neslandsvatn and Nelaug, narrow-gauge tracks have been laid to southern coastal towns such as Kragerø and Arendal, and at Gjerstad station, the blue buses of the Norwegian Railways, or NSB, are lined up to await arriving trains, enticingly offering a swift departure from this inland climate to the small coastal gem of Risør.

Yet by this time the train traffic on the narrow-gauge tracks is over, so the blue NSB buses are also waiting at Neslandsvatn and Nelaug stations, promising a swift departure southward to the coast, while the train, after a brief stop, continues along its astonishingly monotonous inland route, often passing through spruce forests so dense that the branches on both sides strike the windows of the train cars, and it's as dark as if passing through a tunnel, and there are also many tunnels on this particular stretch of track. Emerging from a tunnel, a real tunnel, you look straight down into a chasm, or rushing rapids, or bare blue-grey rocks dripping with moisture even when the sun is shining. But at some indiscernible point the tracks have been laid so that they once again run towards the sea, without the passengers having the slightest clue as they despondently read the station names of Omdal, Grovane and Vennesla before the train suddenly, after five and a half hours, and with the locomotive as frisky as a calf, rolls into the station of the stylish city of Kristiansand with its straight streets, cathedral, hotels, manufacturing companies, central square, and its harbour facing the Skagerrak Strait. For someone who had taken this entire train trip, it must have seemed like a mysterious and largely purposeless journey through the most remote, unassuming and gloomy part of Norway. Even though Singer was supposed to get off in Hjuksebø, after only an hour and twenty minutes, he had great expectations for this journey, especially because his destination was to be his new home.

He arrived well ahead of the departure time and found his reserved window seat in one of the train's many smoking compartments. He would be travelling on the Sørlandet Express. A long, elegant train painted an irresistible yellow. Inside he found himself in a large space with a wide centre aisle and rows of two seats across on either side. The seats were very comfortable, and a knob on the side of the armrest allowed him to adjust the position to whatever felt best, either reclining or upright. Attached to the back of the seat in front of him was a net for holding newspapers, magazines, fruit, drinks, and any food he might have brought along. A foldable tray attached to the armrest could be opened and positioned in front of him when the train hostesses appeared with their carts selling coffee, drinks, chocolate bars and sandwiches. But Singer didn't plan to buy anything from them because he'd noticed that the train also had a dining car. Even though he'd been living from hand to mouth for years – actually his whole adult life – and he didn't like to squander the hard-earned cash he'd acquired from the jobs he'd so conscientiously performed and been forced to take on – earning money that had to last him a very long time, so that he'd grown accustomed to scrimping and scraping until it might almost be said that penny-pinching was in his blood – he decided that since this was the Sørlandet Express, and the Sørlandet Express had a dining car, as soon as they passed Drammen he would walk through the train to have a sandwich and a cup of coffee in the dining car.

So from Oslo to Drammen he sat in a comfortably reclining position and read his newspaper, as well as the latest issue of the magazine *Samtiden*. After passing Drammen, he left his seat and took a look at the luggage area in the front of the car, checking, somewhat warily, to see that his luggage was still there, and then he headed back through the train to the dining car. He reached the car and stepped inside. There were white cloths on the tables. On each table stood a vase of flowers, artificial to be sure, but Singer still thought they were a stylish touch, and very inviting. On each table there was also a freshly cleaned ashtray. In charge of the dining car were two waiters, both wearing white waiter jackets, black trousers, and highly polished shoes; they each stood ramrod straight with a big white cloth draped over one arm, ready to respond to the customers' slightest wish when summoned with a mere wave from the tables. Not many people had settled in the dining car, in fact only two of the tables were occupied – this was no doubt because those who travel all the way to Kristiansand, as most of the passengers do, tend to go to the dining car only later in the journey. I bet the place is packed near Herefoss, thought Singer. He sat down at an empty table and one of the waiters immediately rushed over. Singer ordered an open sandwich with a beefburger patty and a cup of coffee.

The train was travelling along the Drammen River. It was a glorious summer day. The middle of the day. The river was blue. The landscape was meandering and civilisingly inhabited. He had the impression that there was actually a series of villages situated along the Drammen River, and each had its own station and factory. When the train arrived in Hokksund, it stopped there for more than five minutes, perhaps because the imposing train station in Hokksund demanded a longer stop so as not to seem comical. Yet there was no reason the station in Hokksund should be comical, at least as far as Singer was concerned.

After Hokksund the landscape abruptly changed character. The waiter brought Singer's sandwich and his coffee, which came in a silver pot. The sight of that silver coffeepot made Singer restrain the slight irritation he felt because he'd ordered a *cup* of coffee. He was familiar with these sorts of irritations from restaurants in Oslo, but the sight of the gleaming silver pot on the white tablecloth banished all dismay, and he enjoyed his light meal, as the train headed through the Norwegian landscape of woods and ridges, marshes and stillness, forest clearings and farms with hayracks on steep slopes. But mostly forests, spruce forests. He let himself be carried along by the train's rhythm, and by the fairly monotonous landscape, closed-in and dense, that passed outside the train window, lulling him into a sense of inlandness. So it was a strange feeling, suddenly, without transition, to arrive at a town, which the train circled, allowing him to see a church, venerable wooden buildings, streets, and modern-looking shops situated on both sides of a river, with a thundering waterfall, before the train pulled into Kongsberg train station. Afterwards, they continued through the same inland landscape as before, with forests and clearings, scattered farms, ponderous granite crags, steep precipices, slopes, cowberry thickets, and glimpses of timber and livestock. Singer sat there, thoroughly enjoying the journey as he ate his beefburger sandwich and drank his coffee, which he poured from the silver pot, until a voice on the loudspeaker announced that the next station was Hjuksebø. Singer, who had already paid the waiter, stood up and walked back through the train to his seat, grabbed his luggage, and got off the train when it pulled into Hjuksebø station.

Very few passengers got off, and most of them were picked up in cars. Only three passengers remained on the platform when, after a brief stop, the Sørlandet Express, long and elegant, moved off and disappeared around a curve, continuing on its comfortable journey towards Kristiansand. Three solitary travellers waited at Hjuksebø station deep in the interior of Telemark. One of the passengers turned to the stationmaster to ask where to board the train for Notodden. 'Over there, track three,' said the stationmaster in a lilting Nynorsk dialect as he pointed. And there was the train they needed to transfer to. Slightly out of the way. Actually, so out of the way that it was almost hidden behind a long tool shed and thus difficult to spot. Singer and the other two passengers crossed the platform and went over to the train. It was a rickety little train, an old, worn railway carriage with hard wooden benches, but divided into two compartments, one for smokers and one for non-smokers. Singer hauled his luggage into the compartment for smokers and found a seat.

According to the schedule, it was fifteen minutes before the rickety train was supposed to depart, but the station-master announced that there would be a further ten-minute delay because the Sørlandet Express from Kristiansand, which they were waiting for, was delayed. So Singer stepped outside to walk back and forth on the platform as he took a look at Hjuksebø. The station was up on a ridge, with the village and Lake Heddal below. A scent of summer. Lush green grass on the hills and birch-covered slopes. He saw livestock grazing everywhere, on all the hills and slopes. Sheep, high up. And cattle further down. Now and then, long, drawn-out lowing came from the cattle as well as breathless bleats from the sheep, breaking the green silence. The farmsteads rose up, each on its own hill, the buildings painted and well maintained beneath a bright blue sky. Down below, a dusty road wound its way towards the shores of Lake Heddal, which shimmered blue and idyllic. But the only local resident in evidence, after the passengers who got off at Hjuksebø had been hastily carried off in cars, was the stationmaster, in full uniform and cap, holding a green signal flag. Yet from a nearby farm, Singer heard the sound of hammering. He had an expansive view from Hjuksebø station, he could see far into the distance, where the slopes and valleys stretched northward, and way off he could also make out some mountain ridges. But in the far north, all the way up north, there was a strangely incongruous sight. There he could see smoke rising up, and it was unmistakably some sort of industrial smoke. Smoke from factory chimneys way out there in the countryside. That was Notodden, Singer's destination. It was an enchanting sight, he thought. How enticing that faraway factory smoke seems. That's where I'm going, thought Singer. Over there is a town, and that's the goal of my journey. He stared in the direction of Notodden, off in the distance. By staring at that peculiarly placed factory smoke, he felt a quiver of excitement about going there.

Eventually the delayed Sørlandet Express arrived from Kristiansand, with its powerful electric locomotive and its numerous, ultramodern train cars. A few passengers got off and headed for the small train that would take them onward to Notodden; the other passengers had already gone on board, two in the compartment for non-smokers and one in the compartment for smokers. One of the new passengers came into the smoking compartment and sat down right across from Singer. The stationmaster raised his green flag and blew hard on his whistle, and the newly arrived Sørlandet Express, elegant and irresistible, departed the Hjuksebø station. The stationmaster then ambled over to the spur line where their little railway carriage waited and repeated the same procedure, raising his green signal flag and blowing hard on his whistle, and the rickety Notodden train reluctantly set off. It headed along a track across the hills above Lake Heddal so that, when they weren't inside a forest or behind a barren ridge, the passengers could occasionally see the flash of blue far below. The man sitting across from Singer was a younger gentleman. He might have been Singer's age, maybe even a few years younger, wearing a nice summer suit and a tie, and holding a briefcase. He looked up at Singer's luggage in the rack, then asked if he was going to Notodden and how long he was planning to stay. When Singer said that he was in the process of moving to Notodden to start work as a librarian at the town's library, the other man nodded knowingly. He asked if Singer was familiar with Notodden, and Singer said that he was not. It was pure chance that he had applied for a job at the Notodden library and been hired, and so here he was. Then the well-dressed younger gentleman laughed, stood up and shook Singer's hand.

'Adam Eyde,' he said. 'I'm in charge of the bad times.'

Singer also stood up to introduce himself, and then Adam Eyde opened his briefcase. Singer stared, wide-eyed, because the briefcase contained a holder with six slots, and in each slot was a champagne glass. Three of these glasses were filled with champagne and sealed with a plastic lid. The other three champagne glasses were clearly empty, and three plastic lids lay in the bottom of the briefcase. Adam Eyde took out a champagne glass, and now Singer saw that it was an expensive glass made of the finest crystal. Adam Eyde handed it to Singer. He removed the plastic lid of his own glass, and Singer did the same. They were both still on their feet, because neither had taken their seats again after making introductions.

'*Skål*,' said Adam Eyde. 'I'm the head of Norsk Hydro in Notodden, and I'm on my way back from a champagne breakfast at our headquarters in Oslo. Did you come via Kongsberg?'

Singer nodded, and Eyde looked partially envious, partially bursting with glee.

'I always travel the correct way,' he said. 'Via Skien. I take the Brattsberg Line to Nordagutu, and there I change trains to Hjuksebø, before catching the railway carriage to Notodden. The route is somewhat longer, but it's the only real way to travel. For me. And also for a librarian in Notodden. So you know nothing about Notodden?

'Oh, these champagne breakfasts in Oslo,' he sighed. 'Once every quarter, on 31 July, 31 October, 31 January, and 31 April. You may be taken aback when I said 31 April, because there is no 31 April on the calendar, but nevertheless, we at Hydro have our champagne breakfast on 31 April every year, on the day that is generally called 1 May. But at Hydro it's 31 April, and the second champagne breakfast of the year. We come from far and wide, all the Hydro directors, to drink champagne at ten in the morning. After that we each return to our own area, and I, as the director of good old Notodden, stroll down Drammensveien in Oslo to Vestbane station to catch the train via Skien and Nordagutu back to Notodden, but not without first filling my briefcase with champagne for the long journey, which is somewhat of a detour. Did you see the smoke while you were waiting for the train?' he added.

Singer nodded.

'That's good. Because soon you won't see it anymore. It's from the Tinnfoss Ironworks, which we're going to close before the year is out. And that will be the end of smoke over Notodden. Technically we're not the ones who own the Tinnfoss Ironworks, but we're still going to close it down,' said Adam Eyde, giving Singer a sly look. 'It can't go on. There's nothing to be done about it. There's no future in it, if you know what I mean ... Let me tell you about the town you're headed for. Notodden was created by us, and we're the ones who will close it down, in a sensible way; that's actually my assignment. While I'm waiting. Waiting for what, you may ask? Waiting to become general manager of Norsk Hydro. That is my destiny. But first I have to put things in order in Notodden, clean up old mistakes. More about that later.'

Eyde held out his hand for Singer's empty champagne glass, which he put back in the holder inside his briefcase before giving him the last full champagne glass.

'You're drinking it too fast,' he said. 'Look at me, I've only taken a few sips of mine. It's good to *taste* the champagne. Did you notice that it's not cold but lukewarm? Lukewarm champagne is best. At headquarters, we're served cold champagne, from proper champagne buckets, and I drink it, but I look forward to the return trip to Notodden – via Skien and not Kongsberg – and to the lukewarm champagne that will be a treat for my tongue. All true lovers of champagne like lukewarm champagne best, the champagne that's served the day after a party, poured from an open bottle, lukewarm, preferably at breakfast time. Serving champagne cold is merely convention.'

The old railway carriage had made its way down the slopes and was now travelling along Lake Heddal. After rounding a promontory it came to an abrupt halt. Singer looked out the window. The train had pulled into a station, and he saw a rather large brick building that looked the same as most Norwegian railway stations. The sign said: 'NOTODDEN, 31.2 metres above sea level'. They had arrived. Singer lifted his luggage down from the luggage rack, declining Adam Eyde's offer of help, and dragged his two heavy-as-lead suitcases out of the train, dropping them on the platform of Notodden station. He inhaled deeply. How fresh the air was here, deep in the interior of Telemark. And what a glorious summer day! But where was the town? There was virtually no sign of it. A short distance away, off to the right, he saw a big manufacturing plant, but that was all. When he turned round, he could see up on the slopes a number of single-family homes, but surely that couldn't be the town? Right in front of him was Lake Heddal, narrow and unfailingly idyllic. On the opposite shore of the narrow waterway he saw farmsteads. Adam Eyde must have guessed what Singer was thinking because he said that the station was located a little outside of town. The town itself was situated up on a hill above the station but on the slope behind, so it wasn't visible from here, and consequently it was impossible to tell that you were in a Norwegian town; you had to trust what it said there, explained Eyde, and he pointed at the sign on the station: NOTODDEN.

Eyde ushered Singer over to a Mercedes that was parked outside the station. Next to it stood a chauffeur. When the man caught sight of Adam Eyde, he rushed over and reached for one of Singer's heavy suitcases, but Singer said he didn't need any help. The chauffeur opened the car's boot, and as

Singer hoisted one suitcase into it, the chauffeur grabbed the other and with a quick movement placed it inside. Eyde and Singer got into the back seat, and Eyde told the chauffeur to drive to the hotel where Singer had reserved a room for his first night in Notodden.

The hotel was located in town, which the Mercedes reached by driving past the Hydro plant and then taking a sharp turn onto a steep street. As the car made the turn, Singer found himself in the town. They drove up the steep street lined with shops on both sides, and he caught a glimpse of side streets where, because of the way the people were walking, he could partially make out the other streets running parallel to the steep one they were on, and on all sides he saw Notodden. A real town in the heart of Telemark. The hotel stood on the main square, and the Mercedes drove up to the entrance and stopped. The chauffeur quickly got out and took Singer's luggage out of the boot, and while Adam Eyde said he would wait in the car as Singer checked in, the chauffeur carried the two heavy suitcases into the hotel lobby, and Singer followed. He checked in, got his key, and was about to take his luggage and head for the lift, but the chauffeur refused to hand over the suitcases. As was customary in provincial Norwegian hotels, there were no bellhops, so the chauffeur carried the suitcases over to the lift, pressed the button, and when the lift arrived, the chauffeur stepped inside along with Singer, still carrying the two suitcases. They were only going to the first floor, and the chauffeur carried the suitcases all the way to the door of the room and then took them inside after Singer used his key to open the door. Then he said that he would be waiting for Singer in the car, whenever Singer was ready. But Singer said he was ready now, and so they went back downstairs together, walking through the lobby and out to the street, where the Mercedes was parked, waiting for them, with Adam Eyde sitting in the back seat. The chauffeur got in behind the wheel, and Singer climbed into the back, sitting down next to Eyde.

'Home, Kristiansen,' said Adam Eyde.

They drove further up through the town, then took a right and passed a stately and quite modern-looking church from the 1930s, which stood on another square, or plaza, and then they headed into a residential neighbourhood. At the end of this residential neighbourhood was a park, and in the middle of this park was a magnificent white building. It was a grand villa, or maybe it should be called a small palace, majestically fronted by a number of columns on either side of the entrance. The Mercedes pulled in and parked, and the chauffeur got out to open the back doors, first on the side where Singer was sitting, then on Eyde's side. Singer got out. To the left of the grand building or small palace were two big tennis courts, to the right something that was probably a caretaker's residence, although big enough to be mistaken for a substantial home. Adam Eyde said a few words to the chauffeur and then headed for the entrance, with Singer following close behind. He unlocked the door and they stepped inside a large hall with splendid paintings on the walls. Landscapes by Theodor Kittelsen and portraits by Henrik Lund. Adam Eyde set his briefcase on a small table, opened a door, and showed Singer into a stately sitting room with a high ceiling and plenty of space between the walls. Exquisitely decorated with furniture from the first decade of the twentieth century. Along the walls, between priceless paintings by Theodor Kittelsen, Henrik Lund, Edvard Munch, Hans Heyerdahl, Hermann Cappelen, and Lars Hertervig, stood lavish grandfather clocks, radiating antiqueness in all their glory, like soldiers on a parade ground. On the tables were precious vases and centrepieces made of pure gold and pure silver. Placed between them were small treasures glittering with diamonds. Adam Eyde rang a small bell, equally adorned with diamonds, and an elderly woman appeared immediately. She came over to Eyde and politely stood before him with a friendly and enquiring look on her face.

'Shall we have a drink out on the terrace before dinner?' said Eyde, turning to Singer. 'Gin and tonic?'

Singer nodded.

'Two gin and tonics, Mrs Semb, and please set the dinner table for two.'

Adam Eyde led the way out to the terrace. It was at the back of the house, facing an even more impressive park than the one out front. At the end of the park was a balustrade right on the edge of a precipice, as Singer noted. The lawn looked as if it had been treated with emollient that made the green grass sparkle, and it also looked as if it had been cut by hand, with sharp nail scissors made of silver. Eyde invited Singer to take a seat on one of the comfortable and shaded patio chairs grouped under a weeping willow that leaned its branches over the terrace. Mrs Semb arrived with two gin and tonics. To his delight, Singer saw there were ice cubes in his glass; he'd worried that Eyde might prefer his gin and tonic in a lukewarm state. They raised their glasses in a toast and then sipped at their drinks.

'Notodden,' said Adam Eyde, 'is not what you think. Even though you've never been here before and don't know much about the town, it's not what you think. Come on, let me show you.'

He got up and went over to the balustrade at the end of the park, and Singer followed. From there they had a splendid view of the Hydro plant in Notodden, and old Lake Heddal. Eyde pointed at the shore of Lake Heddal closest to them, where a rotting dock stretched out into the water.

'That's Notodden,' he said, with great emphasis. 'Do you see the ship to England? Out there?' Eyde pointed at the horizon, at the far end of the lake. 'No? It must be delayed today! But surely you can see the ship to America? It's that sleek boat over there, at the wharf! The America ship, that regularly travels from Notodden to New York, taking mostly immigrants from here and bringing well-heeled tourists back from New York. What a splendid trip, especially the last stretch into Norway. You see the

America ship, don't you? No? You don't see anything? Can't you see that Notodden is a port? Can't you see you're in one of Norway's biggest seaports way up here in the interior of Telemark? Well, that's what Notodden is. Notodden is a port town. If it's not, then there's been some mistake, and it's that mistake that I have to deal with, seventy years after those in the know realised Notodden was one big mistake. But come over here,' he said, moving a short distance to the left along the balustrade; there he leaned over the framework and craned his neck, then came back and motioned Singer closer so he could do the same.

And that's what Singer did. He leaned over and looked straight down at the Hydro plant, which seemed to rise up towards him quite dramatically as he was leaning over like that.

'What do you see?' asked Adam Eyde.

'I see the Hydro plant,' said Singer. 'It's an impressive sight.'

'But you don't see anything else?'

'No,' replied Singer, beginning to feel an ache in the back of his neck; he also felt a little dizzy.

'Take a good look to your left,' said Adam Eyde. 'Turn your head sharply, yes, like that. What do you see now?'

'Now I see Notodden station,' said Singer.

'Yes, that's exactly what you see,' exclaimed Eyde, 'and yet you aren't able to see any ship to England. So keep looking at Notodden station!' Eyde exclaimed again, as

Singer made a move to retreat from this very uncomfortable leaning-forward position as he stood at the balustrade.

'Notodden station,' Eyde repeated. 'Can you read the date above the entrance?'

Singer tried but could not.

'It says 1909,' Eyde told him. 'That's when it was opened. Okay, let's go back to the terrace, and if we're lucky, Mrs Semb might bring us another gin and tonic before dinner.'

They went back. They took seats on the terrace, and Mrs Semb appeared with another round of gin and tonics.

'Notodden station,' Eyde said again. 'You realise, of course, that it's an end station, right? Maybe you noticed that earlier today when we arrived?'

Singer nodded.

'And that's exactly right,' Eyde went on, 'though it's not, as you may think, the end station for the spur track of the Sørlandet Line between Hjuksebø and Notodden, because that spur track wasn't opened until 1917. We're talking about 1909. Come with me,' he said, and got up again to walk back across the park's lawn to the balustrade, followed closely by Singer. This time he took his glass along, and Singer did the same.

'What you see down there, if you lean out again – no, you don't actually have to do it – is an end station, but an end station for a railway that starts deep in the wilderness. Notodden is the end station for the Rjukan Line. Notodden, the port town. The Rjukan Line was opened right down there – no, you don't need to … – on 9 August

1909, by the first general manager of Norsk Hydro and in the presence of His Majesty King Haakon VII, in the fourth year of his reign. What you're looking at down there is a fairy tale, a Norwegian mountain fairy tale, Mr Librarian. Back at the start of this century, an Oslo engineer bought up the waterfalls on the back side of the mountain called Gaustatoppen, which you can see way up there to the north – beautiful, isn't it? On the back side, in the wilderness, this Oslo engineer bought up the waterfalls. His sole idea was to harness the hydropower so it could be used in industry. At about the same time, a Norwegian physics professor discovered that it was possible to bind nitrogen so that synthetic potassium nitrate, or saltpeter, could be produced. The world's natural saltpeter deposits were in danger of being depleted, and all over the world people were working to develop methods for producing synthetic saltpeter. Norsk Hydro is a result of that competition.

'I don't suppose I need to tell you the name of that Oslo engineer, do I?' asked Eyde, and then paused.

Singer shook his head.

'No, you don't,' Singer replied, 'but if you want to be accurate, you should call him the "Kristiania engineer", because back then Oslo was called Kristiania, and it's a good idea to call a town in a certain period by the name the town was actually known by at the time, and not use a later name, if the town's name happened to change. So call him the Kristiania engineer, that's the advice I can give you, and Kristiania spelled with a *K*, not with a *Ch*; if you're talking about the Norwegian authors Welhaven and Wergeland, they lived in Christiania with a *Ch*, but our Kristiania engineer was from Kristiania with a *K*; people often make a mistake about this,' he said.

'Is that right, is that right?' said Adam Eyde, and he was about to go on, but much to his surprise, Singer interrupted him again.

'I mention this, because it's a problem that we librarians often have to deal with,' said Singer, 'since we catalogue books based on where they were printed, along with the year. A book produced in 1874 by a printer in what is now Oslo will be catalogued under *Chra*, while a book produced by the same printer seven years later, meaning in 1881, will be catalogued under *Kra*, so it's important to keep a clear head when you're looking for books printed in Kristiania, spelled with either *Ch* or *K*, in the previous century,' said Singer, smiling.

'Hmm, interesting, interesting,' said Eyde. 'You'll certainly have to tell me more about that at dinner. But to get back to the Norwegian mountain fairy tale. Back to Norsk Hydro,' he said firmly.

'To make a long story short,' said Eyde, 'Norsk Hydro was founded in order to make use of the physics professor's patent. Norsk Hydro was founded in order to build a power plant in the wilderness on the back side of Mount Gaustatoppen, a plant powerful enough to develop this violent heating process into a viable manufacturing operation. Meaning a new, history-making branch of industry, a modern factory, that would produce something never before produced. Synthetic saltpeter. At a time when the natural saltpeter deposits were becoming depleted, this factory would be located on the back side of Mount Gaustatoppen. On the back side of the moon, I might say, and equally inaccessible. And not only that, it had to be situated in a valley so narrow and closed-in that the sun could hardly reach down into it during much of the year, it had to be cloaked in eternal shadow six months of the year, and it was there, right there, that Norsk Hydro would create its great fairy tale. Because it was there, in the bottom of this valley, and only there, that it was possible to collect this radiant vision of a waterfall, which is what the mighty Rjukan waterfall is. It was there, in the bottom of the valley, that the resources lay, not up above where you can see the beautiful waterfall plunging freely, but down there, at the bottom, where this waterfall could be collected and transformed into something new, into power, into electricity, at enormous temperatures, so explosive that I feel faint at the mere thought of it, even eighty years after the idea was devised for the very first time. Ah, yes,' sighed Adam Eyde, shaking his head with both emotion and resignation upon hearing his own words. He pulled himself together, took a sip of his drink, and raised his glass to Singer, who raised his glass to Adam Eyde before taking a cautious sip of his own.

'But this engineer, whose name you're familiar with, was unable to attract enough international investors to turn his big project into reality, into Norsk Hydro's project. Instead Norsk Hydro purchased another waterfall, a smaller waterfall, at a spot in Telemark on *this* side of Mount Gaustatoppen and started its own project, a test project, and on a much smaller scale. This somewhat smaller waterfall was located near Notodden, a rural community with a steamship dock, two tourist hotels, a Christian teachers college and two shopkeepers. The waterfall would be tamed, diverted into pipes, and the water sent to a hypermodern power station that would arouse admiration all over Norway. In Notodden, near the shore of Lake Heddal, a factory was built that would make use of this power. The Notodden Saltpeter Factory. A test factory, an experiment that would show the international investors that the idea was worthy of a much bigger plant, even something on a huge scale. The plant workers at the power station and saltpeter factory were hired in 1905. In the autumn of 1907 the first trial production began.

'Notodden, 1907,' said Adam Eyde, dreamily, his eyes closed. 'In 1905 a small rural community; then in 1907 everything changed. After that it became a town. A totally new town rose up during the construction period, and it endured. Come over here,' he said and began walking along the balustrade, this time moving to the right. 'Look there,' he said, pointing down. 'Grønnebyen.'

Singer looked straight down. There he saw a strangely uniform housing development. Directly below them, a little to the right, were numerous identical and quite large wooden buildings, each with its own courtyard or garden. The wooden buildings had been erected at regular intervals, neatly lined up, with a grid of streets that intersected precisely.

'Grønnebyen,' said Adam Eyde. 'Homes for Hydro's workers. It was erected there, newly built, in 1907. And here,' said Eyde, as he turned and pointed. 'Do you remember the residential neighbourhood we drove through right before we arrived here? Those big beautiful houses painted white? They were the residences of Hydro's upper echelons, built for the engineers and managers at the Notodden Saltpeter Factory. They were constructed in the beginning of 1907. And the crown jewel of the whole thing was: this!' said Eyde, throwing out his hands to embrace the enormous building before them, and the entire park. 'The residence of Hydro's general manager. It stood here, towering over the Notodden Saltpeter Factory when operations began in the autumn of 1907. That small test factory. It was a Hydro enterprise. And meandering between the homes for Hydro's workers and the homes for Hydro's upper echelons was the centre of town, with shops, a school, a fire department, a police station, and everything else that creates a town, attracted by the Hydro enterprise.

'That must have been a strange year, 1907,' he said pensively. Adam Eyde turned round again to face Lake

Heddal and the Hydro plant as he stood at the balustrade with his guest, Singer, at his side. 'Even before production began – in fact, even before they knew whether or not their experiments to develop a method for creating synthetic saltpeter would turn out to be successful enough to be commercially profitable and to start up production – this town called Notodden stood here, ready and waiting. There was a great hustle and bustle; every day new people arrived with their possessions in removal vans, coming to seek their fortune. There was something so grand about the idea of an industrialised wilderness in Øst-Telemark, it attracted people and ideas from all over. And it was then that the idea of Notodden as a port town also arose. Even before production at the test factory started up, extensive plans for a canal were presented, toying with the idea of a shipping route between Notodden and New York, and between Notodden and London, that self-same England ship I mentioned. This idea did not originate with Norsk Hydro, even though the company was quick to seize upon the proposal, of course. No, the idea came from a bureaucrat. It came from the Waterways director. It was the Waterways director himself who proposed a plan, showing how it would be possible for large steamships to travel from Skien on the coast up through the inland lakes and rivers of Telemark to Notodden at the northern end of Lake Heddal. A large-scale project, to be sure, that would involve building an enormous lock system at Skien and huge masonry and excavation works on the river connecting Lake Norsjø and the waters of Lake Heddal, but it could be done. The Waterways director knew it was possible, in fact it was so possible that he ordered a detailed plan drawn up, and he presented it to the authorities in charge. It was also the Waterways director who fantasised about a ship to America and a ship to England travelling at full steam into Lake Heddal. Norsk Hydro's project certainly stirred up a lot of ideas, got a lot of brains churning, and now even the sober-minded bureaucrats wanted to open the interior of Telemark and connect it to the sea,' said Adam Eyde. '*Skål*,' he added enthusiastically, raising his glass and reaching out to clink glasses with Singer, which they did.

'So, do you see the ship to England now?' he asked. 'Out there?'

Singer looked a bit confused as he scanned Lake Heddal, but he reluctantly had to shake his head.

'What? You don't see it? But you do see Notodden station, don't you? Take a look and make sure you can still see it.'

And Singer, holding his glass in his right hand, leaned over the balustrade and was able to confirm that yes, down there and off to the left he could see Notodden station.

'1909. That's when it was built. That's when the Rjukan Line opened. Everything happened very fast. It was a race against time. All over Europe heavy industry was experimenting with methods for producing synthetic fertiliser, which the world was hungering for. The Notodden Saltpeter Factory was a test factory, put up in all haste in order to convince international investors that Norsk Hydro's method for producing synthetic fertiliser here in the Norwegian mountains was worth betting on. But this method was at the experimental stage. During the entire construction process, they experimented with improvements, often resulting in shattered illusions. But in October 1907 they began building the train station, with the international investors present, so they could see with their own eyes why this was something that deserved their further attention. It went well. They were willing to continue betting on it. In the closed-in and narrow valley behind Mount Gaustatoppen – a place called Rjukan – right before New Year, only two months after the Notodden project had turned out to be a success, they broke ground to lay tracks for a whole new railway line. From Rjukan to Notodden. It was a stretch of tracks through the most remote region a railway line had ever been constructed. In August 1909, the first train travelled from Notodden to Rjukan, with His Majesty King Haakon VII as the guest of honour.

'And with that the port town of Notodden became a reality. Because from the so-called railway dock right next to the train station, the products from the industrial giant near Rjukan would be loaded onto ships carrying them onward, beyond the borders of Norway. To the whole world. That was the most important thing about Notodden. This railway dock. Not the Notodden Saltpeter Factory, which was certainly going great guns and operating at a big profit, but it was and would always be a lesser project in Norsk Hydro's industrial empire in the interior of Telemark. In

1910 a new canal plan was proposed. Now there was a rush to get started on the masonry work, excavation, and construction of a large-scale lock system down in the Skien district so that the loaded steamships from Notodden could get through. Sea and harbour. Hustle and bustle. Can you smell the sea? I certainly think I can smell the salty air of the sea, yes indeed,' said Adam Eyde, though without waiting for Singer's potential confirmation, before taking in a deep breath of the sultry summer air up here in the interior of Telemark. 'But no,' he said, 'it was and would always be an illusion. Yet it was on this smell of the salty sea that Notodden was founded. Alas, how true, how true!' exclaimed Adam Eyde. 'Because all sorts of things began to happen that were not to Notodden's benefit.

'In July 1908 the Norwegian parliament approved the first section of the Sørlandet Line as a stretch of tracks between Kongsberg and Neslandsvatn. This was approved with the laying of two spur tracks, one from Neslandsvatn down to Kragerø, the other as a spur track from Hjuksebø to Notodden. So the Rjukan Line would be connected to the Sørlandet Line. Initially this meant that freight-train traffic could proceed directly from Rjukan to Oslo, or Kristiania, spelled with a *K*, if you want to be precise. But this didn't mean that the idea of Notodden as a port town would be scrapped. On the contrary, as you heard, a new canal plan was proposed in 1910. Such large-scale production was expected from the synthetic fertiliser giant in the interior of Telemark that it seemed like a viable plan to construct both a railway connection to the capital city and a harbour in Notodden.

'At this time the following rail connections existed in our part of Norway: Oslo to Drammen to Kongsberg, which would now be extended to Neslandsvatn, and later to Kristiansand. In addition, a Vestfold Line, or Jarlsberg Line as it was called, from Kristiania to Skien. The tracks of the new Sørlandet Line would go up to Bø in central Telemark, and now under discussion was how the Skien district would be connected to this new Sørlandet Line. Two options were considered, which caused great controversy all over Telemark; it had to do with whether the tracks would be on the west side of Lake Norsjø, or on the east side. Tracks on the west side would go through some of the most populated and fertile rural communities in Telemark, while on the east side they would go through relatively desolate stretches, where there was very little need for people to be connected to the railway, and yet the line on the east side was chosen. Why?

'My dear friend,' said Adam Eyde. 'The east-side line was chosen because that was what Norsk Hydro wanted. Via the east-side line Norsk Hydro would have the shortest possible route between the coast and Rjukan – deep in the interior, hidden away in a narrow and closed-in valley, where the sun doesn't reach for a large part of the year. From Rjukan, via Hjuksebø, to Nordatugu, and from there along the east side of Lake Norsjø to Skien and the newly purchased dock at Porsgrunn. Freight train after freight train, without any reloading, from Rjukan to the coast. The most efficient connection imaginable, on a rail line that had very little traffic. A rail line which Norsk Hydro – for the most part, if you ignore the three or four trains a day travelling to connect with the Sørlandet Express – could have all to itself.

'Goodbye, canal plan. Goodbye, harbour town Notodden. Welcome to the inland town of Notodden, beautifully situated on Lake Heddal. Welcome to a seventy-year-old mistake. Good afternoon, my name is Adam Eyde, I'm the district director of Norsk Hydro in Notodden, and it's my lot to clear up this mistake which has plagued us for all these years. And now, please do me the honour of being my guest; I think we should empty our glasses because I have a feeling that Mrs Semb has dinner ready.'

They emptied their glasses, and Adam Eyde ushered his guest across the lawn, past the elegant terrace and into the enormous luxury residence, where he led the way to a library with a table set for two. They enjoyed an excellent meal. Mrs Semb started by serving a mushroom dish, the first chanterelles of the season, she informed them, hand-picked in Nordmarka by the wife of General Manager Holte on the previous Sunday and sent by internal company mail. Sent this way were both the chanterelles and the main course – fried whiting, caught in the waters of Norsk Hydro's own Frier Fjord just outside Eidanger that very morning and sent directly by internal company mail from the Herøya plant. The fish had been fried in butter churned on the steep valley slopes at Rjukan. The whiting was stuffed with parsley, grown in the soil along Lake Heddal, and the carrots came from the same area, as did the new potatoes. For dessert: the first cloudberries, flown in from Glomfjord. With the food they enjoyed exquisite wines purchased by countless members of the Norsk Hydro family on their visits to duty-free shops in airports around the world. That was also where the cognac came from, while the coffee had been personally chosen by General Manager Holte during a visit to a coffee plantation in Brazil, when he was invited as a guest to the Borregaard wood-processing plant the previous winter. Adam Eyde seemed quite pensive during dinner and said very little. Only when they sat down to coffee and cognac – which they also enjoyed in the library but at a round table next to the fireplace, which of course wasn't lit since it was the last day of the summer month of July – did he become talkative again, exclaiming to his guest and new friend:

'My God, how we have struggled with this mistake! Because we were the ones, after all, who created Notodden, but what were we supposed to do with it? There it was, serving no purpose at all. Or rather, any good we might derive from it we could obtain much more efficiently from other places. Oh, Notodden may well be a mistake, but a mistake that Norsk Hydro has never abandoned. Even our headquarters was here. Where you're sitting right now, that's where the heads of the IG Farben chemical conglomerate in Germany sat and negotiated investments and plans so extensive that they impacted the lives of hundreds of thousands of people. Here. Right here in the mysterious region of Telemark, decisions were made that have meant life and death. No less than life and death. Times change, everything changes, but not Notodden, which is Norsk Hydro's mistake. Norsk Hydro moved its main production to Herøya, its headquarters to Oslo; the company has a large presence out in the world, producing gas at Karmøy and power in Glomfjord, and virtually nothing in Rjukan, but Rjukan is no mistake, it's part of the world that is changing. Rjukan had its days of glory, but Notodden has only been a mistake. However, we will never leave Notodden, we insist on clinging to our mistake. We're closing down everything here, but not without putting something else in its place. That's my job. Through the years we've kept our biggest mistake in our thoughts, and never abandoned it. Keep in mind that we could have left Notodden way back in 1917, when the Bratsberg Line was finished and Notodden was left with an ordinary train station on the stretch between Rjukan and Eidanger. We could have abandoned Notodden when we transitioned to the electric-arc process in 1928, but did we do that? No. That's when we installed our first ammonia factory here. It's true we intended to show IG Farben that it was possible to use other production means than the Haber-Bosch method, in case they thought their patent entitled them to it for all eternity. And we convinced them; once again Notodden astonished the international investors – well done, Notodden – but did we later shut down the ammonia factory because we were focusing big-time on ammonia production in Rjukan, where the natural conditions were better? No, we did not. We continued on in Notodden with the ammonia factory that really could have been moved, lock, stock and barrel, over the mountain to Rjukan. Or to Eidanger. We allowed it to stay in Notodden. Later we built a sack factory here, the factory was supposed to produce sacks for all the products we produced around the world. And when plastic replaced the paper sack, what did we do then? We opened a plastic-sack factory for our products of course. It wasn't a given that it should be located in Notodden, but we put it there. And not only that – at about the same time we bought an entire Respatex wall-panel factory in Drammen and moved it to Notodden. And where did we put the central warehouse? Since you are an enlightened man and librarian, you would naturally say in Herøya, but that's not what we did. We put it in Notodden. Which meant that right up until the 1960s we had almost a thousand employees on the payroll in this remote part of the country. And you have to ask yourself: Why, why? It certainly hasn't been because of an insatiable greed for profit, I can assure you of that. But I think it's about time for a drink,' cried Adam Eyde delightedly. 'Now that it's evening and getting dark, let's go and sit on the terrace and have a whisky. We'll help ourselves,' he said, going over to a lovely escritoire, which he opened to reveal a bar. He took out two tall highball glasses and poured two whiskies, handing one to Singer, and then they strolled out to the terrace in the warm summer evening, where dark had now fallen. But Adam Eyde couldn't settle down; once again he felt the need to take Singer over to the balustrade, and there they stood, looking down at the present-day Hydro plant and peering out at dark Lake Heddal. The factory was lit up, emitting a steady humming sound.

Earlier, when it was bright daytime, Singer's ears hadn't been aware of the humming sound coming from the factory. But now that it was dark and the lights were on down below, he heard the humming sound.

'The Factory,' said Adam Eyde, and his voice had an oddly dreamy quality to it. 'What's left of the Factory. Listen hard, because the humming will soon fall silent. In a couple of years we'll shut down the rest of the Factory too, and then Norsk Hydro will be out of Notodden. But we'll be leaving our mark behind. We're planning a different type of industry here. Plus a museum of industry; it will be Norway's most impressive museum of industry, a monument to Norsk Hydro, to energy production and bold dreams, even to what is inconceivable. Maybe we should call it the Museum of the Inconceivable, what do you think about that? Yes, this is Notodden, with a dormant train station, an imaginary England ship out there and a shut-down manufacturing plant, which altogether constitute the Museum of the Inconceivable. Well, let's go back, because

I'm certain that by the time we've slowly walked across the lawn and reached the terrace, our glasses will be empty and we'll need another drink.'

And he was right. No sooner had they reached the bottom of the steps leading up to the terrace than both Adam Eyde and Singer had emptied their glasses, and Eyde took both glasses inside to pour two more, while Singer took a seat on the terrace in the warm summer evening, here in the middle of Norway. Eyde came back with newly poured drinks, and they toasted each other. But Eyde was restless and took Singer along for another walk across the lawn. This time they didn't stop at the balustrade, but simply turned around and went back the way they'd come, and when they reached the terrace again, Adam Eyde turned and set off on a new stroll across the lawn in the park of the luxurious residence while he chatted animatedly about himself and his interests.

'Data!' he said. 'Information technology! A museum! Art and culture! Education! Science! That's Notodden's future, and that's what we're going to give to the town, which is no small thing, let me tell you. They signify what's modern. Notodden will be the centre of everything modern. For the twenty-first century. Our parting thank you, that's what it will be. Or our thanks for a good ride. The mistake from the beginning of this century will rise up and buzz with the sounds of the new era. Slightly quieter sounds, but it will still buzz and simmer here, just like in the good old days! Fashion!' he said. 'We need to bring in boutique fashion companies. They can sew the Hydro logo onto teen clothes here. Notodden can become a design centre. Norsk Hydro has its contacts, we can make it happen. The Paris of the North. The fashion centre of the North, it's all a matter of thinking boldly and making use of the good will that a worldwide corporation possesses, and then we'll make it happen. What do you say to that? Would you like to have the National Library here? Just tell me if you do. No? Well, then they can put it in Mo i Rana instead, it'd be nice for them up there. But what's a shut-down coke factory compared to eighty years of Norsk Hydro? No, Notodden should get the National Library. You don't think so? Well, well, I suppose they need to make a living in Mo i Rana too, but damnit. The Notodden National Library. We'd call it the Notodden National Library, the name has a certain ring to it. What? You don't agree? Well, all right.'

Adam Eyde walked back and forth across the lawn in front of the enormous luxury residence where he lived, with Singer at his side. Singer was smoking a cigarette. The tip of the cigarette glowed in the dark of the warm evening. This was way back in 1983. It was a time when directors tolerated cigarette smoke, even if they'd personally given up smoking long ago, and when it was natural for someone like Singer, even in the presence of a Hydro director and at a Hydro director's residence, to light up a cigarette without first asking permission, even indoors, as he'd done at dinner, though it's true that an ashtray of solid silver had been discreetly placed next to his plate. Now he was walking next to Adam Eyde and having a smoke and holding a whisky glass in his other hand. The two of them kept pace with their drinking and emptied their glasses at the same time, at the moment when they were only a few metres from the terrace steps and the huge, illuminated luxury villa.

'I think we should have another,' said Eyde, 'but let's take a seat indoors.' Once again they sat down in front of the fireplace in the library, each with his newly poured, or newly mixed, whisky and soda, with lots of ice.

'So, in a few years I'll be able to leave this place,' said Adam Eyde. 'By then the new Notodden will have been created, and I can leave. Where will I go? Back to headquarters, of course, though that's not a given, I could actually picture myself moving to another company, preferably abroad, for that matter. But I've got it into my head that I want to be the new general manager of Norsk Hydro. Just wait, you'll see. I'm the one who'll lead Norsk Hydro into a new century. By then I will only be in my early fifties, at my peak, if I may say so. Not old, not young, in mid-life, and strong. You don't believe it? Oh, don't pretend that you believe it, why should you, just because I say so? But pay attention and you'll see. If Norsk Hydro, in the year 2000, does not have a boss who's on fire, then I won't have been the one who was chosen. It's as simple as that.' So said Adam Eyde with a little smile as he emptied his glass in one sustained swig.

'Another?' he asked, pouring himself one more while allowing Singer time to drink up before taking his glass and pouring one for him as well.

'Books,' he said. 'You must have read a lot of books. A strange occupation. Sitting and reading. I often do it myself, though maybe not that often, when I think about it, at least not the sort of books that you undoubtedly read; but when, on rare occasions, I do sit down and read a book, then I quickly find myself thinking about what it is I'm doing, and I think: Jesus, are you sitting here and reading? Don't you have anything else to do? Reading just for the sake of relaxation doesn't come into the discussion, crime fiction is not for me, it has to be something more than that. But even that isn't enough. Life is too short. Too exciting. It's *here* that things are happening. ... But we do need books. Especially philosophy. Did you know that every business executive tries to find a philosopher to be his successor? I swear it's true. General Manager Holte is looking for a moral philosopher. That's what he would prefer, but it'll probably be someone with an MBA, or maybe a lawyer. I happen to have an MBA myself, but I'm fascinated by philosophy. Do you think that's strange? Our work has to do with philosophy. There is no one, other than the great philosophers themselves, who comes closer to philosophy than we do. That's why General Manager Holte would prefer to see a philosopher succeed him. Trying to find a philosopher, after all, is a way of summing up your own life and activities. That is how you end up in philosophy.

At least you do if you've been head of Norsk Hydro for twenty years. A general manager of Norsk Hydro looks back in order to choose his successor, which is a way of looking forward, isn't it? By looking back in that manner he is looking forward, and seeing himself, what he has actually been, and what he is – he now acknowledges that he's been living under a sign of philosophy, without having had the chance to cultivate it personally, in a theoretical fashion, but he's been living it, living it to the fullest, in his daily activities. General Manager Holte would prefer to have an actual moral philosopher as his successor, and that says the most about him. But he'll probably choose one of us; anything else would be a breach of the rules of the game. But someday someone will have to breach the rules and point to reality. Maybe I'll be the one. Maybe I'll be the one to choose a philosopher as my successor as general manager of Norsk Hydro. If so, that'll happen sometime around 2010. But it won't be a *moral* philosopher. General Manager Holte is mistaken when he thinks that large international corporations need moral philosophers to be in charge; it's not that simple. That's not fundamental enough. For my successor I want a philosopher who asks fundamental questions. A fundamental philosopher. A philosopher of language. Ludwig, who finally returns home. Wittgenstein, you know, a Wittgenstein who returns to the greatest thing of all. And what is that? It's running large companies, that's what. Nothing else can make your heart swell with greater pride, or cause your mind to stand still, gaping with awe. Or make you fumble for words. Wherein lies the secret? It's called a company, sir. It's called being in charge of a large concern, the language is already in place, as if spontaneously invented. All that's necessary is to study it. Where is the secret, to which the fundamental philosopher can find his way and present it to us, in his capacity as general manager of Norsk Hydro anno 2010? What is it that occupies us? Financial calculations. Budgets. Trimming the organisation. Cutting costs. New areas of interest. Reorganisation. Mergers. And what is the guiding principle? Profit? Yes, of course, of course. But why do we constantly need greater profit? Couldn't we say: no, right now the earnings are so good that we're managing just fine. We can sit back for a while and let the wheels roll on as we observe the whole operation. Never mind an ammonia factory in Notodden, we're doing fine, and things are going well in Herøya, so never mind. Why don't we do that? What sort of laws dictate our behaviour? I think I know where to look, I think I could provide guidance to our fundamental philosopher. He should look to the law of gravity. It's all a matter of a single, rather abused word, and that word is "cheap".' The concept of "cheap", that's what could make us better understand our civilisation. It's one of the dual pillars of truth. *Cheap. Cheap enough.* Yes, "cheap enough" is the key. It's the watchword that fundamental philosophy should use in order to enter philosophical heaven, where the answers to the big questions glitter in self-evident radiance. *Cheap enough.* That's what makes the practical world, to which we are witnesses, the world as it is and not something entirely different, or even slightly different. So it's not a spaceship up in the air above Lake Heddal at night. New York's skyscrapers – have you seen them? You haven't? Well, then you have something to look forward to. It's the most magnificent sight on this planet. But what is the truth behind this impressive sight? It's the land prices in New York, which for natural reasons are so astronomical that they have to build up. *That is cheap enough,* that's how something looks that is cheap enough. Can't you just picture it? Oh, wait,' he said and abruptly got up. He looked around, searching for something, and finally found what he was looking for, a piece of white paper, and he sat down again.

'Can't you just picture the photograph of New York,' he said, 'and the caption underneath: *Cheap enough.* But that's only one pillar. There's also a second pillar, and together they form the two pillars of a formula, which would be the full caption under the photograph of New York's impressive skyline.' Adam Eyde wrote something down on the piece of white paper, rather secretively, using one hand to hide the words from Singer as he wrote. But when he was done, he handed the piece of paper to Singer, who read: CHEAP (ENOUGH) and (MERE) LUCK.

'It wasn't that easy to work it out. Plain *cheap* and *luck,* sure, but something gets lost in that. I could also write: *Cheap enough* and *mere luck,* but it's really more than that. The way I wrote it, that's how it needs to be written. New York. It's mere luck. In a place with sky-high land prices, the soil is such that it's possible to build upward. If the soil conditions in Manhattan had been different, how would New York have looked today? And imagine if the land prices had shot up at a time when the technology didn't exist for building skyscrapers, even though the soil would allow for it. How would New York have looked today? No, this is the second pillar guarding the heaven of truth, the philosopher's promised land,' said Adam Eyde. 'Oh, excuse me,' he added. 'Here I am, babbling away and I didn't notice that your glass is empty.' He grabbed Singer's glass – because Singer had actually finished off his drink while Eyde's was still half-full – and went over to the bar to get him another whisky.

'What is cheap,' he said as he handed Singer his drink and then sat back down, 'what is cheap is the law of gravity; it's burdensome for us, yet tremendously simple, and at the same time difficult to understand fully as the enormous driving force that it plays in a person's life. Precisely something that a fundamental philosopher, whom I believe has to be a philosopher of language, can sink his teeth into. There's a lot of new territory, waiting to be described. By researching the concept of "cheap" or "cheap enough", I think you can come up with a philosophical conceptual apparatus that will make our understanding of life more closely approach life itself, the dynamics of life. It's a key concept, and explains what drives the work itself, creating the great enterprise. But it has to be juxtaposed with (mere) luck, because otherwise it would be too mechanical to become a truly great philosophy. Luck, that unpredictable element that has to do with chance and boldness. The concept of cheap (enough) can give you insight up to a certain point that is crystal clear right before the decisive moment occurs, like a lightning bolt out of the blue. At that decisive moment it's a matter of luck. Take Ivar Kreuger, for instance. Have you heard of him? He already had a monopoly on matches, so what did he do? Did he raise the price so somebody else might come up with an idea for producing an alternative light source, such as butane lighters? No, he kept the price the same, but he took out four matches from each box, which contained fifty. Nobody counts the matches in a box of matches; he took out four, which meant that, with this simple operation, he made a bigger profit, comparable to Sweden's total national budget, meaning what it cost the Swedish nation to run schools and hospitals, offer services for the poor, administer communications, the mail and telegraph service, the universities, and provide maintenance for the former world power's countless grand edifices, as well as pay the salaries of all the government officials and civil servants. Not to mention the Swedish army, the Swedish navy and the Swedish cavalry. The sum total of all of this was what Kreuger could stuff into his own pocket, and without anyone even noticing. That is *cheap enough*. But Kreuger lacked something else, when it came to the decisive moment. At that decisive moment he ended up firing a bullet into his own forehead. Because he didn't have luck. If he'd only had luck, the world would have looked different; we don't know how, but it would have. Regardless of the calculations, regardless of estimates and precautions, insurance and double insurance, no one can foresee everything. Something unforeseen will always occur, and then what counts is having luck. Without luck, even the mightiest of financial empires will collapse. It's here that having the philosopher as head of a large enterprise comes in. Ludwig Wittgenstein's homecoming. The merging of the mightiest industrial giants within a field is, of course, one way of reducing the unpredictability of luck, but it turns out that even that is not enough. The secret structures of luck are mightier than that. But with philosophers in charge, you have a management group that works with that very element, and they can reduce the horrors it spreads, and increase the gentle rain trickling over the blessed. I'm talking, of course, not about moral philosophers, but fundamental philosophers, meaning philosophers of language, those who research the foundation of speech and thereby also have access to what we cannot express in words. It's with philosophers – meaning people who have a deep knowledge of this unpredictable element in life, which is, in fact, so active, it's what makes the world look precisely the way it does – that large companies will find natural leaders, and so the rest of us, MBAs, lawyers, engineers, computer experts, statisticians, can modestly put our special expertise at the disposal of these natural leaders. Oh yes, this is what I believe. I'm convinced that this will make its way to the forefront. By 2010.'

Adam Eyde had become gripped by his own words, as he excitedly strode back and forth in the library. Suddenly he realised that there was no more whisky in his glass, which he held in his right hand as he strode back and forth, and so he stopped.

'Let's have a drink,' he said, looking at Singer, who at that very moment was emptying his glass. 'A drink,' he repeated. 'And a midnight snack.' He went over to the bar and poured two more whisky and sodas, then handed one of the glasses to Singer and set the other down in front of his chair. He disappeared into what Singer assumed was the kitchen and came back a few minutes later with two small plates, two forks, and a can of fish balls. He opened the can with a can opener, then they ate the fish balls right from the can. They used their forks to fish out whole fish balls and stuffed them in their mouths. Between bites they took swigs of whisky.

'Marvellous,' said Eyde. 'A marvellous conclusion to a festive day. It has been incredibly pleasant for me, all of this, getting to know you. I really must say. But now I'd better let you go. I have to get up early in the morning,' he said, glancing at his watch. 'I'll get Kristiansen to drive you back to your hotel.'

He accompanied Singer through the rooms and out to the front hall. In the hall he caught sight of an escritoire and went over to pull open a drawer. He took out some papers and said:

'Wait here a sec,' and then left. A moment later he was back, and he was holding a stack of papers in each hand. He put one pile in the drawer and stuffed the other in an envelope, which he gave to Singer.

'Take these,' he said. 'It's my system for betting. It doesn't really have anything to do with philosophy; it's all about calculating the odds. Betting on football scores is a matter of skill, and that's when my modest expertise comes into its own. When I'm abroad – for instance in Lausanne – and my colleagues and contacts are out on the golf course, I sit in my hotel room and work on this. I can't stand golf, which of course puts me at a disadvantage, considering my ambitions, but if it's not possible for me to be named general manager of Norsk Hydro without being willing to trudge around, lugging golf clubs, then so be it. Anyway, this is my system. I'm giving you a copy. If you use it, you'll get rich. The big system may be too much for your wallet, but if you make use of the little system, things will go your way.' For a long moment he stared at Singer, who stood there, holding the envelope he'd been given. Then Adam Eyde briskly turned on his heel and moved towards the front door, with Singer following.

Eyde opened the door and paused in the centre of that ostentatious entrance with the heavy white double pillars on either side; Singer stood slightly behind him, and the light from the enormous luxury villa flooded out from the open door. They glimpsed the Mercedes parked under several big oak trees. When the villa's front door opened and light flooded out, they heard the slam of the car door, and now they glimpsed the figure of Kristiansen standing alongside the car in the dark summer night. Followed by Singer, Adam Eyde headed for the Mercedes and its driver. Eyde asked Kristiansen to drive Singer to his hotel, and while the two men said their goodbyes, Kristiansen stood ready, holding open the door to the back seat. Singer got in, Kristiansen closed the door, climbed in behind the wheel, and turned on the engine. As they drove off, Singer turned to see if he might be able to wave goodbye, but Adam Eyde had turned round and was on his way back to the house. They drove through night-quiet Notodden, illuminated by street lights, both in the residential neighbourhood and in the centre of town. Not a soul in sight. The Mercedes pulled up in front of the hotel, and as soon as the car stopped, Singer grabbed the door handle wanting to get out before Kristiansen could come round and open the door for him. But he couldn't open the door, it had been automatically locked. Kristiansen got out and came round the car to open the door. Singer climbed out, offering his sincere thanks for the lift, to which Kristiansen replied with a polite smile.

The next day Singer went to see his new workplace, the Notodden library. And with that he began his new life. He ended up staying in Notodden for years, the whole time as librarian at the town's municipal library. But an event like the one that occurred on the day he arrived in Notodden never happened again. He never revisited the enormous luxury villa belonging to Norsk Hydro. Occasionally, rarely, when he was out for a walk he might pass by the place, and then he'd cast a glance at the villa as he passed at some distance and think about the peculiar evening he'd spent there as a guest, many years earlier.

He had nothing more to do with Adam Eyde. It's true that he caught sight of him a few times in the centre of Notodden, the first time about six months after the man had so suddenly and surprisingly entered Singer's life, in the carriage of the little train at Hjuksebø station, waiting to leave for Notodden, and subsequently laid claim to him in his own home, for an entire evening, until the late hours of the night. The first time Singer saw Adam Eyde again after that evening, he was surprised and thought: Jesus, that's him, that has to be him. But he saw him from far away and wasn't completely sure about that. Later they once ran into each other on the same pavement. Adam Eyde gave him a friendly greeting, and Singer responded in an equally friendly manner, but neither of them stopped to exchange a few words; they simply continued on, in opposite directions. This happened several more times over the coming years, until Adam Eyde disappeared from Notodden. Singer never saw Kristiansen the chauffeur again, not him or the Mercedes, nor Mrs Semb, though he probably wouldn't have recognised her if he'd run into her on the street.

Yet even if he hadn't passed Adam Eyde on the street, even if they hadn't greeted each other in passing, he couldn't have dismissed his experiences in the Hydro villa as a dream, at least not after a few years, because Eyde's predictions for Notodden's future all came true. The last Hydro factory in Notodden was shut down the very next year, in 1984. In 1985, passengers who took the Sørlandet Line and changed trains in Hjuksebø could no longer see factory smoke off in the distance if they looked inland towards Notodden. And the new Notodden sprang up, just as Adam Eyde had foreseen. Art and culture. Data and information technology. Expertise and education. All of it came true. Except maybe for the fact that Notodden did not become the new fashion centre – otherwise everything fell into place, one thing after another. Hydro's old ammonia factory became a museum of industry; in addition, Hydro's offices were turned into a business park, dubbed *Hydros næringspark*, or the Hydro Business Park, where one modern niche company after another moved in. And at Hydro's transformer station, which was built in 1907 in the middle of the residential neighbourhood for Hydro officials, no less than Telemark Teledata took over, uniting the local with the global, like a spear point that resembled electrical sparks, a forward-shooting bolt of lightning. In that sense it was almost reassuring for Singer, now and then, on rare occasions, to catch sight of Adam Eyde hurrying along a pavement in the centre of Notodden – for instance in 1987, three years after Hydro had shut down its own operations – as if he were a man from the past who had come back to haunt the place and would not stop until all his promises were kept, and the enormous Hydro villa at the top of Notodden, with its view of Lake Heddal, could put down roots for all eternity, as the monument it had always been.

Yet after 1987 Singer couldn't remember seeing Adam Eyde. Sometime afterwards he must have disappeared for good. But Singer did not forget him; his first evening in Notodden had been too peculiar for that. And besides, he'd received a gift from Eyde. He kept it in the envelope that had once been handed to him. Sometimes he would take the betting systems out of the individual envelopes and study them as he slowly shook his head. But he never made use of the systems in order to seek his fortune, neither the big system nor the smaller one that was more suitable for him.

When he woke up the day after he'd been Adam Eyde's guest at Hydro's enormous villa in Notodden, he didn't give it a thought, that was already an event he'd left behind in a dreamlike glow. The only thing on his mind was that today he would present himself at his new workplace at the Notodden library. He was about to begin his job as librarian in Notodden. He quickly got dressed, wolfed down his breakfast, and rushed off to the library, which wasn't far from the hotel. He introduced himself to the head librarian and the rest of the staff. And that was the start of his new life. He moved to a neighbourhood, the so-called

Tinnbyen area, where he rented a studio apartment in the basement of a home belonging to an upper-level municipal official, and every day he would walk to his job in the centre of town, though at different times of day, since his work hours varied; it was a shift schedule, requiring him to take either a morning or an afternoon shift. Singer quickly became immersed in his work at the library, just as he had expected and hoped. He'd come to Notodden to live incognito. Using his full name, of course, but hiding from the thirty-four years that had clung to him, comprising the life he'd lived so far. He'd put all those years behind him and had no desire to revisit them, and that was why he'd started on his belated training to become a librarian, a three-year course of study at the College of Library Science, where, in addition to the formal training, he had also taught himself how to make anonymous the life for which he felt such a thirst. A new life, a new future, that was what he looked forward to. He'd always been fascinated by the possibility of disappearing. To start fresh, in an unfamiliar town, where no one knew him and had no idea where they stood with him.

It wasn't long before Singer adapted to the daily routine at the library in Notodden. It's true that the head of the library, a somewhat older woman, and a couple of the other employees did regard him with a certain suspicion initially, because he was a relatively young man, and so they assumed he was an up-and-coming type who consequently would try to interfere with all the arrangements that had been made, and which they thought he would deem, if not outright old-fashioned, at the very least insufficient, and in need of updating. But gradually they realised that this was far from Singer's intention, that he hadn't come to Notodden to start his career within the library field but instead to do a basic job well while drawing as little attention to himself as possible. Since he also turned out to be friendly towards everyone, and sarcastic about the boss when she wasn't around, he was well liked by everyone, even the boss; at least that's what he thought, or assumed to be so.

It was astonishing how quickly Singer felt at home in Notodden. The library work – including cataloguing, classifying and other internal duties, as well as dealing with the public at the counter, where he received books brought back by the patrons and stamped the new books they borrowed – proceeded without any trouble whatsoever. He quickly settled in, and he liked seeing himself in this situation; in fact, he enjoyed it. Routine work, conscientiously performed, was something he'd always liked. The meticulousness, the feeling of being present in purely routine operations fascinated him, and that's when he felt more in tune with himself than he normally felt or had reason to feel. It was the unthinking, purely automatic nature of sticking to what was routine in a situation, the near absent-mindedness of it, that could bring out the jesting, almost amiable side of him as he stood behind the counter in the Notodden municipal library. He might cheerfully joke with the book borrowers, sounding witty, in fact immeasurably witty, so that the book borrowers simply had to surrender whenever he enthusiastically proffered his witticisms, which simply poured out of him, requiring no thought on his part. Or he might frown in what appeared to be the deepest concentration when book borrowers, now and then, asked for his advice if they wanted to research a certain topic, or if they asked him for the name of a book they were looking for, though they couldn't recall the author's name or the title, but it contained a very specific scene, which, as it turned out, had become distorted in their memory, something Singer found out after asking enough questions to be able to determine that there was only one book it could be; and what joy he felt when he turned out to be right, a joy he felt especially because the book borrower was so happy that they'd found the book after all, because it was this book he, or she, had in mind even though he, or she, had been so badly mistaken, according to the book borrower him- or herself, when it came to remembering the scene he or she had presumably remembered so well; the scene was actually not like that at all, but like this, as presented here, which he, or she, realised now that Singer had practically conjured forth the book for him, or her.

And so that was how the days passed in Notodden. He lived a simple, well-ordered life. He familiarised himself with the town and adapted to his new routines. He found a certain cafe where he ate his daily dinner, found his way to the route he should take to and from his job, subscribed to *Teledølen*, the local newspaper, even though he could have made do with ploughing through the paper at work; he looked for and found an alternative route he could take to and from work, for a change of pace, and he frequently went to the cinema. He preferred to do this after finishing the so-called afternoon shift at the library, because when he was done with his work for the day, after he'd made everything ready for the following day's morning shift and was able to close up, then he had just enough time to slip into the last showing, just before the film started. Once he didn't get in because it was sold out. It was a very popular and much-touted American film, so tickets had been in high demand. After that, he made it a habit to look in *Teledølen* to see what film was playing at the cinema in the evening, and then he would assess whether it was a film that might sell out. If he thought it might, he would leave the library for a few minutes to go over to the cinema to buy a ticket in advance. Subsequently, he was never again stopped at the door because the show was sold out. Yet this led him to wonder whether he might have set the standard a bit too high, causing him, too often, to assess films as being so popular that they would sell out even if they didn't even approach that level of popularity, so that the women who worked in the ticket booth of the Notodden cinema might find it strange that he constantly came over to buy his ticket for the last showing even though there was no reason whatsoever to assure his place in that manner; on the contrary. And for that reason he decided to take certain chances, as he phrased it, by purchasing a ticket in advance only to the obviously top films, those that everyone was talking about, those that were mentioned in all the Oslo newspapers, with big film stars in the lead roles, and there weren't very many of those. In fact, there were so few of those types of films that he eventually stopped leaving his job during work hours to buy a ticket in advance for the last showing, but he did not stop looking in *Teledølen* to see whether a really big film was going to be shown in the evening. And if that was the case, then he made sure to buy a ticket in advance.

So, that was how Singer's life in Notodden had begun to take shape. It was a new life, yet everything had begun to fall into patterns, a specific rhythm, which was what he sought and also felt fairly certain he had found. He was content. He was in hiding, and yet he had a great deal of freedom of movement. Singer in Notodden. Fresh air and wind. He took his walks to and from work, alternating between the two routes, which were, in fact, identical for large stretches of the way. But he also did a lot of walking in his spare time, strolling along the streets in town, and also in surrounding areas, and out in nature, for instance up near old Tinnfoss, near the dams, or along the ridges above the town, or on the flat stretches out towards the Heddal stave church, a long and intrinsically pointless Sunday hike, but with a sensible goal in mind. He wandered around, listening to the town's metaphysics, as they'd said at the College of Library Science. Trying to absorb the smell and dust from the three-storey brick buildings in the centre of Notodden, juxtaposing this with the shop windows and advertising signs of the 1980s. He had a sense of the time in which he was living, here in this town. He enjoyed himself. In mid-August he could now and then catch the first whiff of autumn in the air, a slight trace of chill in the mild breezes, and Singer found himself thinking that he was looking forward to the autumn, to the brittle creaking of ice early in the morning on Lake Heddal and on the Tinn River, which ran through town, looking forward to the frost and the leaves falling from the trees; and when this happened, he thought to himself: Autumn has arrived, and I've been looking forward to it, and he sensed it in his nostrils and took a deep breath of the chill autumn air, that raw current of Telemark in the air, here in the middle of Notodden.

He would eat lunch at specific times, either right before he had to start the afternoon shift, or right after the morning shift. That came naturally, since the cafe where he ate wasn't a restaurant but a simple cafe that closed at 6 p.m. If he wished to have dinner after the library had closed for the evening, he had to find somewhere else to eat. But he never did that; he'd found this cafe, and that's where he ate every day, except on Sunday, when the place was closed. Always alone, but not always at the same table. He hadn't selected a specific table that he called his own, he chose a seat at random, and that could be anywhere, depending on where the other cafe guests were seated. If on the rare occasion the place was full, then he would pause, holding his tray in his hands, and scan the room, then go over to a table occupied by a solitary man, or woman, but preferably a man, and ask if the other chair was occupied, and if not, would it be all right if he sat down. One time, as it happened, a colleague from the library came in as he was sitting alone at a table, eating his food. This person, a woman, sat down at his table. She was only having a cup of coffee, and while she sat there, she invited him to a party on Saturday. At her home, hers and her husband's. Singer immediately accepted, trying also to give the impression that he was grateful to be invited to a party at the home of his colleague; he thought he owed her that much, because she no doubt thought he probably didn't yet know many people here in Notodden, and that was why she'd thought of him when she was arranging the party. She certainly didn't need to do that. Singer wouldn't have been offended, or hurt, if afterwards he'd heard that she and her husband had given a party and he wasn't invited, even though other colleagues had been. If all his colleagues had attended, then of course it would have been a different matter, but she hadn't invited all of his colleagues. There was actually only one other librarian present, aside from the hostess and Singer.

Most of the other guests, both male and female, worked at the teachers college. But also present was a young lawyer, who had settled in Notodden to set up his own practice. He was married to an artisan who made pottery and was now looking for suitable premises for a ceramics workshop. Much of the evening was spent trying to suggest possible locations that she, the lawyer's wife, might want to take a closer look at. That may have been a little too much local colour for Singer's taste, since he wasn't yet very familiar with the town and its premises, but he enjoyed himself and made use of the opportunity to ask about the address each time certain properties were mentioned if he didn't already know where they were located. In this way he became more familiar with the town, in a very local fashion, as he internally memorised the names of the properties where such and such premises were located, names that were frequently not official names but the ones used by locals, names he wanted to learn now that he'd moved here to put down roots.

Singer enjoyed himself at the party given by his colleague and her husband. In general he handled himself well in social settings, it was just a matter of taking a few simple precautions and then manoeuvring from there. For instance, never take the innermost seat in a room, because, if you needed to get up, you could do so only by causing a great deal of trouble for the other guests, who would often have to move their knees and contort their bodies, even on certain occasions get to their feet and move aside so that you could slip past. Of course, this applies only if you're new to the group; if you're part of a group where you know everyone, or at least most of the other guests, beforehand, then it's not so important. Because then you've been incorporated into a form of routine self-regulation among friends, which means that it's not so important if N or B has to move his or her knees or contort his or her body to allow you to slip past. But that is not the case when you're with a completely new group of people. Then your body, your own sphere, is noticed in an entirely different way. The greediness of the other guests towards you personally is all too palpable if, in such a situation, you have to get up and manoeuvre your way past them, causing them to twist and turn, and therefore pay careful attention to this man, Singer, who, tall as he is, has stood up and made his way past.

For that reason Singer chose his place with care on such occasions, when he had the opportunity to do so. If he didn't have the opportunity, but instead had to take the innermost seat in the room, either because he was specifically assigned to that seat or he ended up there by accident, he would stay seated all evening, without showing any sign of what was going on inside him. Yes, Singer had mastered the social life, it was no trouble for him to take part; in fact, now and then he even looked forward to the idea that on Saturday he was going to a party, just as on that evening in Notodden when he was invited to the home of a colleague and her husband, which had gone exceptionally well.

His social life was actually looking pretty good. Pleasant parties at the weekend, and a good relationship with his colleagues, including his boss, on weekdays. The people he had the most difficult time interacting with were actually the library patrons, or at least some of them. Those who, after he'd helped them once in a witty or most obliging manner, came back and made it known to him, either through gestures or even through direct remarks, that he, or she, was practically on first-name terms with Singer. He didn't like that, and he would behave quite stiffly. It wasn't because the book borrowers recognised him that he felt the need to retreat into formality. That was quite nice, and he liked being recognised, since, after all, he'd tried his utmost for them, with either his jokes or his willingness to help; he appreciated the fact that they at least showed that they recognised him. But what he didn't like was being recognised with the expectation that he should display a specific quality, in this case either that he was witty or that he was self-effacingly eager to be of service. Even if, in his blessedly routine work, he might greet them with an absent-minded joke on one occasion, that did not give them the right to conclude that he was one of their witty acquaintances, or one of their extremely obliging acquaintances, who now came rushing over, so self-effacing, to be at their beck and call in terms of everything a library patron might require of books from the Notodden library's abundant shelves and secret chambers in the basement. At times his stomach would knot when book borrowers came over to the counter, carrying books they wanted to take out, and they would speak to him with an overly familiar and cheerful tone, offering some so-called clever remarks that person-ally amused them greatly, and then look at him expectantly, waiting to hear his response. The connection between these ever so stupid, asinine jokes and the expectant look accompanying them seemed to him a terrible intimacy that he hadn't invited, and he refused for all the world to get roped into it. And if anyone thought that it was only men who excelled at saying stupid, asinine jokes accompanied by expectant looks, rest assured that Singer would disagree. It was just as likely to be women, both young and middle-aged, who might assume that same attitude with regard to the new librarian at the Notodden library. But in such circumstances, Singer did manage to defend himself. He, whom they regarded as a witty man, the cheerful knight of stupid jokes, would not respond to their advances; instead his manner would be reserved, correct and distant. The situation was worse with those who thought they saw in him someone who was an extremely obliging and devoted gentleman. He couldn't react in a dismissive way with such people; instead he was forced to play the role they seemed to perceive as his. There were two library patrons, in particular, who individually had decided that Singer was so amiable and so knowledgeable and so unselfishly devoted, that they simply refused to allow any other librarian to help them if he happened to be present in the library. One was a middle-aged woman who was a voracious reader of novels; the other was an elderly gentleman who was keenly interested in history. Singer had helped each of them, on separate occasions, extract themselves from the labyrinthine warrens into which they'd wandered because of mix-ups and misremembered details, and led them to the books they were so eager to find, since they could no longer recall where to find them in all the bookcases made available, at no charge, to book borrowers in the Notodden library. Hence Singer was able to step forward and help the middle-aged woman away from the *M* shelves where she was desperately looking among novels by Somerset Maugham, trying to find the characters she knew she wanted to find, and he resolutely led her over to the letter *G*, where, under the name of John Galsworthy, she found the first novel in *The Forsyte Saga*, which was what she was actually looking for; not necessarily a brilliant display of librarianship on Singer's part, but the middle-aged woman was so impressed and grateful that from then on she refused help from anyone but Singer. This was also the case with the elderly gentleman who had got lost in an impossible scenario, which he fully understood was impossible, but he couldn't find a way out because he wasn't aware that Bavaria was the Latin name for what is called Bayern in Norwegian, and instead he'd mistaken it for Batavia, the Dutch colonial capital in the East Indies, and in this way he'd ended up in a state of complete bewilderment, confusing the Kingdom of Bavaria, with its mountains and King Ludwig's fairy-tale castle, with East Indian frigates on their way across the oceans of the world in the first half of the nineteenth century. With a simple intervention Singer was able to free the elderly gentleman interested in history from his books about the Dutch naval vessels and put into his hands what he was actually looking for, a biography of mad King Ludwig of Bavaria, a gesture that greatly touched the elderly gentleman. And from then on he too refused help from anyone other than Singer. Singer found this annoying. He found it uncomfortable to be subjected to their appreciative attention. Especially because it occurred in the presence of his colleagues. He couldn't find any way to avoid attention except by getting his colleagues to side with him and against the middle-aged woman and the elderly gentleman. He openly acknowledged to his colleagues that he found the attention of these book borrowers quite annoying, and that he was trying to avoid them. He made a point of trying to slip away whenever they arrived, retreating to some remote bookcase, preferably at the very back of the library, and subsequently playing a form of hide-and-seek with them until, at last, unseen by the middle-aged woman or the elderly gentleman, he was able to escape from the book-borrowing area and go into the office on the other side of the corridor. This prompted amused approval from his colleagues, and they started warning him. 'Karlsen just came in,' they might whisper, or 'Barbro Tuven is here,' so that he'd have time to retreat to safety, by either hiding in the office or going down to the basement where he always had some odd jobs to do, since that was where the library's true treasures were kept. In this way he demonstrated to his colleagues that he had a far better and much more relaxed relationship with them than with the book borrowers who had presumed they knew him and had attached a specific and praise-worthy quality to his dubious person.

Singer in Notodden. In the process of living his life, and still with certain expectations in his blood. For Singer, a library was layer upon layer of stored materials, dusty books. The library was a labyrinth, and the cataloguing system was a way of relating to the labyrinth. Being able to master it was a great pleasure for him. Dusty books, each in its place within the labyrinth, and whoever knew the code could simply go down to the basement and find the most precious of treasures. The fact that Singer had ultimately decided to become a librarian was partly because he was attracted to the notion of being a guardian of the books. That was how he liked to picture himself. And so his deepest, in fact his most satisfying, affiliation with the profession he'd chosen was of a metaphorical nature. Guardian of the books. He found traces of this notion in reality in the library's basement, where the discarded, dusty and forgotten books were stored. Unfashionable curiosities were stowed away and catalogued on shelf after shelf made of steel posts and sheets of aluminium.

Upstairs, in the circulation department and in the reading room, the metaphors and ideas of social democracy reigned. Yet Singer's strongest connection was to the dusty, yellowing books in the basement; in the real world upstairs it was one of his basic duties to keep the books dust-free. Books were not supposed to smell of dust, you should be able to open them, and fresh air should pour out from the pages. There was also the constant airing out of the Notodden library! At least once an hour a vigorous airing out would occur, which was good for both people and books; now and then it was Singer who did the airing out, although only rarely, because there were plenty of others who were happy to throw open the windows. He found himself in a strictly social-democratic institution, and it was in the clean air of the place that he spent his days, dutifully and self-effacingly tending to his job. The truth was that he was never the one who did the airing out, but since there were plenty of others who thought about doing it, and then actually did it, his colleagues assumed that he, as a matter of course, also did it. In a sense he was prevented from doing so because of his own metaphorical attachment to what it meant to be a librarian. But otherwise he fitted in beautifully with the social-democratic landscape in which he found himself. The interior was welcoming, practical and free of dust. Not a single dust mote could be found on the light-coloured wood, on the armrests of the chairs or on the chair seats, nor on the tabletops, which were made of the exact same light-coloured wood. The library was bursting with health. In a social-democratic way they had united reading with health. This was instantly noticeable when you entered this temple of reading. A thirst for knowledge is healthy. That it's necessary has been known for a long time, but it's also healthy. A good book is good for the heart! (thought Singer). Actually, they found themselves in a solarium. Books are sunshine for the mind. The circulation department and the reading room looked more like a tanning salon than a library, at least in the way the library had been preserved in Singer's metaphorical consciousness. Singer's task, he thought, was to provide a brain massage for the middle-aged women and elderly men. Plus direct the artificial sun of reading towards the younger generations who came to gather material for their so-called special projects, which seldom had anything particularly special about them, as far as Singer could tell. So, these were the sorts of thoughts that might occur to Singer, thoughts that he might also mention, in jest, to his colleagues. Because of this, his colleagues regarded him as a radical, and for this reason those who were radicals themselves thought they had found an ally in him. But they hadn't. He was just joking. Whenever the conversation turned to politics, he would quickly withdraw into himself. He didn't participate in the big social-democratic debate about how the library system should adapt to the new times. It was well known that social-democratic modernisation began in the library. First the Library was modernised, then Society, and finally the whole Party. As early as 1983, libraries in Norway were modernised. As early as 1983, when Singer arrived here, it was common practice at Notodden library to place smokers at the bottom of the waiting list for the most popular books. Tobacco and books do not go together, cigarette smoke damages book pages, and therefore it's preferable to loan popular books to non-smokers. Then the books will last longer, and more people will be able to enjoy them. Smoke settles not only in wallpaper, but also in the letters of the alphabet, creating a bad smell. In the Notodden library, they were all social democrats, including Singer. Yes, Singer pretended to be a social democrat, it was to his advantage to do so because then he was left in peace and could sink into himself when the others discussed politics.

Singer wasn't especially interested in politics, but he tried to hide this as best he could. He kept up with politics, but it was mostly a kind of game for him. He might vote in an election, but it was mostly so he could follow along on election night, happy when his party did well and disappointed when things went badly. He never watched campaign debates, only the TV news broadcasts on election night, and he would go to bed when the party leaders arrived at the studios of the Norwegian Broadcasting System to analyse the election. But before that moment, he was actually keenly focused on the election results, tensely following the reports from the smallest of towns and the most distant of counties, and keenly following the shifting prognoses regarding the distribution of parliamentary seats by party. He had never considered getting involved in politics, the thought had never even occurred to him, he wouldn't even have bothered to laugh if anyone had asked him whether he'd consider getting involved in a political issue. Politics did not concern him. He discussed politics with friends and acquaintances, and his colleagues as well, and they probably weren't aware of his indifference, because occasionally, in spite of everything, he might display a great involvement in the form of sarcastic remarks and counter-arguments. If his friends and acquaintances or colleagues had analysed his involvement, they would have noticed that they never heard Singer express admiration for any politician or for any political view. His involvement was expressed only in remarks about the banalities and phoniness of politicians. That was what provoked his opposition. He especially reacted whenever politicians were illogical, meaning when they supported or opposed an issue which they, if they had followed their basic premises or fundamental political views, could not have supported or opposed. Then Singer would laugh, and he was merciless in his mockery of such humbug. He could understand why politics were important, because they had to do with how society should be governed, and that was certainly important, because he had no doubt that society shapes all of us. But he couldn't see that it had anything to do with him. Societal consequences just didn't reach deep inside him. Yet even if they did, on rare occasions, he would still take an indifferent stance towards them.

Singer had a similar attitude towards history. He was fully aware that the human being is a historical creature, but he still couldn't see what that had to do with him, in any fundamental way. This may seem like a rather peculiar viewpoint, because, unlike politics, Singer was keenly interested in history. He'd always read a lot about history, and he'd also thought along historical lines whenever he tried to understand a certain phenomenon having to do with the human condition. But he wasn't able to put himself in a historical context. He couldn't see his own life as a historical example. The truth was that he was neither a societal nor a historical example. Or symptom, if you will. He was not a societal symptom, nor a historical symptom. And by that he meant not only that he reacted against being a societal subject, or a historical subject, but that he also had a great dislike of thinking of himself as such. He'd given this a lot of thought. And his conclusion was and would continue to be that even though it might seem quite self-contradictory when he denied the objective reality he attributed to everyone else, both in the present and in the past, he continued to hold on to this view because the subjective indifference with which he regarded the fact that he, from an objective viewpoint, was also a creature of society, was so all-encompassing that it robbed him of the joy of any objective attachment to anything outside himself. If object-ive realities existed, they were nevertheless not strong enough to touch him in any way.

Singer thrived in Notodden, and in his new job. He had what he called a calm, good life, possessed of a certain rhythm, meaning regularity. In September, Ingemann, who was his childhood pal and still his best friend, arrived for a visit. At the time Ingemann was employed by the Riksteatret, a Norwegian touring theatre company, with a role in a play, quite a funny comedy, that was making a guest appearance in Notodden. Before the performance,

Ingemann visited Singer, and after the performance they met at the Telemark Hotel, first in the restaurant, and then the two of them sat and talked in Ingemann's room until far into the night. Singer was a little worried about Ingemann, who had turned thirty-four, like Singer himself; he had to make do with minor roles instead of lead roles with the rather antiquated Riksteatret. He even tried to broach the subject with his friend, but Ingemann merely laughed and said that Singer didn't know the art of acting or the professional ethics of genuine actors. Half in jest, Ingemann donned his costume for the evening's performance, which he kept in a suitcase, and intoned Hamlet's famed monologue for his friend. Even though Singer felt a little uncomfortable, he did think this scene, meaning the scene of Singer and Ingemann in a hotel room in Notodden, was captivating. Afterwards he said his goodbyes to Ingemann, walked home, and climbed into his own bed in the basement studio apartment that he'd rented from an upper-level municipal official in Notodden.

Two days later it happened. Singer fell in love. In late September, after he'd been in Notodden for barely two months, on an evening just before closing time, two women came into the library and practically made fun of him. Perhaps not him personally, but they came in and were joking around, obviously aware of his presence as he stood behind the counter and accepted the books that were being returned and stamped the books that were being checked out. He knew one of the women from before; she was the lawyer's wife, the artisan who had monopolised an entire dinner party hosted by Singer's female colleague and her husband as they all suggested suitable premises for her ceramics workshop. He didn't know the other woman, but she was clearly friends with the lawyer's wife, and like the lawyer's wife, she was about thirty, or twenty-eight to be precise. Both women were in high spirits, laughing and talking to each other more loudly than was customary in a library, where, by long tradition, peace and quiet are supposed to reign because, in spite of the fact that the 1980s were far more cheerful and freer in social interactions than in previous decades of our century, this freer style had not slipped into our libraries – in this particular area, but not in other areas, the libraries have preserved a somewhat old-fashioned tone, which seems to be ineradicable. So the two women were breaking with the library's ineradicable old-fashionedness, which made them seem younger and freer, meaning bolder, than they actually were. Singer wondered whether they'd been drinking wine. They took a book from one of the bookcases that stood slightly to the right of the counter where Singer was standing, and they put their heads together to study the book, turning a few pages and pointing as they tittered like little girls. Singer happened to know full well what sort of books were in that bookcase; they were books about the local history of Telemark, a subject that, as far as Singer knew, provided no basis for that sort of merriment, in any way whatsoever. And so this girlish giggling surprised him, it made him a little uncomfortable. While they were carrying on in that manner, the lawyer's wife cast a glance at Singer, met his eye, and greeted him, without any sort of girlish gesture or giggling at that moment, giving a brief, friendly nod of her head. Singer returned the greeting. Then the two women put their heads together again and continued on as before, unaffected. After a while they apparently tired of the book and stuck it back on the shelf, then moved away, treading lightly as they headed further into the library, out of Singer's view, just as he was out of their view, yet Singer had to suppress an urge to rush immediately over to the bookcase they had left to see which book they had been looking at, enjoying themselves in such a girlish way. There were few book borrowers in the library that evening, only two or three people, and one of them came over to Singer carrying a whole stack of books, which Singer would now have to check out by stamping them as well as the man's library card. That's when he heard the two women making a racket behind his back. Behind him was a wall partition, and on the other side of the partition was a bookcase that held the library's books on psychology and the science of religion. Again he heard them making fun of something they'd found on the shelf, and now it wasn't girlish giggling but pure laughter, pure female laughter, the laughter of one of them sounding a little darker than the other's, which was thinner, like a jet of cool water.

A little later he saw them again as they passed him on their way to the library reading room, where the newspapers and magazines were on display. There they sat down, each of them taking a newspaper, he noticed, before they re-emerged and came over to the counter, where Singer was standing. The lawyer's wife spoke to him, saying how much she'd enjoyed the party, and then: 'So, this is where you work,' as if it was a big surprise to find a librarian working in a library. And maybe that thought occurred to her, because she suddenly began to laugh, and then the other woman laughed too, and even Singer found his eyes blinking merrily behind his glasses at the thought that it was certainly surprising to run into a librarian in a library.

'Well, we're not going to borrow any books,' she said then, throwing out her hands. 'We just dropped in because it's so cold outside. We're going to the cinema,' she told him. 'We had some wine in the cafe, and we finished long before the film is supposed to start, and if we'd had another glass, we would have been a little too tipsy, so that's why we came over here instead. And there you stood,' she said, giving him a merry look.

Singer gave her an equally merry look, and as he did so, he noticed the other woman staring at him. She stood a few steps behind the lawyer's wife, looking straight at him. An odd gaze. Direct, calm, and she didn't look down or away when she noticed that Singer saw that she was looking at him.

They left. There were still two people in the library. He announced that the library was about to close, and they brought their books over so he could stamp them.

Then he closed up and headed straight for the cinema, as he'd done so many times before, and slipped inside just before the film started. It was dark inside the cinema, but after his eyes had grown accustomed to the dark, he began looking around the cinema's sparsely occupied darkness to see where the two women were sitting. He wasn't able to find them, though he guessed where they were sitting, but when the lights came on, it turned out he'd guessed wrong. So he rushed out to the lobby, where he paused to look around as he tentatively peered at the other film-goers who streamed through the lobby and out to the street. That's when he saw them, and they immediately saw him.

'So you were going to the cinema, too?' said the lawyer's wife.

Normally Singer would have felt uncomfortable about such a remark, which in a sense might be interpreted as exposing all-too-obvious motives and hopes; Singer was, after all, a man well into his thirties, but this time he didn't care. He simply said yes, and a moment later he heard himself asking, quite affably, whether it might be the right time to drink the bottle of wine they had refrained from drinking before the film. So together they went over to a popular new restaurant, a little further away, called Bistro. That was how he made the acquaintance of Merete Sæthre, the friend of the lawyer's wife and a woman whom he had already begun to glorify, and for a long time would continue to do so.

Can a man like Singer fall in love? Yes, he can. But can he, under the influence of this love, move in with the one he adores in order to sleep with her and eat at her table, which they will now share? Yes, he can. That's what Singer did, though it was hardly advisable, and you might ask how it's possible for a man like Singer to get involved in this type of merciless intimacy, which requires that he stand there, naked, erect with a naked body, which concealed nothing, in front of a naked woman flaunting herself before him.

But that's what he did. Over the course of a couple of months he gave up the basement studio apartment that he was renting from the upper-level municipal official and moved in with Merete Sæthre, in a townhouse apartment in a residential neighbourhood on the same slope where the teachers college was located. What sort of clock was ticking inside the thirty-four-year-old librarian that caused him to do this? He moved right into that vulnerable and intimate sphere, with open eyes. Into an unfamiliar apartment with a number of qualities that were not his own. With a woman who, in this book up until now, has been described only as a friend of the lawyer's wife. To live with this unknown woman, as her husband. With this woman, who also happened to have a small child, two years old, from a previous relationship.

Because that was what she had. Two years earlier, Merete Sæthre had given birth to a daughter, Isabella. At the time she had just returned to her hometown after spending more than ten years away. She had trained as a ceramicist in Oslo and abroad, and she'd also worked as a ceramicist in artist collectives in Helsinki and Copenhagen, among other places. While on a study trip to Germany she'd got pregnant by a man who was practically a stranger. She'd met him in Karlsruhe, he was a Norwegian who happened to be travelling through on his way to Zurich. He refused to acknowledge Merete Sæthre's pregnancy and wanted nothing to do with the future world citizen. He went to live in Latin America, which was something he'd planned to do well before Merete Sæthre happened onto his path. And so Merete Sæthre moved back to Notodden and gave birth to her child there. For a brief time the mother and daughter lived with Merete's parents, both of them teachers, before she, with generous help from them, found this townhouse apartment, which was where Singer now moved in.

It must have been a drastic change in Singer's life! He had barely grown accustomed to his new life in Notodden before he ended up a man with a small family of three: husband, wife, and a little child! Did he know what he was getting into? Of course he knew what he was getting into, he went into it with open eyes. Dazzled by Merete Sæthre's very being, he moved towards her with pleasure and took his place as the husband in her little family. Not only did he glorify her, but she must have glorified Singer as well. In any case, during that autumn Singer was eagerly preoccupied with getting a driving licence, which he succeeded in doing shortly after the new year. Of course it was because of the strong urging and steady encouragement from Merete that he took this step, and even achieved his goal. Not for a moment had he ever considered getting a licence or driving a car; he'd managed quite well without it, but Merete had insisted, she claimed it was essential to have a driving licence if you were going to live in small Norwegian towns, there was no getting around it. Besides, she was looking forward to seeing him as a driver, sitting behind the wheel of a car; that was a sight she would enjoy, and she was looking forward to it. Singer behind the wheel. And so: with a little shrug, merrily delivered, Singer trooped over to see his new teacher, the driving instructor. So that Merete would be able to see Singer behind the wheel of her old Lada station wagon. And that was what she saw shortly after the new year, and after that Singer could often be seen driving around Notodden and the surrounding area. Behind the wheel of the old Lada station wagon. Next to him in the front seat was his wife. In the back seat, in an appropriately designed child's seat and securely strapped in was little Isabella. They went for Sunday drives, even when the roads were icy, up to Tuddal and to the foot of Mount Gaustatoppen to go skiing. Sitting behind the wheel, Singer focused his attention on the narrow, winding roads. This is Singer, a glorified version of the Singer we know.

At home they spent a lot of time in the kitchen. Merete Sæthre liked to cook, spending a lot of time turning the simplest and cheapest ingredients into the most delicious dishes. If this had generally been a happier, not to mention a more light-hearted, book, then at the very end of the book there should have been a section with Merete Sæthre's best recipes; unfortunately that's not going to happen, for reasons that we'll soon explain. During her stay in Helsinki, Merete had developed a taste for Russian cuisine, and during her stay in Copenhagen she became a lover of Italian cuisine. She loved pasta and liked to make her own. She made pasta with her own hands, from scratch, utilising only a very sharp knife. At first Singer sat and watched her; he sat on a chair and liked to watch the way she deliberately set to work with her elegant fingers at the kitchen table and kitchen counter. But eventually Merete insisted that he should help. They should cook together. That was how Singer became a wizard in the kitchen. He learned to make the most delicious dishes. He, too, could make pasta from scratch, with his own hands, and utilising only a very sharp knife. As a husband he also decided to buy his own pasta machine, imported from Italy and procured by Ingemann from a specialty shop, not in Oslo, but in Copenhagen. Merete loved the fact that he'd bought that pasta machine. They didn't use it often, but there it sat, and they could look at it sitting there, all shiny steel, as they kneaded the dough and cut it with the very sharp knife, and now they had two knives. Singer also learned to bake bread. Yes, he became a real wizard with bread dough, inventively using the rarest of herbs in the yeasty dough. You should have seen him at work in the kitchen, wearing a simple and rustic apron as he leaned over the roasting oven, opening the door and taking out the most delicious of breads that had risen perfectly. Or as he lifted the lid off a pot and breathed in the delightful aroma of a hearty meat soup that had simmered for hours, made from a marrowbone, or as he made one of the heavenly sauces in which he eventually took such pride. Or why not show him making pierogi?

Yet in scenes like these, as time passed, you might often find him alone in the kitchen, because even though he and Merete cooked together for parties or at weekends, it was left more and more to him to cook their meals on a daily basis. Not always, far from always, but quite often Singer would have the kitchen to himself as he stood there conjuring forth a minestrone soup, or a spaghetti Bolognese, or how about a carbonara today, which is not – as Singer might have been inclined to think six months earlier – an Italian word for burger patties, but instead an exquisitely ordinary spaghetti dish made with egg yolks, a dash of cream, and bacon. Sure, spaghetti carbonara today. And by the time Merete and little Isabella came home to the townhouse apartment early in the evening – after Merete had spent a long day in her ceramics workshop and then picked up her daughter from the home of her parents, who in turn had picked up the child at the day care centre, because her parents were so good about babysitting so that Merete could have some relief – the ingredients had already been mixed and the spaghetti was boiling.

And while Merete takes off her daughter's outdoor clothes and then she and Isabella both settle in, Singer sets the table, turns off the boiling water with the spaghetti, which he drops into a colander, where it rests for a couple of seconds before he pours it into a bowl. Then he mixes the ingredients with the spaghetti, and voilà, the dish is done and he sets it on the table, at the very instant that Merete and little Isabella come into the kitchen, hungry after a long day. They sit down at the table. Is anything missing? No, everything is there, even the parmesan cheese – genuine parmesan, bought in an exclusive cheese shop in Oslo, and personally delivered by Ingemann at Singer's request, in connection with his visit two weeks earlier. Singer can take off his rustic apron and sit down at the table, where Merete is already sitting with her little daughter, who is seated in a high chair. Truly, this is the real Singer. The man who finds himself incognito in Notodden.

There's no doubt about it. Under the influence of his love, Singer has undeniably changed. You would hardly recognise in him the man who was previously described in this book. If you see him now, he's a person who has been created and kept going by Merete Sæthre. Yes, you can safely say that the Singer we now see is a man created in the image that Merete Sæthre has of him. But we also need to add that this is Singer's own choice, freely taken. He is a man created by Merete Sæthre's image of him, but not without a certain delight from the adoring man himself.

In other words, he is a man who is reaching out towards the glorified figure of himself that a woman, who loves him, has created for him, a figure he wishes to inhabit fully and completely. He grabs the car key that is lying on the table in the hallway, steps outside, and goes over to the car. He opens the car door, gets in behind the wheel, sticks the key in the ignition, and honks impatiently for the others who are still inside the apartment. He's waiting for them, and now he sees them come running. This is the figure of Singer, glorified by Merete Sæthre. Her eyes are sparkling. How they sparkle as she sits down at the table, where a huge portion of spaghetti carbonara is steaming in the bowl on the table, and with a look of satisfaction Singer takes off his rustic apron and he too sits down.

Her eyes may continue to sparkle, but he can't join her in everything. He can't reach out towards her image of him in those areas where he can't see any glorification of himself, but on the contrary sees something else, something threatening, something calculating and false, although he can also see how tempting it might be, if it had been possible to inhabit this other figure fully and completely. He'd like to be a glorified figure of himself, created by her image of him, but he cannot, nor does he want to become her dream hero. If he'd been able to, he would have done it, because then he would have taken the last step, and that would have been marvellous in its lunacy, but he can't do it.

There were a number of things he couldn't do. He could teach himself to cook and even teach himself to enjoy cooking, for her sake, but she was not allowed to tamper with his wardrobe, or lack thereof. On that score he was adamant. She had to make do with a couple of shirts given as Christmas presents and/or birthday presents; on those occasions she was allowed free rein to find him something in accordance with her own sophisticated taste, go ahead, but there was no question of completely changing the way he dressed, and Merete did realise this, however reluctantly.

'I like you best the way you are,' she said, with a spark-ling smile, even though his appearance hardly appealed to Merete Sæthre's refined taste. But she sparkled never-theless. She loved someone who was her complete opposite. Of course. Singer understood this. He realised that he had to stand his ground if he wanted to keep his old wardrobe, and also refuse to get new glasses.

The woman in love had a hard time keeping her hands off his glasses. At first she wanted him to wear contact lenses.

'You do?' asked Singer. He actually felt offended and said as much.

'No,' she then replied. 'No, I don't. But new frames. New frames for your glasses, that would be exciting.'

But Singer made it clear that he didn't think new frames would be at all exciting. For his part, he didn't give a shit, he didn't care whether his glasses were round or rectangular, steel-framed or plastic; for that matter he could have easily allowed Merete Sæthre to find him completely new and up-to-date frames. That would have pleased Merete, although not in the long term. And so Singer clung steadfastly to what he had; his old appearance was perfectly fine, also in terms of what was in front of his eyes, and in that way he underscored that he had not been reborn, that he was his good old self in the midst of intoxicating love, no matter how much his life had otherwise been turned upside down. And he thought she liked this. Doing the opposite would have made her regard him with suspicion: who exactly is this man behind the guise that I've given him? Now she had no doubt that Singer was his good old self, although she had no idea what constituted that.

A rustic, masculine apron when I bake bread, that's fine, spaghetti carbonara, that's fine, and a refined shirt for my thirty-fifth birthday as well, but otherwise: my good old suit, in the same boring and anonymous style as before. Do you understand? Yes, Merete Sæthre understands. This is his personality, which makes her sparkle, even though she would have dressed him in something she regarded as truly handsome.

It was not the fancy or ultramodern that Merete Sæthre was looking for, but something individual, something distinctive, something more exciting or bold in colour choice. She didn't care whether the colours matched but she wanted them to be bold and refined. She would have liked to see him in bright red trousers, for example; Singer was sure of that, and he knew what that looked like because he'd seen men walking around wearing bright red trousers, and that wasn't for him. And honestly, it would have been impossible, it would have been a breach of something deep-seated in him, something he wasn't able to breach. All the things that he actually did for her were not a breach of something deep-seated in him, they didn't make him seem conspicuous in his own eyes. They were unused aspects of himself, somewhat unremarkable and little-noticed aspects, but he had no problem with summoning them forth and behaving in a way that would please her, as well as himself. The man behind the wheel. The bread baker. The man who prepares dinner for his little family. Dinner for his little, bogus family. These were new aspects of himself, which he regarded with a sense of disbelief and almost humorous astonishment whenever he thought about it. He was content with the life he was living, under the influence of love. Added to this was a secret satisfaction that was a blatant extension and realisation of Singer's purpose in moving to Notodden. Now, as the husband in a nuclear family of three, with the car in the parking space outside the townhouse, Singer was living in complete hiding in Notodden. If his purpose was to come here as an anonymous librarian in order to live incognito in Notodden, he had now, in this surprising manner, completely succeeded. No one could find him here, he had disappeared without a trace from whatever or whomever it was he had wished to disappear from, or so it seemed to him, evoking a deep sense of contentment in his heart.

Merete Sæthre was a ceramicist. It was in this capacity that she could be introduced in this book, as the friend of the lawyer's wife. Merete Sæthre and the lawyer's wife were such good friends in large part because they were both ceramicists, and they were now looking for premises in which it would be suitable for them to share a workshop. The lawyer's wife had recently arrived in Notodden and hadn't yet started up her work, while Merete Sæthre had been working here for more than a year, albeit in rather makeshift and miserable premises. Nevertheless, she immediately invited the lawyer's wife to share her kiln until they each found something better. After a while they realised that they got along so well that they could look for a workshop together. That was what they were now searching for. Together they trawled the town, and they never passed up an opportunity to tell everyone under the sun what they were looking for. Singer found it a constant source of amusement that the premises they had discussed so thoroughly on the evening he attended the dinner party, hosted by his colleague and her husband, were the premises where not only the lawyer's wife but also his future wife would be working. And on that evening Singer had associated nothing with his future wife, he didn't even know that the lawyer's wife, whom he'd only just met, had a female friend.

The lawyer's wife and Merete weren't the only ones searching; Singer (from his foothold in the library) and the lawyer, in particular, also helped them search. Many people will now claim that since Singer married Merete Sæthre, the author should provide the name of the lawyer's wife (Merete's best friend). There is much to be said for such a viewpoint, and it can now be revealed that the name of the lawyer's wife is Merete Holtan, and that her husband is the lawyer Nils Hartvigsen. Attorney Hartvigsen spent a great deal of time tracking down premises, potential sites that had attributes worth investigating, especially in terms of finances. And in the end, he happened upon an overgrown and moss-covered brick building in a declivity or hollow down by the Tinn River, close to the centre of town, close to the hill leading up to Villaveien, slightly to the right; Attorney Hartvigsen had turned and headed down yet another slope, at a slight angle, and there it was. The place was for sale for next to nothing, they practically received a finder's fee for having found it at all, but the renovation would be expensive, of course. So expensive that Attorney Hartvigsen was compelled to reveal that he was actually a carpenter. Not only that, he was actually a mason as well. Not to mention what a hard worker he would be. So what about Singer? With a modest expression Singer admitted that he might not be a carpenter, or a mason, but he was certain that he would be an excellent assistant and an exceptionally hard worker. So they set to work with volunteer labour. Attorney Hartvigsen sawed, and Singer held the wood, while the two women gathered all the creative people in Notodden – and in our day there were an extraordinary number of them – to do one thing or another. And Singer held, and Singer carried, and Singer did everything he was asked to do, moving among all these creative people who hammered, painted, sewed, carried and installed the electrical wiring, and he was reticently present the whole time, until the new ceramics workshop of Merete & Merete was ready, a point of pride for the old industrial town in the middle of the country.

The moss-covered, over-grown building had become a ceramics workshop, and also a gallery space and shop. Most of the square footage was allocated to the workshop, but both the gallery and the shop were important parts of the business, because it was here that other ceramicists besides Merete & Merete could stage exhibits, and not only ceramicists but also painters, sculptors, weavers, graphic artists and photographers, who in ever-increasing numbers settled in Notodden, and in the surrounding countryside. In other words, Merete Sæthre suddenly found herself holding a central position in a creative and artistic setting, as its prime mover, along with her friend and namesake. Ideas flourished, and new artists were constantly arriving. People appeared who called themselves installation artists, and in the late 1980s a pale young man showed up, calling himself a video artist and computer operator. The gallery space of Merete & Merete was immediately put at his disposal for a Christmas exhibition. Notodden had never seen anything like it, and people flocked to the premises to see the exhibition with their own eyes, doing so without making the usual derogatory remarks about art and artists in our day. And while the exhibition was still going on, Merete and

Merete were in the process of planning a performance exhibit, and for that occasion they were in the process of training three interested teachers from the Notodden Teachers College to become live works of art. But in between all this, they fired ceramic pieces in the kilns; the two women turned their pottery wheels, forming pots with practised hands and confident, tasteful looks, and out of the kilns emerged one ceramic piece after another, to be then carried over to the small shop from which they made their living.

But neither of the two women ever lost her grounding in reality. They never lost their sense of the basics, which means knowing that it's the human hand that draws. That is the basis for everything, and Merete Sæthre and Merete Holtan always took their sketch pads with them. They primarily drew objects. Pots, plates, glasses, which had to do with the profession they had chosen and from which they made their living. Yes, they were meticulous about drawing their own products after taking them from the kilns. Surely it's unnecessary to explain that these ceramic pieces became the basis for their drawings or sketches. But the two women also took their sketchpads along when they went out in nature, or were among other people. One of the places they liked to frequent best was the old stadium right near the teachers college, or the University College of South-East Norway in Notodden, as it would soon be named. Their walks to the stadium took the form of family outings. The lawyer, Nils Hartvigsen, and Singer would often accompany their wives, and little Isabella often went along too, and the lawyer's wife, Merete Holtan, was pregnant, so she carried her own little child in her womb. They would sit down on the old decaying wooden benches, and the women would get out their sketchpads. Then they would draw hammer throwers, because this stadium had been turned into Norway's only hammer-thrower stadium. Hammer throwing is a traditional Olympic sport that unfortunately struggles with big problems; such a major sport has to be characterised as dying, or at least threatened with extinction. This is because hammer-throwing competitions in our audience-friendly time are regarded as potentially dangerous because a single athlete once lost control of his hammer, which ended up in the stands. And as the name indicates: we're talking about a hammer. That's why the hammer-throwing competitions today take place before virtually empty stands, because they start and even finish before the actual athletics meet begins. And the hammer throwers perform in a cage, though it's open in the direction they throw, and this is done to underscore the safety of the spectators, even though they haven't yet arrived, but if anyone should be present *solely* to watch the hammer-throwing competition, then these cages in which the athletes perform are in use for their protection.

So hammer-throwing competitions did still exist, and it was still possible, for the most enthusiastic of the sport's supporters, to witness them in person, and it was still an Olympic sport, after all, it was even quite popular in Eastern

Europe. In Norway there was also a tradition for this sport, which demonstrates great strength, though it had now ended up so far down in the doldrums that it was doubtful it would ever become popular again. Because it's not enough to be allotted a few hours in advance of an athletics meet every once in a while, for an athlete to be dubbed in the traditional way, as in the past, the Norwegian national champion, and preferably also club champion of this noble sport – you also have to be able to train. You can't become an athlete in a sport without training in that selfsame sport. And it wasn't that easy. Because who wants a hammer thrower, even in a cage, to be given free rein inside a sports arena, which, in democratic fashion, is filled with other athletes, both children and youths, as well as active adults and old people who are running, jumping, and playing football, joyfully expressing themselves, while at any moment a hammer weighing seven kilos might strike them in the head? Nobody. Except in Notodden. Notodden had extended a welcoming hand to the devotees of this mightiest of all masculine field sports. The town had placed an entire stadium at their disposal. The only one in Norway. Notodden was itself in the doldrums at that time, as it tried to make the difficult transition from an industrial community to a more modern town; not because the modern was considered preferable but because it was a necessity, since the industry was going to be shut down, no matter what. Perhaps as a protest against this, but a protest that at the same time acknowledged this as a necessity, a hand was extended to

Norway's hammer throwers, inviting them to Notodden, where they could train and even hold their competitions. Not only that, they were offered admittance to the Notodden Teachers College, or the University College of South-East Norway in Notodden, in either the athletics department or the carpentry department. Actually, in any department at all, although it was thought that the athletics department, and especially the carpentry department, where students were trained as vocational teachers, would be particularly suited to hammer throwers. But in that respect the town was mistaken, because seven of the ten hammer throwers still left in Norway chose the computer and telecommunications department, while only two chose the carpentry department, and the tenth hammer thrower wanted to be an economist after his athletic career was over. Ten new people arrived in Notodden and would be paying for lodging, food, clothing, entertainment, etc., and along with that, salaries would be earned for teachers at the university college as well as the students themselves. Every little bit helps. A hammer-thrower milieu also enhances spending of a few kroner, while at the same time creating an image. An image of Notodden, in Notodden. At the Notodden hammer-thrower stadium, young men train in the most strenuous of all field sports, a traditional event from the twentieth century, involving muscles and technique. Long before Hydro's museum of industry rose from Hydro's shut-down factory area near the shores of Lake Heddal, ten muscular athletes were hard at work in the heights above the town, in their hammer-thrower cage. We remind you that the symbol on Notodden's coat of arms and seal is a spark. The sight of these hammer throwers attracted the interested gaze of the ceramicists at Merete & Merete. They couldn't get enough of this sight, which they tried to put down on paper. When they suspected that their interest in hammer throwers might be misunderstood and seem overzealous, they brought along their husbands, and occasionally Merete Sæthre's little daughter as well. The two women would sit on the lowest decaying bench with their sketchpads on their laps, trying to capture the hammer throwers' movements: the rotation, which was probably not easy to accomplish in reality and certainly not on paper. Often the two husbands would take seats behind them, sitting erect and staring at the hammer throwers as long as Isabella wasn't fussing, but that didn't last long. Then Singer, at least, would have to get up and try to entertain Merete's daughter in some way, often by taking her the long way round to the nearest ice-cream stand, and on those occasions Attorney Hartvigsen would frequently go with them, because by then the hammer throwers had noticed that the husbands were there too, that this was a family outing, and so it didn't really matter if they were gone for a while. At least it made no difference to the women, who barely noticed that the men had been gone by the time they came back. They were eagerly immersed in their creative endeavour, trying to capture the movements of the hammer throwers on paper. This was their hobby.

They studied the hammer throwers' feet firmly planted on the ground as they rotated the hammer; the hammer throwers' hip movements as they rotated their bodies; the elasticity of their muscles; the hammer throwers' outstretched hands as they released the hammer and it flew off. And the athletes bellowed. Because hammer throwers bellow as they release the rotating hammer, which flies through the air in an arc and lands in the gravel, making an ugly wound, about sixty metres away (if it's an acceptable training throw made by quite a good Norwegian hammer thrower). A terrible bellow issues from the throat of the man in the cage. A primal bellow, uttered in complete freedom, as part of a public sports event.

Gradually the two women became more and more preoccupied with drawing that bellow, that face, and the open mouth as the men emitted it. The massive rotation ending in that bellow, which fascinated them beyond measure. But no matter how much they tried, they never succeeded in capturing the bellow on paper, and after a while Singer began to suspect that it wasn't really all that important to them, that it was mostly an excuse for hearing and seeing what was going on. But he didn't voice his suspicion, nor did the lawyer, who no doubt harboured the same suspicion. In this way, the two men who accompanied their creative wives on their outings to Notodden's hammer-thrower stadium drew closer. Perhaps it would be an exaggeration to say that a friendship developed between them, it depends on how you define friendship, but there's reason to believe that Singer and Attorney Hartvigsen drew closer than many others who call themselves friends. The lawyer still had his head full of new plans, which he described to Singer as they sat behind their wives on the decaying wooden benches where the women were capturing the actions of the hammer throwers on paper. Or while they were walking or jogging through the area. Part of the new plans had to do with further developing the company of Merete & Merete, in which both men were involved, after all. Both men drove station wagons; the lawyer had a Volvo station wagon, while Singer had a Lada. Two types of cars with differing status, you might say, yet both were station wagons, for the simple reason that both vehicles were suited to the ceramic needs of their wives. They required station wagons to transport all the basic materials that with time would become ceramic vases, pots and mugs.

Things had gone well here in Notodden for Attorney Hartvigsen, a young lawyer with his own practice. He had bought an old mansion with a view of the narrow, peculiar and idyllic Tinnfoss Canal, a house that had previously been the residence of an operations manager for Tinnfoss Paper Factory, long since closed down. Singer and Merete Sæthre had no plans of their own to move out of their small apartment, or for that matter to replace their Lada station wagon, and perhaps that made Attorney Hartvigsen feel a little uncomfortable, because he was constantly pointing out that the former residence of the operations manager was mortgaged to the hilt. For that reason he might assume a rather worried expression whenever he and Singer met up at the Notodden hammer-thrower stadium. But that didn't prevent him from coming up with new plans. He was thinking that the entire old paper factory, with its rubble and debris, should become an arts centre in which the ceramics workshop of Merete & Merete, with its shop and gallery space, would be the crown jewel, so to speak, as he explained to Singer. Which meant the workshop needed to be moved over there, and as soon as possible, before anyone else had the same idea and took possession of the best buildings. Singer envisioned himself as the eternal assistant to the carpentry-skilled Hartvigsen, and he couldn't help uttering a little sigh.

Yes, one little sigh in an otherwise happy time. But this would soon change. Soon that little sigh over the fact that Singer was condemned to act as the eternal assistant for the energetic and carpentry-skilled lawyer would seem like a breath of fresh air from a happier past. Only a few months after the scene just described, we find Singer has lapsed into broodings from which he will never emerge. It happened gradually, but eventually it became all too noticeable. And it was something that the relationship between Singer and Merete Sæthre could not withstand. We have to be able to make this statement without discussing any question of guilt, or any other pertinent topics that the two of them had plenty of time to consider, though fortunately in private. Here we will make do with stating that after two years their relationship had noticeably deteriorated. Let's say that they had a two-year grace period, two years in a bubble state together. But as we've seen in Singer's case, being in this relationship was not without ulterior motives, peripheral motives that clung to this individual and caused him – under cover of finding himself in a relationship, in a marriage, actually – to live out entirely different schemes and assumptions than those that were exposed to the light of day. Most likely we have to assume that the same was true of Merete Sæthre. If pointing this out means initiating a discussion about the question of guilt and deception, then any relationship between two people, which is established on the open assumption that it's a love relationship, must be based on guilt and deception. For that reason, anyone who has ever loved has also felt subject to deception. Even when you glorify and are glorified in return, you still live an unglorified inner life lying in bed next to the one you love, who sleeps so soundly, often sweetly, as Singer would have claimed.

So who is she, this Merete Sæthre, who has lain down to sleep next to the brooding Singer night after night? We know very little about her, nor will we find out much more. She is not the main character in this novel; it's doubtful that she could have been the main character in any novel of a certain quality. It's possible that a number of female readers will protest, finding what little we've learned about her to reveal a courageous, strong and exciting woman. Someone even possessed of a sense of humour. That's no doubt true, but the fact that you're a strong, courageous and exciting woman with a sense of humour does not, unfortunately, make you a character in a novel. In this novel she is subordinate to Singer, playing the role of a minor character, and that's not Singer's choice but the choice of the author who is writing this book. For Singer, in real life, Merete Sæthre was at that time a main character, but that's not what she is in this fictionalised description of what – it has to be underscored – is the only extant description of Singer's life, and most likely also the only *possible* description. Because it has to be admitted that at this point in the story it may seem mysterious that Singer could be the main character in any novel at all, regardless of quality, but here it can be divulged that it's precisely this mysteriousness that is the topic of the novel, and attempts will be made to turn this into reality. As a way to turn it into reality, it might be tempting to defer to Merete Sæthre and ask her about her view of the change that occurred in Singer over the course of a couple of years. We have to assume that what she tells us are things that she has, on numerous occasions, also mentioned to Singer himself.

He has grown distant, Merete Sæthre would say. She has tried again and again to make contact with him, but he doesn't seem to respond. If she were asked about his brooding, she would say that it wasn't really that important, she accepts that he is a brooder by nature, even though at the time she met him she called it being thoughtful, which is what she believed him to be, but he actually was a brooder, and that's something quite different, because he gave off a

stifling air of despair, and it's no good living around something like that. Because even when he wasn't brooding but
spending time with her and Isabella, taking part in ordinary
daily activities, he behaved like a shadow to the extent that
he was even a shadow of himself. He was always friendly
and tried to do his best for them, but he did it with so little
joy. As if there were no longer any joy left inside him. She
pointed out, or would have pointed out, that he had lost
all cheerfulness in his soul. Because previously he did have
a cheerfulness in his soul, she noticed it the very first time
they met, in so many little things, the way he did something,
often with some reluctance, as if he didn't have complete
faith in what he was doing, but he did it all the same and
with a slight laugh, like the time she made him get his
driving licence. But now he did everything with a distant
air of routine. He does things, even with great thorough-
ness, and he often asks whether he should do such-and-such,
but he does them only for the sake of doing them. He
doesn't really care one way or the other whether he does
these things or not. And it's not that he would prefer to
do something else. Or that he would like to do nothing at
all. He wouldn't have preferred to refrain from doing what
he does, yet he takes no real interest in doing it, even
though he asks whether he should do it or not.

It seems likely that in this context Merete would start
talking about his averted face, even though it's no secret
that Singer always averted his face. When Merete, and
Isabella, came home for dinner one day when Singer had

worked the morning shift at the library and so was responsible for doing the cooking, they found him standing in the kitchen with an apron tied around his waist, stirring the pots, setting the table, then telling them that dinner was ready, and asking them in an amiable and interested manner how their day had gone, but then he didn't listen to what they said, he didn't listen! That's what we can imagine her exclaiming. And he stood there with his gaze averted as she, or Isabella, began to describe how their day had gone, and then she might have shouted: 'Look at me!' and then he would turn and look at her in astonishment, and in that instant she could see a trace of merriment in his eyes. But was it only a mask? Which he swiftly assumed before turning towards her? Perhaps because she had shouted so loudly, and in that way awakened him, so that he abruptly woke up and thought, good lord, I'd better put on my merry mask right now or else I'll be in trouble! Was that possibly how it was? Can we picture Merete Sæthre brooding when we bring up the matter of her husband's distant attitude? At the very least it would have made her suspicious about almost every word and gesture he might offer that wasn't connected to this distant attitude (these joyless routine movements), but to the other person, to the Singer she knew from before. For instance, one evening she picked him up at the library after he'd worked the afternoon shift, and in the car he said: 'Oh, I have such a craving for spaghetti with pesto. Could we make that for dinner?'

At first that made her so happy, not only because he'd suggested they make that particular dish for dinner, but also because he'd said he had a *craving* for it; but then she couldn't help scrutinising him every second as they made the spaghetti together, trying to see whether she could observe something that showed, or proved, that it was merely something he'd said because he thought it would please her, and it was not something he'd said because he really did have a craving for spaghetti with pesto, as well as a craving to cook the food together with her. And of course she ended up finding what she was looking for: a trace of distance, a reminder of his joyless interior, maybe for only a second but enough for her to think – no, for her to know – that this too was a mask that he'd assumed, a mask that for a moment had cracked to reveal the same distant attitude that ruled all of his steps, and eventually all of hers as well.

For Singer, not a single word of this would have come as a surprise. Although he hadn't heard such words expressed very clearly, he'd still heard enough to know the lie of the land, and even if he hadn't heard more than the shout 'Look at me!' he still would have known. Yet Singer was caught in his own labyrinth, from which he could not get out, nor did he want to get out, maybe *because* he couldn't get out. Occasionally, while he was working at the library and performing his routine duties, he might think: If only my whole life would be like this, it would be no big deal. But when he was at home or together with his little family in some other setting, then he would notice that his own preoccupied state was not to be borne, not by anyone. He had no wish to break up his marriage, he would prefer to stay in the marriage, which meant in spite of the fact that he'd made himself into a more or less unwelcome guest at home, he made no attempt to leave; on the contrary, he settled in more comfortably, even though he knew this was impossible. He wished he could banish the distance he felt and his state of mind, but even that was something he could not manage. In spite of all the brooding, what preoccupied him didn't even have to do with the big questions regarding the meaning of life, the nature of existence, or what we associate with the absolute otherness, and similar questions that we rightly categorise as profound questions requiring profound and preoccupied thoughts from all those silently asking themselves these questions; instead, the thoughts preoccupying him were completely random, for instance when he further speculated about something he'd read in a book or a newspaper; or he might sit preoccupied and brooding about a current political issue, eagerly discussing it with a fictitious opponent as he tried out his arguments; not to mention the times when something simply got his thoughts moving, randomly, without purpose or intent, like abstract figurations, obscure meaningless rhymes and word combinations; or some sudden destination might pop into his mind, a place to which he immediately travelled in his imagination. But in spite of what was unnecessary and futile in all of this, he couldn't manage to tear himself loose, even though he realised the possible consequences that this type of transparent and glass-like thought process, as he now and then called it, with great pain, might lead to, both for himself and for others. He couldn't manage to tear himself loose in order to 'Look at her!' as she wanted. At the library he checked in books and checked out others as he stamped them. He catalogued new books, inspected old ones, and took a keen interest in the new computer system, in which everything was to be entered, and which heralded a new era and completely new routines. But he could not 'Look at her!' Why not? Because he regarded it as an impossible demand and assumed she knew this. When she shouted like that, she was shouting for an obligatory action on his part, and when he therefore turned towards her, she knew that she was seeing a Singer who was looking at her in an obligatory way, and that his non-evasive amiability was a plea to be understood in a different manner. But if she didn't want to understand, and be understood, in this different manner, there was little he could do, and that too she knew, or so he assumed, in a glass-like way, which combined with other glass-like ways of relating to life, in this distant attitude of his, which was his way of living and withstanding that which he, perhaps all alone in the world, experienced as unbearable.

But then, eleven years ago, on a winter day in February just like today, a young hothead lost his patience in a long line of cars on the E-18 and made a foolhardy attempt to pass. But he didn't make it past the whole line before he saw oncoming traffic racing towards him, and since there was no space for him to slip into, he stomped on the brakes, but he braked so hard that he lost control of the car on the slippery road and swerved and crashed right into another car with a violent bang that made people in the nearby houses in that small but densely populated area rush to their windows. In that screeching bang of a crash the young hothead died, but he also took with him into death the driver of the other car, the thirty-two-year-old Merete Sæthre. And as a result, T Singer, at the age of thirty-nine, became a widower, and the six-and-a-half-year-old Isabella became motherless.

The funeral for Merete Sæthre was held in the chapel of Notodden cemetery, where she was afterward laid to rest, in a snowdrift. The chapel was packed during the funeral, and in the front pew sat Singer and his stepdaughter Isabella. Next to them, in the same pew, sat Merete's parents, her brother and her sister-in-law. Behind them sat other relatives, along with a large group of Merete's friends and acquaintances, some of whom were also Singer's friends and acquaintances, including Merete Holtan and Nils Hartvigsen. All of his colleagues from the library were also in attendance, and the library was closed. Ingemann was present; Singer saw him and spoke to him at the reception that followed at Villa Bergly.

This meaningless death seemed doubly meaningless to those closest to her because it had happened at a place where they thought it surprising for Merete Sæthre to have been at all. She lost her life in a car accident on the E-18, but at that moment she should have been on the E-11, somewhere between Drammen and Kongsberg, because she'd been in Oslo and was supposed to be on her way home to Notodden. The E-11 wasn't simply the fastest route, it was the only route, unless you intended to take a big detour, which is what Merete Sæthre had apparently decided to do. This irregularity made Merete's death even more incomprehensible than it would have been, and her parents in particular couldn't let this go; they kept circling around it again and again, even though Singer tried to console them by saying that Merete had previously taken a detour on the E-18 and then turned inland, either at Sande or Holmestrand. This might have been understandable on a summer day, but not on a grey winter day, when almost nothing was visible, everything seemed erased in a grey-white haze. But maybe that's what had attracted her, said Merete's brother, Per Christian. The silence of the winter landscape. Her parents accepted this, maybe they even thought it was a lovely notion, which for a moment muted their pain, even though Merete never got that far, she never entered the winter landscape between Sande and Kongsberg, or Holmestrand and Kongsberg; instead the thread of her life was abruptly severed in the middle of the E-18, near a densely populated area. And by the way, the area was Sande, and when Martin Sæthre, Merete's father, realised *that*, he was able to determine that the accident occurred right before Merete would have exited the E-18 and headed into the enticing, winter-silent landscape along the R-32. This made the randomness of Merete's death even more painful. A hundred metres, that was all that had separated her from life, a hundred metres that she could have covered by driving a little faster, a hundred metres that the hothead in the fatal vehicle could have delayed reaching by losing his patience some seconds later. Then Merete would have slipped onto the R-32 and enjoyed the silence of the grey-white landscape past Hoff and Hvittingfoss and from there along Numedalslågen, the river now frozen in the wintertime. In that sense, Merete's death might be experienced as triply meaningless and in truth a terrible injustice, struck down as she was by blind chance, though there had been three crystal-clear opportunities to avoid this happening.

In spite of the triple coincidences at play when it came to Merete's precious life, coincidences that kept circling through their minds, Merete's parents had to think about the future. Merete had left behind a young child, after all. What was to become of little Isabella? Singer said that she should live with him, as before. Merete's parents said that she was not his child, she was Merete's, and therefore he shouldn't think it was his duty to care for her. But Singer said that he did see it as his duty, and there was nothing to discuss. Isabella's grandparents on her father's side were also present at the funeral, but their son had relinquished any responsibility for Isabella, which meant that her paternal grandparents had no claim to assert. Merete's parents said that life had to go on, and that it might be best for the child if she lived with her own family; even though they were close to sixty, they were in good health and had plenty of energy for taking care of a grandchild. They didn't picture her growing up in their own house, since they might fall ill or in some other way become incapacitated in the coming years, but she could live with Merete's brother, Per Christian, and his wife; then she'd grow up among siblings – her cousins, a boy of eight and a girl of five – and still have close contact with her grandparents, who would daily welcome her into their home, because Per Christian Sæthre and his wife also lived in Notodden, and they were both teachers. So all the arrangements had been made for Isabella, and she would have a good upbringing, if he, Singer, after thinking things through, should find it difficult to take care of her. Even though he now said that he would take on this obligation, as Merete's husband, he didn't need to do so. But Singer repeated that Isabella should live with him; she was Merete's daughter, after all.

And this was something they couldn't deny. When Singer put it that way, they couldn't for a moment allow themselves to doubt that he was voicing the express wishes of the deceased. They couldn't allow themselves to imagine that their deceased daughter would not have wanted her husband to take care of her daughter and continue to provide her with the home that was hers. At the very least they could not allow themselves to doubt this, because Merete had never said anything to the contrary. Since Merete hadn't personally revealed to her parents what her marriage to Singer had been like, especially during the last year, they couldn't say anything, or even think anything different. And there was nothing to indicate that Merete had said anything; maybe they had sensed something, but she hadn't said anything to them. That much Singer could tell. Their desire to take in Isabella wasn't based on any knowledge that the relationship between Merete and Singer was on the verge of dissolving, but rather on a feeling that the death had decisively parted their daughter from Singer, who was left behind so painfully isolated, without any real connection to what Merete had left, meaning Isabella, their grandchild. Out of sheer instinct they now regarded Singer as a foreign body in relation to them, and especially in relation to their granddaughter, and they opposed seeing her grow up in the home of a man who was indifferent to her, even though she had lived with this man for more than four years now, but under the secure protection of her mother. Should this stranger, Singer, become her guardian, instead of allowing her to grow up under the natural protection of her own family? But out of consideration for the deceased, they didn't voice these kinds of thoughts. When their daughter's widower quietly and firmly made it clear that Isabella should live with him, as she had before, Berit Sæthre, Merete's mother, could do nothing except say through her tears: 'Before you were three, but now there are only the two of you left. You two must stick together.'

With these tearful words brimming with emotions impossible to comprehend, Isabella was left in Singer's charge. With these words Berit Sæthre tried, as did her husband, to draw closer to Singer in their sorrow. The man to whom they now handed over their granddaughter seemed to them deeply sincere because he was honouring their daughter's memory by taking on this obligation, which he certainly didn't need to take on. Berit Sæthre wept, and her husband wept, and Singer himself wept, embracing first Berit Sæthre and then Martin Sæthre. In the background stood Merete's brother, Per Christian, and his wife Henriette, and they too were deeply moved. There was a sincerity and a closeness among them that cannot be described in words, because it is impossible to comprehend this scene. Yet it was utterly necessary, because they were acting in the presence of death and the demands that death makes on those who have been affected, when it strikes close, involuntarily and mercilessly. Death makes us social animals. Never are we more animal-like; we are swallowed up – skin and all – by what is instinctual. We are encoded, just like a dog or a cat is encoded, and just as much trapped by our instincts as they are, and yet it's our behaviour governed by this code that separates us most decisively from animals, because this code is sewn into the human consciousness, which now, at our most weighty and least comprehensible moment, automatically governs our steps and determines our behaviour within a disciplined and socially acceptable context. Singer, from the moment he received word of the death, had acted automatically with regard to the great sorrow he was now forced to bear. He had behaved appropriately, without having to think about it. He had automatically said the right words and done the right things. He had behaved with a subdued and frozen grief, which occasionally, as in this scene, might be transformed into a violent outpouring of tears as he received other people's sincerity and their fumbling attempts to draw close. He was completely subordinated to this social, instinctual discipline. He was the carrier of a human code, which demanded to be manifested in precisely the way he manifested it, by means of exclusively voicing formal phrases and expressing conventional emotions in the most banal and sentimental manner, because death will not tolerate anything else. Plain and simple. Death will not tolerate anything else. It demands that we surrender, without inhibition, to our helplessness. Singer knew this; in fact, he knew it so well that every time during this period when he was tempted to observe himself from the outside and watch from a distance to see how he was behaving (which was something that had always come naturally to Singer), he regarded this opportunity for self-observation with horror, and literally chased it away, fully aware that if he'd allowed the vision of himself to slip inside, into his consciousness, if only for a brief moment, he would have been committing a mortal sin.

This scene took place in Singer's home, in the townhouse apartment, after the funeral and reception. Berit and Martin Sæthre, along with their son Per Christian and his wife, had gone home with Singer so they could all be together, alone, after the official programme was over. Closeness in grief. The others were finding it difficult to tear themselves away and leave Singer alone with Isabella. They were reluctant to let the thirty-nine-year-old widower be alone with his grief on the day of the funeral, wanting instead to stay and share it with him, even until the next day dawned. Berit and Martin Sæthre suggested that they stay overnight, but Singer said that wasn't necessary. They weren't sure whether this was merely politeness on his part and said that it might be difficult to have responsibility for Isabella on this particular night when he was so shattered by so many other thoughts. But Singer said he would manage, it was just as well to look to the future at once, it might even make things easier to do so. Yes, perhaps it would make things easier to do so, repeated Berit Sæthre, and again tears flooded down the heavy make-up on her rough cheeks. And again Singer embraced her, and again he felt tears streaming down his own cheeks. And in that manner they said goodbye. And Singer was left alone with Isabella. He took off his dark suit and changed into ordinary clothes. His stepdaughter was sitting on the floor, next to the table in the living room, next to one of the table legs, wearing beige tights and playing with a rag doll. Occasionally she would get up to find something and twirl around, and then he saw that her tights were sagging, having slipped down and formed baggy rolls around her ankles, and he went over to her and picked her up as he pulled her tights back into place. Then she sat down on the floor again, next to the table leg, and resumed playing. After a while Singer happened to think of something, and he glanced at his watch, but it was too late for any children's programmes on TV, it was past time for that. For a moment he thought he ought to say, oh, looks like we forgot to watch the kids' show on TV, but he thought it wouldn't be appropriate to say something like that, and since Isabella hadn't said anything about the kids' show on TV, he thought it would be best not to mention it at all. Instead, he made dinner, but Isabella had eaten so much all day that she wasn't hungry. Instead she was allowed to play a little longer until Singer said it was bedtime. He went with her up to her room, and when she was under the covers, he read to her for a while. Then he said good night and went back downstairs, but he left the door to her room ajar so she'd be able to call to him. And she did several times, and each time Singer went up to see to her until she fell asleep.

Singer sat alone in his own living room, surrounded by the familiar objects that had been his daily setting, his private home, for more than four years now. He was exhausted but tremendously tense. He sensed a great uneasiness, and he didn't dare suffer it alone. He had to talk to somebody. So he called Ingemann at the Telemark Hotel. Ingemann had told Singer during the reception that he'd booked a room at the Telemark Hotel in case Singer felt a need to talk to him. But when Singer called the hotel, he was told that Ingemann had checked out because something had come up and he needed to return to Oslo that very evening. Ingemann was no longer employed by the Riksteatret but had started as a freelancer and often did work for NRK, the Norwegian Broadcasting System, mostly for radio but also sometimes for TV, and Singer assumed that it was in this connection that he'd been forced to go back to Oslo tonight.

Singer hung up the phone. He was pensive. Not because Ingemann had left but because he realised when he heard that Ingemann was gone, it wasn't Ingemann he wanted to talk to. Actually, it *was* Ingemann he wanted to talk to, but that was because he didn't dare talk to the people he should be talking to. Ingemann couldn't have done anything but listen to him and now and then offer encouraging remarks; that would have been reassuring, but that was not the reason that he now needed to talk to someone. He should have talked to Nils Hartvigsen, the lawyer. Not because he was a lawyer, but because he was married to Merete's best friend. He was the person he should have talked to. He would ask him whether he knew that he and Merete were going to get a divorce, whether Merete had told them, or told her. Of course she would have mentioned it to her best friend, in some form or other, as a fact or as a possibility. So he needed to call Nils Hartvigsen, but he couldn't bring himself to do it.

For that reason the same thing happened as so often happened with Singer. He got lost in his own thoughts. In his thoughts he invited Nils Hartvigsen to come over, and then seated him in a chair right there, next to his own armchair, while he himself got up to pace back and forth in the rather cramped living room of the townhouse apartment as he talked to Nils Hartvigsen, who in his imagination was sitting in a chair, occasionally offering some remark, and – this was something Singer emphasised – Nils Hartvigsen was able to avoid putting on that sympathetic expression, displaying great solicitude, speaking in that subdued tone of voice people assume when talking to a newly widowed man, and instead he was as upset as Singer was, although hopefully for different reasons, because otherwise there was no use in him sitting there, in Singer's imagination, to listen to what Singer was saying.

'Did you hear that Merete and I were going to get a divorce?' Singer began. No, that wasn't how he'd begin, because he knew that Nils Hartvigsen knew, and only in reality could Hartvigsen have denied it, but he wasn't actually here, merely his imaginary figure was present. And the imaginary Nils Hartvigsen couldn't offer him any reply to this question, either in the affirmative, as Singer believed he would, or in the negative, which is what he hoped. He couldn't talk to the imaginary Nils Hartvigsen, and so he sent him away. Instead he happened to think of the husband of his colleague who had hosted the dinner party well over four years ago, and whom he'd often met since then, and whom he liked very much. He thought he should call him and ask him to come over for a visit, because he needed someone to talk to. He was certain that he would come over immediately, considering the circumstances, but if he did come over, and Singer began talking about what he wanted to talk about, then he was afraid that the husband of his colleague would feel uncomfortable, because even though Singer liked him very much and could imagine telling him just about anything, they weren't exactly friends, and what Singer wanted to confide in him were things that it was difficult to confide in anyone other than your closest friends; and so the husband of Singer's colleague would feel uncomfortable because Singer regarded him as such a close friend, which was not how he'd ever thought of Singer. So Singer decided not to call him but instead invited him over as an imaginary friend. What prevented him from actually calling him was the fact that he was not a friend in reality, but he could just as well invite him over in the capacity of an imaginary friend. And that's what he did. The man came over, sat down in the armchair on the other side of the coffee table, and Singer, who would soon get up to pace back and forth in the cramped living room of the townhouse apartment, got right to the point and said:

'Do you know that Merete and I were going to get a divorce? And then this happened. If this hadn't happened, we would have been living apart very soon, and continuing our lives separately, Merete and her daughter here in Notodden, and me somewhere else. Now Merete's dead, and I'll go on living here together with her daughter, Isabella, as her stepfather. What do you say to that?'

The other man, the husband of his colleague, didn't answer. He paused to think for a long moment before replying.

'How awful, Singer,' he said.

'That Merete's dead? Or that we were going to get a divorce?'

'Both,' said the other man. 'Both. I have to say it's awful. You must be feeling just awful right now.'

'Yes,' replied Singer, 'I feel awful. But why, why? Those two things have no connection. The fact that Merete and I were going to get a divorce, that's something we'd both agreed on, and it may be sad, in a way, but it's not really awful, is it? We had agreed to get a divorce. Things just couldn't go on any longer between Merete and me. So why do you call that awful? Okay, I'll tell you why, it's because she's dead. But the fact that we were going to get a divorce and the fact that she's dead have nothing to do with each other. The fact that she's dead doesn't make the fact that we were going to get a divorce awful. It's nothing to get upset about. But you're still upset, aren't you?'

'Yes, I'm upset,' said the other man. 'I have to admit it.'

'But they have nothing to do with each other. Don't you see, it's pure coincidence.'

'Yes, I know that,' said the other man, 'but I still feel shaken. I feel so sorry for you.'

'When you heard that Merete was dead, did you also think it was awful and did you feel sorry for me?'

'Yes, but in a different way. I would have said that I felt such sympathy for you. But not sorry for you, I think that's how it is, I have to admit,' said the other man.

'Admit. Feel sorry,' said Singer pensively.

He got up from the armchair and began pacing back and forth as he talked to the imaginary man sitting in the other armchair.

'But that's wrong. Surely you must realise that. You know there's no reason to feel sorry for me. We both wanted to get a divorce, it was decided. Then Merete was killed in a car accident. I'm completely blameless. It was the other driver who is the guilty party. He's the one you should feel sorry for, if you can. I am not to blame.

'How strange that I even have to say that,' Singer went on. 'To you sitting here, I have to say that I am not to blame.'

'I didn't say that you're guilty,' replied the other man. 'You're the one talking about such notions. I simply said that now that I've heard you were going to get a divorce, her death seems even more awful.'

'Why? Oh, don't say it, I can say it myself. Because of the guilt I'll have to live with, right? But I have no reason to feel guilty.'

'No, you have no reason to feel guilty,' sighed the other man. 'That's not what I mean. It's the fact that you're robbed of the grief that I assumed you felt, and that I had such sympathy for, until I heard that you were going to get a divorce because the two of you could no longer live together. Listen here, what I mean to say is, it was awful to hear that you had decided to get a divorce, and then Merete gets killed right afterwards, those are two sad things. Even though they can't be compared, of course,' he added, possibly in an attempt to offer solace.

Singer sat back down. He sat there for a long time, staring straight ahead.

'Death is too shitty,' Singer said. 'It's impossible to comprehend. Not only intellectually but also emotionally. It makes us such liars. Everything we say, all the facts, become distasteful when we're confronted with death. If I told you what I'm feeling now, you'd be sick to your stomach. I've only told you a tiny piece, given you a small, precise bit of information, meaning that several weeks before Merete was killed, we had decided to get a divorce. That the man who received word of her death, in his capacity as the one closest to her in this life, was in reality, by virtue of a mutual decision, a man who would ostensibly no longer be in her life. And it makes you uncomfortable to hear that, this simple, precise bit of information. I should have kept it to myself. Yes, I know that, but I had to confide in somebody. Confide? Why do I say confide? There's nothing to confide. And yet I'm confiding in you. I shouldn't have done that. Because when I do that, something despicable emerges. Not because Merete and I were going to get a divorce. But because I'm saying it now, after Merete is dead, and before we got divorced.'

'These are difficult matters you're dealing with,' said the other man, the husband of Singer's colleague. 'Wouldn't it be best to wait a while before thinking about them? Allow yourself a little distance first?'

'What you're accusing me of is that I didn't love her. You're accusing me of no longer feeling any love at seeing her. That's why you feel sorry for me. And it's true, I didn't feel any love at seeing her anymore. But I still feel grief.'

'I know you feel grief,' said the other man. 'Yes, I can see that; you're sitting here completely heartbroken with grief, that's why you're talking the way you are.'

'Yes, but I don't feel any personal grief. My grief is general, if you can understand what I mean. When I tell you about my grief, are you willing to listen?' The imaginary man nodded. And Singer went on.

'I picture Merete's face in front of me, at the moment of death. Her expression of disbelief as she realises what is about to happen. It's not hard to imagine, it's almost impossible not to imagine it. A person has only a few expressions to display to others, after all. Just think about how you form an image of another person, there are maybe three or four typical expressions, no more. It's the other person's distinctive character, captured in an image. I knew all of Merete's expressions, and I had stopped loving them. Truth be told, her expressions no longer told me anything. But the look of disbelief on her face, her expression at that moment when it happened – that stays with me. And it makes me feel grief. General grief. Because that face, that expression – I can't reconcile myself to that, not even now. They contain a nothingness there's no use trying to remove. For me. The wear and tear between us cannot be erased. Merete's expression from that first period when we fell in love, for example, I can't re-create it, and her disbelief from that time, the same that I'm now picturing, at the moment of death, no, I can't re-create it. The wear and tear is what I see, the irritation, it's there, even in the horror. Do you understand?'

'No,' said the other man. 'No, I don't think I can follow you on that path. But I'm listening.'

'You will understand me if you try,' said Singer.

'In that case, I can't try,' said the other man. 'But I'm here, and I'm listening.'

'So I don't feel any personal grief,' Singer went on, after another pause. 'But Merete's face as she dies, as the thread of life is brutally severed, and she knows it. I can imagine that, and I feel a stab of pain. Confronted with death, I'm so helpless, and in a completely shattered way. What in the world is a human being when confronted with death? What does this illogical state that I'm in actually mean? That I feel a pang of guilty conscience because my wife is dead, and we were going to get a divorce? There's no connection, and yet you can hear the way I'm talking, maybe you can even hear how you reply. Both things are the result of a bad decision. But it's not something we can regard sensibly. It's there, the bad decision. We, or at least I, have no problem accepting it, but it's there, and we have to accept it. Does this have anything to do with the human condition? Even though we see the bad decision, that doesn't stop its effect. It exists. Confronted with death, we are shaken to our core by something we know is a bad decision, a stupidity of elementary logic. Because that is what it is. It's stupid, it's too stupid. And yet it shakes me, and you, I can see that, you're just as scared as I am by what I'm saying. Is this the equation? In that case, I don't understand it. Perhaps it's wrong. I'm not to blame. Do you hear me? I am not to blame.'

'Yes, I hear you,' said the other man, the imaginary man. 'And I didn't say that you're to blame. You're the one who is blaming yourself.'

'But you're still shaken?'

'Yes,' said the other man, 'I am.'

'Why?' asked Singer. 'Tell me now in your own words why you feel so shaken about what I'm saying. It would be of great importance for me to know.'

Silence descended. Both of them sat in silence, lost in their own thoughts, almost as if they'd dozed off, because by now it was very late at night. When Singer looked up and glanced over at the other man, he saw that he was no longer there. He was gone. Singer was horrified.

'Come back!' he shouted. 'I have a lot more to tell you. I've hardly even begun.'

Fortunately, the other man came back and calmly sat down in the armchair again.

'Go on,' he said. 'I'm listening.'

'Isabella will live with me,' said Singer. 'What do you say to that?'

'That's nice of you,' said the other man, 'because you didn't have to do that. She's not yours, after all.'

'Are you being ironic?' asked Singer warily.

'No,' said the other man, 'although it's an irony of fate that you are now going to take care of Isabella. If Merete had lived, you would never have had to see her again.'

'What do you mean by that?' asked Singer.

'Nothing,' replied the other man. 'I'm just pointing out an ironic fact.'

'Yes, it's strange,' said Singer. 'Because, as you say, I didn't have to do this. On the contrary, you might even say. Merete's family would have been glad to take her in, they've even said as much.'

'Do they know?' asked the other man.

'Know what?'

'That you and Merete were going to get a divorce.'

'No,' said Singer. 'I couldn't tell them. Not now. And I don't think Merete has – I mean, had – told them about it either. They know nothing about it.'

'So they're living under a happy illusion that everything was fine between their deceased daughter and her husband, now a widower?'

'Yes.'

'Isn't that rather difficult for you to deal with?'

'Not really,' replied Singer. 'It's something that I have the least difficulty dealing with.'

'Ah, so that's how it is. Even though you know that if they'd known about it, they wouldn't have let you take Isabella, at least not without a protest. Her parents would have found it unacceptable for you to keep the child; you must realise that.'

'Yes, I realise that. But I couldn't tell them. It was too late to say anything. Since Merete never managed to tell them, for one reason or another, I can't tell them now that I cared so little for their deceased daughter that I was thinking of moving out. Or, vice versa, that she cared so little for me that she was just waiting for me to move out of her home. Well, maybe the latter was something they could have tolerated hearing,' Singer added with a little smile. 'But I thought it would be too difficult to say that.'

'You thought it would be too difficult to say that? Meaning you didn't want to hurt them?'

'Well, as I said, if I'd told them, truthfully, that Merete was just waiting for me to move out, then it wouldn't have been as hurtful. No doubt it would have come as a shock to them, but they would have felt sympathy for me, and I could have simply left. But it was terribly difficult for me to say those specific words. You have to believe me, it may sound banal, but that's how it was. I couldn't bring myself to tell them. And so I'm left with Isabella.'

'You're left with Isabella?' exclaimed the other man. 'That wasn't necessary. It wasn't even right for you to keep her. When they said they wanted Isabella to grow up within their family, to live with her uncle, you could have simply nodded and said that was probably for the best. You could have told them that you didn't feel capable of taking care of her, or something like that, and you were happy to leave Isabella in such safe hands.'

Singer nodded.

'Yes,' he said. 'You're probably right. But I didn't do that. And why didn't I? I don't know. That's what I'm trying to understand. Actually, I do understand, but I can't say it.'

'You can't say it?'

'No, I know why, but I can't find the right words. What I know, and can say, is that within a few weeks I was supposed to have moved out of this apartment. For good. The thought of that doesn't make me feel bad. It didn't make me happy, but I accepted it. I would have done it because I wanted to start a new life, approaching the age of forty as I am. I was actually looking forward to it. When I divorced Merete, her daughter Isabella would also disappear from my life. I wouldn't have had anything more to do with her. I was fully prepared for that, she had never meant anything special to me. When I was out of her life, she would quickly have forgotten me; maybe she'd have a vague childhood memory of me, so hazy that she could hardly place it other than as a shadowy image in her subconscious, which her mother could have no doubt told her was the man she'd been married to for a brief time in the eighties. And I had nothing against this, ending up as a hazy shadow in the world of her imagination, almost as nothing; I actually liked the idea. Oh, just think if Merete hadn't died right now but three months later instead, then we would have been divorced, and I'd be living in a different town, maybe Fredrikstad, because I have a job advert from the Fredrikstad library lying over there on the desk, but I didn't have time to send in an application. That would have cancelled out everything. Then I could have shown up at the funeral, discreetly sitting down in one of the middle pews and leaving right afterwards, without going to the reception, because it would have been enough for me to attend the funeral. "Singer was there too," they would have said. "Yes, Singer showed up, he came to offer his condolences, he seemed very moved." And then I could have gone back to Fredrikstad and my new life.'

'You can do that now,' said the other man. 'You can go to the parents of your deceased wife, let's say in a week or two, and tell them that, after further consideration, you've decided you can't take on the responsibility for Isabella after all. That won't be hard to explain, and Merete's parents will be very happy. Then everything will be rectified, in line with the real circumstances.'

'Yes,' said Singer. 'I could do that. That's probably the right thing to do. I realise that. I'd be released from constantly pointing out that I'm not to blame and that there's no connection between the fact that Merete and I were going to get a divorce and the fact that Merete died in a car accident. The divorce meant that I would have had nothing more to do with Merete and her daughter. The car accident means that Merete died, and is gone, and her daughter grows up within her mother's family, which is only natural, and that I have nothing more to do with her. You're right. I'm free, I can shake off this grief and move on. But I don't want to do that.'

'Why not?'

'As I said: I don't know.'

'No, that's not as you said. When you said that earlier, it was because you couldn't bring yourself to tell Merete's parents that you and Merete were actually going to get a divorce. You won't have to tell them. You don't have to tell them anything, except that you think Isabella, in spite of everything, belongs with her natural family and not with you, since you doubt you'd be able to give her the care that a young child needs.'

'I still don't know. Maybe I can't bear the thought of simply going my own way. Leaving all this. I could do it, in fact I ought to do it, but there's something telling me I shouldn't.'

'And what's that?'

'I don't know. But I'm scared. Scared to do what I'm saying I ought to do.'

'What I'm saying is simply that it's the decent thing to do. Shall I repeat that? It's the decent thing to do. I'm not begging you to do this, no, I'm merely suggesting that you do it. Do the decent thing. What you want to do is not the decent thing. Do you understand?'

'Yes.'

'And what's your answer?'

'That things will stay the way we decided.'

'But don't you understand? Your wish to take care of Isabella isn't valid. Your wish plays no role, because the truth is that it's now known that the deceased wanted you to leave, and that's what is so hair-raising, not only that you won't leave and will stay here, but that you will also let her daughter live with you, as if nothing had happened. You are deriding her memory. And that is now known. You should know that.'

Singer slumped, turning pale at the words the other man had spoken.

'I had a feeling you would say that,' he replied. 'But it's late at night, and I have to try and get some sleep before Isabella wakes up. So I have to ask you to leave. Go, please go, there's nothing more for you to say. I have my duty, and you have yours. You've said your piece, I've listened to you, and I thank you for it. But now I need to sleep, because, as I said, I've taken on an obligation that requires my attention.'

The other man got up. He stood there in the middle of the cramped living room, pompous or formidable, there was something dismissive about him that underscored the formidable or pompous nature of his appearance.

'It's a terrible burden you've taken on,' said the other man, 'and one day you'll come to regret it, and then you'll know there's nothing to be done about it. Nothing. If only you cared about the young girl,' he exclaimed as he vanished into thin air, being the imaginary person he was.

Silence. Singer sat slumped in his armchair. Suddenly he gave a start, as if he'd abruptly awakened after sitting there, dozing off, and he shook his head in bewilderment. He glanced over at the armchair, which was empty. He was alone, alone with himself, you might say.

He thought he should go upstairs and go to bed. It was three in the morning, after all, and he needed to sleep. But he couldn't manage to tear himself away from the armchair; he sat there thinking about what the other man had said. That was quite a salvo, thought Singer. Good heavens, and he was supposedly a man in whom I have a great deal of trust and would actually like to have as my friend, he thought, shaking his head in resignation. It really wasn't all that unexpected, logically enough, I should add, thought Singer. But I have to admit that for a moment I was tempted by his suggestion. In a way it would solve everything. Everything would work out if I followed his suggestion. But he could have left out that part about me not caring about the girl. I didn't say that, I said that she didn't mean so much to me that I couldn't accept having her disappear from my life, as a natural consequence of the divorce, and so it wouldn't lead to any sort of irremediable sorrow, that's what I said, but that doesn't mean I don't care about her. There's a small but crucial difference. Yes, there's a difference, damn it! thought Singer, almost upset. Not care about her! In spite of everything, I'll be responsible for her for the next twelve years. I'll be past fifty by the time I can think about myself once again. That's clear. He could have thought about that before he started flinging out accusations based on a poor understanding of what I actually said, thought Singer.

And that was how the night passed. Singer stayed up, slumped in his armchair, thinking over and over about his new situation and how he'd ended up in it, of his own peculiar free will. In a confrontation with death. Someone else's death. Someone who had parted from him well in advance.

February nights are long and dark, although not nearly as long and dark as December and January nights; in mid-February the light both day and night is like the light at the end of October, and actually a little brighter because October usually has no snow, but in February the night-time darkness is illuminated and reflected off the white, cold, let's even say the caved-in and greyish snow; but it's still a long time before there's daylight when you wake up, this was something to which Singer could attest with his own eyes as he sat there. At seven in the morning he could begin to make out that it was dawn and not dark night. And it was also time for him to hear Isabella stirring upstairs and then running barefoot into the bedroom where his cold bed stood. There she'd find an empty bed, with the coverlet neatly spread on top, as if the person who had slept there was already up; or the bed might also arouse suspicion that it had been abandoned by the person who hadn't slept there at all. And so, making a lot of noise (so Isabella would hear him), Singer went upstairs and called to her even before he'd made it all the way to the top step; yes, he called to her when he was slightly past the midway point on the stairs, so that when she heard his voice, or preferably his heavy footsteps, and had turned round to run barefoot towards the sound, she would see him as he climbed the last step and came towards her.

And so began the life of the widower, soon to be forty, as the sole provider and parent of the six-and-a-half-year-old girl, Isabella, who was not his, but rather the daughter of his deceased wife. He continued to live in the townhouse apartment up on the slope, not far from the teachers college, or the University College of South-East Norway in Notodden, as it would soon be called, and not far from Isabella's grandparents. Isabella understood and didn't understand that her mother was dead, and life went on, as they say, in its usual, daily grind, even though six months after the incomprehensible car accident the girl might come rushing into the bedroom and be surprised that her mother wasn't there, just for a moment, before she again remembered that her mother was gone for good; but after a while this too stopped, at least from the end of August when she started her first year at the school. She also spent a lot of time at the home of her grandparents, as she'd always done; Singer and the Sæthres took turns picking her up from day care, and she often stayed the night with her grandparents, so you might say that Singer and the Sæthres also took turns delivering her to the day-care centre, even though it was most often Singer who drove her there, usually on his way to his job at the library.

Initially Singer was the object of a great deal of attention from his colleagues, and also from Merete's artist friends. Every now and then both Singer and his stepdaughter would be invited to dinner in the middle of the week by his colleagues and others, most often those who had children of their own and preferably children who were more or less the same age as Isabella. Then they would sit there, Singer and his little stepdaughter, in the kitchen of an unfamiliar home, and eat meatballs with mushy peas and creamed cauliflower and drink water or juice, surrounded by the family who lived there, in the midst of their friendliness.

Singer's days were busy, filled with work, housework and caring for a seven-year-old girl, cooking, laundry and everything else that makes up the everyday life of a single dad. This meant that life's routines crept in and overtook and forced into the background the shocking event that had occurred in February, and the subsequent rituals of grief which then had to be endured. At the library he soon resumed his old place, and his colleagues and the book borrowers got used to seeing him again in his usual role as a dutiful and obliging librarian, and not as a forty-year-old man who had been struck and felled by misfortune. In a way there is reason to believe that the friendly reserve that characterised Singer's conduct also seemed suitable or appropriate for his new status as a widower and parent to a seven-year-old girl who was not his. In any case, it was easy to offer him sympathy and, as mentioned, invite him home for simple, weekday dinners, which included fish dishes such as fish gratin and smoked haddock and poached cod with bacon and creamed carrots, since it was thought that a newly widowed man might not be vigilant enough about giving his stepdaughter the essential proteins and vitamins contained in a fish dinner. Isabella, during these fish dinners at the homes of Singer's colleagues, would pick at the food and not eat even a bite more than she strictly had to, which served to underscore this fact, for both the hosts and Singer himself, who nodded and smiled, and said that the fish gratin or smoked haddock or poached cod with bacon and creamed carrots was tasty. It was important to teach children to appreciate the food, especially at a time when there were so many prepared frozen foods of insufficient nutritional value. But in all fairness, after Singer and his stepdaughter had been invited for a simple fish dinner, they were often invited back, perhaps two weeks later, and then they'd be served meatballs and creamed cauliflower, with a lot of gravy, and lingonberries, which Isabella liked much better. On Sundays they usually ate at the home of Isabella's grandparents, and Isabella's uncle and aunt and two cousins were most often there too. It has to be admitted, however, that Singer was more relaxed when he sat in the kitchen belonging to one of his colleagues than during these family dinners, when he was always wary, and not without reason.

In the same way he was also wary when it came to Merete's old milieu, which was connected to the ceramics company of Merete & Merete. Merete Holtan had told Singer that the name Merete & Merete would continue and never be changed, no matter what form this company or workshop or art gallery might take in the future, and no matter how it was run or who ran it, whether she did so alone or together with someone else, a replacement for Merete Sæthre, or possibly and preferably as a collective of three or four or five people, though still keeping in mind the goal of moving to the old location that had once belonged to the Tinnfoss Paper Factory. Singer, feeling quite moved, had thanked Merete Holtan for this, yet he'd otherwise avoided as much as possible spending any time in the old milieu of his deceased wife, even if it was to be called Merete & Merete for all eternity. The person he was most wary about was Merete Holtan herself, and her husband, Attorney Nils Hartvigsen, but also others with whom he thought Merete Sæthre might have had a close relationship – either by happenstance or on a more permanent basis – and he tried, as best he could, to avoid meeting them, especially on any social occasions. This was not all that difficult to do, because everyone understood that Singer didn't feel up to socialising that spring, or during the ensuing summer. And when autumn arrived, he had actually slipped so far away from the milieu in which he'd participated in his role as Merete Sæthre's husband that people no longer automatically thought of him in social contexts.

Worse was trying to avoid meeting the lawyer and the lawyer's wife, or Nils Hartvigsen and Merete Holtan, or Nils and Merete, if you will. He couldn't avoid them completely, especially because Merete & Merete also had a business side that required his attention.

What distressed Singer whenever he met Nils Hartvigsen and Merete Holtan, either together or separately, was the fact that they never gave the slightest sign that they knew anything. They behaved towards him, both together and separately, in exactly the same way Singer would have imagined they would have behaved if Merete Sæthre had never confided in her friend and namesake Merete Holtan that she was going to get a divorce, which Singer found to be most unlikely. This was true of their behaviour towards him when he met them at the funeral, and it was also true of the following period, when he met Attorney Hartvigsen at his office, and it was true of the subsequent months, when they constantly exhorted him to come over and visit them in their mansion down by the Tinnfoss Canal, frequently calling to invite him over. Even after a year had passed, they behaved in exactly the same way, as if they knew nothing, and this was true when he happened to run into Merete Holtan on the street and they exchanged a few brief remarks, or the time that Attorney Hartvigsen showed up at the library to borrow books; this was right before Easter, and he took out a stack of crime novels, and, as usual, they ended up chatting, discussing one topic or another, ending with Nils Hartvigsen spontaneously inviting him, and Isabella, to come to their newly purchased cabin on Lake Bolke for Easter, whereupon Singer regretfully declined, saying that he had already planned to spend the Easter holiday with family at home, with Isabella's grandparents and his brother- and sister-in-law and their children.

Singer couldn't rid himself of a suspicion that this was some sort of calculated game on their part that had been planned, since they were so similar in how they behaved towards him – whether it concerned a brief encounter with her, or a long conversation and the subsequent spontaneous invitation from him. But why? What did they hope to achieve through this? Singer didn't like it, and he became more uneasy as time passed. In the period immediately following the funeral, he could have understood this to be some type of tactful approach, but now, well over a year later? If they knew something, why did they pretend they didn't know anything? What in the world were they trying to express? Surely they couldn't be ignorant of the fact that Singer assumed that his deceased wife must have confided in her best friend? It couldn't be denied that when the second Easter arrived after Merete Sæthre had died in a car accident and Singer had taken on responsibility for her daughter, Singer felt more hounded than ever.

It didn't make the matter any better that he was living in Merete's townhouse apartment, among her things and her furniture, with her photographs displayed on the shelves. Out of consideration for Isabella, everything was to remain the same, this was Isabella's home. For Singer, however, it became more difficult to bear than he'd thought. While Merete was alive, even during the last period when everything was falling apart, you might say, it hadn't bothered him that he was living in her home, among her things, marked by her taste, among objects that were indicative of her personality. But now that she was gone, he found it bothersome. He was seriously thinking about moving to a different apartment. Here in Notodden. He would take along all the things that had been in Merete's possession and that her motherless daughter had grown up among: paintings, curtains, furniture, drawings and photo albums, photographs hanging on the walls, the kitchen table, the stove, refrigerator, everything. The mere act of placing them in a different setting, in new rooms, seemed to him a complete liberation from a shattered past, to be quite blunt. The mere act of having a different route to walk, or drive, to work at the library seemed to him, when he thought about it – and he thought about it often – to be something close to happiness; he'd imagined himself going out the door of his new, unidentifiable apartment and down a totally new, unidentifiable street to the Notodden library in the centre of town.

What Singer was waiting for, and expecting, was the gossip. He was waiting for the moment when Nils Hartvigsen and/or Merete Holtan could no longer keep their secret, or they no longer wished to keep their secret, and they cracked. Or, to be more precise, this might have already occurred long ago, in fact it was just as likely that this was the case, so Singer was now waiting for the consequences to appear because they had cracked. And they weren't the only ones who might crack. For all he knew, Merete could have confided in others, who sooner or later would crack, and probably much more easily than Nils Hartvigsen and Merete Holtan. Because when it came to the lawyer and his wife, Singer had reached the conclusion that they probably did not want to hurt him. If they had wished for a confrontation with him, because of everything they knew, they would have forced a confrontation long ago. Since they behaved as they did, Singer could just as well take this as a sign they had been initiated into and were aware of his conspiracy. He nevertheless kept his distance from them because he didn't want to hear them admit that they had been initiated into and were aware of this conspiracy; he would have found such an admission on their part to be extremely painful, he couldn't bear the thought that they should openly share his knowledge – the three of them conspiring in an all-too-dubious knowledge. He actually didn't think they should share his guilt, to put it plainly; the longer he thought about what that involved, the more he held it against them because they might harbour certain thoughts they were trying to convey to him, assuming, in such a blatant fashion, that they knew everything. He pictured spending the Easter holiday in their cabin at Lake Bolke, together with the two children they now had, and Isabella, and how, in the evening, after the children had gone to bed, they might approach him and confide in him, in an almost intimate manner, with great sincerity in their voices, saying that they understood him so well, and even though they knew what Merete's last wish was, meaning the separation, they understood him so well when he in this way tried to, and practically succeeded in, demonstrating his reconciliation with her; in fact, they were certain that she too would have understood. This is what he imagined them whispering to him up in the cabin on Lake Bolke where he'd never been before, and he bristled at the thought of how painful that situation would be. That was what he imagined, and he found it extremely painful. So painful that he avoided them and kept them at a distance, even though it was stupid of him to do this, because he was then at a high risk of letting loose the gossip. Because if he'd kept them close, become a friend of the family, so to speak, that would have prevented them from letting loose about him. With him as a friend of the family, they would have been his co-conspirators, and most likely would have kept quiet. But now, a year later, without having had any contact with him, and having admitted as much, they would have given up in a way, having realised that Singer never wanted to see them, and thus he would have lost importance for them, with the result that it would be much easier to loosen their tongues. Consequently they would no longer keep the secret that they shared but instead tell a strange story, which was both true and had taken place and was continuing to take place, in Notodden. Most likely they hadn't planned to tell this story, maybe first and foremost out of consideration for Merete Sæthre, but it would take only one of them, inadvertently, to mention it once, and all hell would break loose for Singer. If Merete Holtan just once, under the influence of wine, revealed what she knew to a friend, that would be the end. Then the story would spread. And it wouldn't be just one person that Singer was counting on to keep the story quiet. There would be at least one more person. Nils Hartvigsen could also give the secret away, under the influence of wine, during some social occasion among creative and witty people over at the Merete & Merete ceramics workshop, as they happened to talk in passing about Singer, who was quietly continuing his life, as a widower and the steadfast provider and stepfather for the daughter of his deceased wife. Two tongues that might wag in Notodden, at least two tongues. He didn't know how many others Merete had confided in, maybe not so many, but there could have been one more, he had to consider that, one or maybe two more. Sooner or later they would become loose-tongued. The chance of that happening increased as time passed, because the tactfulness that death, in spite of everything, instilled in a person would naturally diminish as the months (and years!) passed, and they would involuntarily become more loose-tongued. It was enough if someone in whom Merete had confided should spot Singer on the street and say, almost spontaneously, to the person she was with, as she saw Singer: 'How strange that he would take care of Merete Sæthre's daughter when they were going to get a divorce … ' Maybe word had already spread, though Singer hadn't yet noticed. Maybe the gossip was spreading from one to another, right at that moment, because a person in whom Merete had confided just before she died, now a year later, had caught a glimpse of Singer on the street, maybe even when he had Isabella with him, and all of a sudden she thought about what Merete had told her, and then it slipped out, inadvertently, as a question, and then word spread further and further. It meant that they were talking about him, discussing him and his relationship with his deceased wife and his stepdaughter, in numerous places when Singer was not personally present, nor was he aware of what they said. Because that's how it is with the person who is the subject of gossip, what's said will remain unknown to the person in question. For a long time. Word spreads along the most peculiar of pathways, but always detouring around him. Though not necessarily detouring around those who must not, at all costs, hear what's being said. Sooner or later someone who shouldn't hear about it will find out all the same, by accident. So it's possible that Per Christian Sæthre might have been told everything, both he and Henriette, his wife. And then it wasn't far to Berit and Martin Sæthre. Even though it might take a while. But sooner or later it would happen.

That might have been the situation at precisely the moment when Singer and Isabella went to dinner last Sunday: Per Christian and his wife Henriette knew. Berit and Martin Sæthre didn't. Not yet. Per Christian was reluctant to tell them, but he was sitting there knowing, and he spoke to Singer, asking him to pass the gravy, and as Singer passed it to him, he looked at Singer with a woeful expression and then at the unfortunate child, Isabella, who was an innocent victim. Studying his brother-in-law, Per Christian wondered what Singer was really like inside. Yet he said nothing. Not now. ... But there will be more dinners after this one. A dinner at Eastertime, for example. Singer and Isabella will come strolling over to the home of Isabella's grandparents to have dinner on Maundy Thursday. With Per Christian and Henriette and their two children. With Berit and Martin Sæthre. Singer and his stepdaughter. Singer notices the mood seems a little tense among the adults, but no one says anything. After dessert the children leave the table while the grown-ups have their coffee in the living room. That's when it happens. Suddenly Martin Sæthre straightens up, clears his throat, and looks right at Singer, as Berit Sæthre also looks right at Singer, with the same expression, while Per Christian and Henriette lower their eyes, and Martin Sæthre asks bluntly: 'Is it true what they're saying?'

No! That couldn't happen. And maybe it wouldn't happen, and so far it hadn't happened, in spite of the fact that a year and three months had passed since Singer took over responsibility for Isabella. But as long as he felt as if he were living with the fear that it might happen, he found himself in an unbearable situation and he needed to escape. After a year and three months, he'd come to the conclusion that the fear of being exposed hadn't diminished or disappeared, it had actually increased, and he saw no prospect that this would change, and so he needed to escape. Not only from the townhouse apartment but also from Notodden and its environs.

But he was stuck. He didn't have the money to escape, at least not enough to leave with Isabella and start fresh somewhere else. The townhouse apartment wasn't owned by Merete but by Merete's parents. And even if they would transfer the deed to Isabella, the sale of a townhouse apartment in Notodden – where at the time it wasn't exactly a seller's market but quite the opposite to a high degree – would not bring in enough money to invest in adequate living quarters somewhere else, especially in Oslo, which was where he now wanted to go. He'd even applied for a position at the Deichman Library in Oslo, a temporary one-year position with the possibility of the job extending and his gaining permanent employment, and one day in May he received word that he'd been hired. Nor did the ceramics workshop of Merete & Merete bring in any income for him, as the heir to one of the Meretes. The investments that had been made still entailed a relatively large debt, which Nils Hartvigsen had, however, taken on, at no charge. In other words, Singer owned nothing, and he was prevented from leaving due to the economic conditions and housing prices. He'd been hired for a position at the Deichman Library, but he couldn't take it because he had no chance of finding an apartment in Oslo.

That was when he happened to think about the envelope he'd once been given by Adam Eyde. It contained Adam Eyde's system for football betting, the big and the little system, and he'd occasionally taken a look at it, with some amazement, although he'd never made use of either system. Now he got out the envelope and opened it. He found the little system and studied it. He got himself some betting cards and filled them out, according to Adam Eyde's written instructions from six years ago. Even the little system cost him dearly, several hundred kroner, but if three specific games went as Singer (or Adam Eyde) had wagered, then he'd be a sure winner. He waited tensely for Saturday to arrive. For once he sat in front of the TV and jotted down the betting scores. The system hadn't worked. He'd lost. He tried again the following week. Again he lost. He skipped the next week because he had to wait for his next pay cheque before he could take another chance. By now he couldn't stop himself. He filled out the system for the third time, and this time it worked. Singer won what was for him an unbelievably huge sum. After that he played the little system once again. And it worked again. This time he also won what was for him an unbelievably huge sum. He now had a fortune that he could invest in a place to live in Oslo. Solemnly he put Adam Eyde's system back in the envelope, sealed it, and put it back where he'd taken it from.

He got in touch with Ingemann and asked him to go out and look for an apartment for him. He explained what sort of apartment he wanted, the number of rooms, the street, the neighbourhood, with a lift, fireplace, etc., etc., and a few weeks later Ingemann called to say that he thought he'd found an apartment for him. It was a four-room apartment in a building from the 1920s, located on Suhms gate, a street in the Majorstua district. Singer asked him to send over the prospectus by express mail, and when he received it, he immediately made an offer. As a result, his offer was accepted because his was the highest bid and no one else wanted to make a higher offer when they were invited to do so.

This was in June. He spent the summer in Notodden. He'd been dreading the summer beforehand, because summertime in the townhouse neighbourhood was all too open, all too deliberately sociable for Singer to thrive in those surroundings, especially as the sole parent of an eight-year-old girl. The townhouse summer was a standing invitation for socialising, in which the barriers between apartments disappeared and everyone thrived in the company of others, with unfamiliar children running into your kitchen for a drink of water, or running past outside as you sat there with a bare torso, surrounded by sun-worshipping housewives lying on blankets in their patch of lawn, without barriers, soaking up the sun, and the children wading in little inflated swimming pools, and cheerful fathers who were on holiday, and who got an unannounced visit from people they knew, and then your own neighbour cheerfully welcomed them and forced them to sit down and chat, so that Singer had to get up too, his torso bare, and go over to them, because that's where his neighbour's visitors were sitting; in short, it's what Singer could participate in only by summoning all his forces and, by means of a ferocious act of will, behaving in a gentle and pleasant manner, in a setting that was utterly foreign to him. But this year was the last time, and the thought that he was about to leave for good kept him going, and he sat there with bare torso and breathed in the fresh summer breeze in upper Telemark, longing for autumn to arrive.

Their departure was in late August. Up until the very last minute Singer felt exceedingly tense. He was actually more tense than ever before, because if it turned out that someone had been loose-tongued and the gossip had spread, in secret and in a big arc around him, then he had to figure that now, if not before, he would be confronted with this gossip, because it had become known that Singer and his stepdaughter were moving to Oslo where Singer had taken a position as a librarian at the famed Deichman Library. But nothing happened. Singer took his leave from the Notodden library, where he was feted by his colleagues and wished good luck. He and Isabella said goodbye to the Sæthre family, who thought it was a shame, but they realised that Singer's new position was a step up and an offer he couldn't refuse (and, in fact, that might have been true, although it wasn't as obvious a promotion as they seemed to think, since their view was well bolstered by Singer's own description of his new job).

Moving day arrived. The big removal van arrived at the townhouse, and the removal guys emptied the apartment. They took most of the furnishings; some Singer had given to Merete's parents, some he'd thrown out, but most went into the removal van. Isabella needed to be surrounded by familiar things in her new home. They stood and watched as the removal van drove away, packed to the brim with all their possessions. It headed for Oslo, and Singer and Isabella would follow that same day. Singer and Isabella now drove over to her grandparents' house, where the entire Sæthre family had gathered. They sat down at the table in the garden to have a farewell meal. Then they said their good-byes. When Singer shook hands with Berit and Martin Sæthre he thought: Now, now it'll happen. But nothing happened. Isabella's grandparents talked about the autumn break, which they were so looking forward to, because then Isabella would come to visit them. The same with the Christmas break, because then Isabella (and Singer) would again visit them. In general, it was in the cards that Isabella would spend as many of her holidays as possible in Notodden, and Singer had repeatedly told them that of course she would. It took a long time to say goodbye, but eventually they got in the car and drove off.

Yet Singer didn't head straight for the highway that would take them to Oslo; instead, he drove into the centre of Notodden, past the church, and into the area that was formerly reserved for Hydro's upper-level managers; there he parked on a quiet side street. Together with Isabella he walked up to Hydro's magnificent executive residence and crept past it to the park area behind the house. He took Isabella over to the balustrade where he'd stood with Adam Eyde on the day he arrived in Notodden exactly six years and one month ago. That's where they now stood, and Singer lifted Isabella up onto the edge of the balustrade. They stood there staring out at Lake Heddal, and Singer seized the opportunity to tell Isabella the story about the England ship. He'd never told it to her, or anyone else, before. Afterwards they walked back, sneaking past the magnificent Hydro villa, hoping they wouldn't be seen by the people who were undoubtedly inside, and then they headed back to the side street where Singer's car was parked.

It was a small Japanese car that he'd bought after receiving the insurance money for the old Lada station wagon, which had been written off in the accident. Singer unlocked the door and climbed into the driver's seat, then opened the front passenger-side door and told Isabella to get in. She was taken aback but did as he said. When they drove away from her grandparents' building, Isabella had been sitting in the back, as usual. On one previous occasion he'd driven up to her grandparents' building with Isabella sitting in the front, but they'd pointed out that this was irresponsible. Apparently a child had to be twelve before being allowed to sit up front, and Singer, not wanting to get into an unnecessary argument, had made sure that Isabella sat in the back from then on. But now she took her place up front next to him. He fastened her seatbelt, and they drove off.

To Oslo! The capital of the kingdom of Norway. With Singer at the wheel, they drove to Oslo. They took the usual route via Meheia to Kongsberg, and from there towards the Drammen River, following it to Drammen, and then took the E-18 to Oslo. First through mountainous terrain typical of Telemark, then the forested and bleak landscape of Buskerud, then along the former glory of the Drammen River, and through the unassailable Drammen, and finally through the tollbooth at Lier and out onto the real E-18. It began to rain when they were driving along the Drammen River, which turned dark with stripes of the gentle August rain, and as they passed through Drammen, dusk fell; and at the tollbooth at Lier the lights were on and it was getting dark. Singer had switched on the windscreen wipers, and that was how they drove towards Norway's capital.

The main entry to Oslo consists of a four-lane highway, two lanes in each direction, and there was a steady stream of cars moving in both directions. They drove towards Oslo. Singer sat behind the wheel in the midst of a stream of closed-up cars in the rain, and with the sound of the windscreen wipers, and the glare from all the tail lights of the cars in front, reflecting red on the rain-drenched asphalt, and with the yellow headlights from the equally closed-up cars coming towards him on the other side of the guard rail; and then, as they came to the suburbs of the big city, the lights from the tall buildings became visible, and at one place a panoramic view appeared of the slopes of Oslo, glittering in the rain-wet lights up ahead, at the same time as yellow lights above lit up the road, as if they were chandeliers of cold neon, and Singer felt a wave of anticipation about what was now going to be his life. As he sat there like that, behind the wheel of a car in the midst of a stream of other cars, on a two-lane road feverishly rushing towards something unknown, something big and indefinable, he had a rare sense of irresistible freedom, as he sat securely armoured behind the wheel of his car with a very sleepy eight-year-old stepdaughter sitting beside him on the front seat, bewitched by the lights of the city they were now entering.

And so began Singer's new life. Together with his stepdaughter Isabella. They lived in an apartment on Suhms gate, not very far from the building of the NRK, the Norwegian Broadcasting System, and even though they couldn't see the building from their apartment, they saw it immediately when they came out onto the pavement and looked to the right.

'If anyone asks, you just have to say that you live right near the NRK,' Singer told his stepdaughter.

The apartment consisted of four rooms: living room, dining room, Singer's room and Isabella's room, as well as a kitchen and bathroom. Dark parquet floors, a fireplace in the living room, and a balcony facing the heavy traffic on Suhms gate in the evening sunlight. The apartment was furnished with the old furniture from Notodden, though arranged in an entirely different way. A lot of things were also stowed in the storage room in the basement, and quite a few new things had been purchased. Including a large crystal chandelier, which was so expensive that for a moment Singer wondered whether he should once again open the envelope containing Adam Eyde's systems, but he restrained himself. The chandelier was hung over the dining table (also newly purchased) in the dining room, where they ate their dinner every day. Yes, Singer and Isabella always ate dinner in the dining room, never in the kitchen. The kitchen is where the food is prepared, Singer claimed, and when it's ready, it's carried on a platter into the dining room and placed on the dining table, and then you sit down to eat. Food should be eaten in the dining room. That's why it's called a dining room, he explained to Isabella. He taught Isabella to help him carry the food into the dining room. Then they would sit down at the table. The two of them, with Singer on one side of the table and Isabella sitting quietly across from him, on the other side. After the meal Isabella would help Singer clear the table, and then Singer would sit down in an armchair to think, while Isabella disappeared to her own room to play, preferably with her doll's house.

During the first weeks Singer spent a lot of time taking Isabella around Oslo so that she'd become familiar with the big, and for her possibly frightening, city. The buildings were so much bigger than those she was used to, and it was possible that they might seem oppressive to her. There was much more traffic on the streets, and the pavements were much more crowded. In general, everything was much bigger and more intense. For example, there were plenty of beggars, and every now and then drunks would appear, and the eerie wail of sirens resounded through the streets, and all of a sudden the traffic would stop except for a vehicle with flashing blue lights speeding among the halted cars; they were police cars with howling sirens, or ambulances on their way with accident victims or deathly ill patients, or on rare occasions fire engines responding to an alarm. It was to this new world that Singer wanted to introduce his stepdaughter, because from now on she would grow up here, and she would regard this city as her own.

From now on Isabella was an Oslo girl, just as Singer was a forty-year-old Oslo man, holding a responsible position at the venerable Deichman Library. Isabella had not had any desire to move to Oslo, but when she was told that was what would happen, she accepted the decision without protest. He'd heard her tell others that when the summer was over, she was going to move to Oslo, and that's where she would go to school, but he hadn't been able to discern anything in her voice that might indicate she was looking forward to this, nor that she was dreading it, or that she didn't want to go. Maybe she wasn't sure herself, maybe she had no words to express what she was feeling about this move, other than knowing it was something that occasionally happens to children. Even though the move meant she would be torn away from the entire life she'd lived so far, there was nothing to indicate that she was in any way distressed. These things happen.

Singer showed her Oslo. He did so on Thursday afternoons, when the shops stayed open later than usual, until six or seven o'clock, and for that reason the streets were crowded with people rushing to and fro, a restless bustling that Singer thought Isabella should experience because it was the pulse of the big city. Otherwise they would stroll along the streets in the quiet of Sunday afternoons; then the mood was different, then the city stretched before them, naked and pure, like some sort of structure within which it felt good to roam. Singer showed Oslo to Isabella. The big city's pulse and its pure structure. They would leave the apartment on Suhms gate and head down to Majorstua. From there they took either the blue tram through the city, via Bogstadveien or via Frogner, or they took the metro. The first time they took the blue tram via Frogner, but even as they were waiting for it, Singer thought that he was looking forward to taking Isabella on the metro and watching her as they travelled underground in the dark even though it was the middle of the day. And that's what they did the next time. They waited at the Majorstua station and watched as the red train came towards them on the tracks, then stopped – and they got on. Suddenly it was dark, the red train sped through the dark, they heard the train humming, but outside the window it was completely dark. Then suddenly: a station. In the middle of the dark, underground, a station appeared where people were standing close together on the platform, down here, deep underground, staring straight ahead at those sitting inside the cars. And there was a strange light from the underground stations; Singer saw that Isabella thought it was strange, though she didn't say anything, nor did she press her nose against the windowpane. After that the train again disappeared into the tunnel, and they rode for many minutes in a narrow and cramped darkness before they once again entered a carved-out, lit-up station underground, where the train stopped, and they got off and walked effortlessly up into the day, to the open streets of the city, to the air and the sun, or possibly to grey clouds.

Or they took the blue tram, sitting on board and allowing themselves to wind their way leisurely through the city, travelling along the predetermined laid-out tracks. Up in the light, through Oslo's streets, from north to south, from west to east, through the city's structures, past the tall buildings and all the people they caught clear glimpses of, moving around the centre of Oslo on this afternoon before the shops closed at seven. Singer showed Oslo to Isabella, it was the city that would become hers. The underground stations. Allowing themselves to be conveyed by the blue tram. The Steen & Strøm department store, that six-storey building filled with merchandise on every floor, where they rode the escalators up all six floors and back down again. People everywhere, and merchandise. Things. All sorts of things. Singer was easily overwhelmed by them all, and then he grew so tired, worn out, even despondent, that they couldn't stay long inside Steen & Strøm, only long enough to ride up the escalators, all six floors, and back down again.

Singer showed Oslo to eight-year-old Isabella. He showed her the sea lions in front of the National Gallery, and the heraldic lions in front of Storting, the parliament. Statues of famous men, including the Norwegian author Henrik Wergeland. He showed her the Royal Palace, seen through a tram window on Drammensveien, as the tram headed down towards the National Theatre. He showed her the Royal Palace seen from Karl Johans gate, where it towered at the top of the hill. He showed her the Royal Frederick University. The parliament. The National Theatre. The National Gallery. The city hall. The main train station. The Plaza Hotel. The Hotel Viking, which was the Olympia Hotel in 1952, and which had now been given a new name, though Singer didn't care for it. The Grand Hotel, with the Grand Cafe, where everyone from Notodden goes whenever they're in Oslo, along with everyone from the towns of Porsgrunn, Sandefjord, Larvik and Moss. The Hotel Continental with its elegant Theatre Cafe, where Singer had once dined. He showed her the fake towers at Frogner. The decorations on the building facades. The American Embassy. Norsk Hydro's headquarters. The university library. The famous bronze doors of the Gyldendal Norsk publishing company and the equally famous black mailbox of the Aschehoug publishing company. He showed her the equestrian statue of Karl Johan, seen from behind, meaning from the backside of the palace in Parkveien, and through a gap in that same palace. And just before 7 p.m. he was able to show her the crowds outside the big cinemas on Klingenberggata, the lit torches in front of the revue theatre called Chat Noir, and the neon lights. Singer was very animated, he pointed and showed her everything. He showed her the sea, or at least brought to her attention the smell of the sea; he showed her the slopes above the city, in particular Ekebergåsen, and it was as if he were saying the whole time that all this would be hers, it was here she would grow up and live her life.

He tried to show her that Oslo was a magical city, since that was how it now appeared to him, having returned after several years' absence. For that reason he took her to secret places, unexpected small stone stairways that connected various street levels. He showed her underpasses and hidden alleyways that were shortcuts allowing a person to save numerous metres by seeking it out and then slipping through. He showed her building courtyards that sometimes had small gardens. He showed her Oslo Harbour. On one Sunday they walked the entire length of the harbour, from Frognerstranda to Containerhavna in Bjørvika; it was a long walk that Isabella completed with an inscrutable look on her face. He showed her the east side of Oslo where all the foreign workers lived and where highly foreign-looking Asian women wearing silk clothing wandered around, and they visited the shops run by immigrants where Singer offered Isabella a chance to taste exotic fruits, which she did, saying they tasted good, although without asking for more.

Several times they passed the places where Singer had previously lived or worked, but Singer didn't say that's where I lived, or that's where I worked; he would cast an amazed glance at these places, whether it was the dilapidated buildings, the Gyldenløve Hotel, the printing plant for the newspaper *Dagbladet*, or for that matter the premises of the College of Library Science, and he was amazed because these places were now of so little importance to him, as if they'd never had anything to do with his life, and he found no reason to initiate Isabella into a life to which he person-ally felt so little connection. On the other hand, he did point out the beautiful entrance of the Deichman Library – the massive stone staircase and the pillars – and the distinctive grey-green elegance of the building in faux classical style. He told her that this was where he worked. Isabella looked in the direction he was pointing but didn't say a word. The library was open, and for a moment he wondered whether he should take his little stepdaughter inside so that she could see his workplace, but he decided not to. Instead, he pointed towards Regjeringskvartalet, the government section of town, but not really at the specific buildings, so as to emphasise in passing that it was from here that everyone living in Norway was governed; however, he didn't want to conceal the fact that these buildings were the seats of power (as was the nearby courthouse on the other side of Regjeringskvartalet), and he did want to point out the sandblasted symbols on the facades, decorations or figures, which he told Isabella had been done by Picasso. That's all he said. Just that name: Picasso. So she would remember it. So she would remember it, fixing the name in her memory all on her own, hopefully, as something she would think about when she lay in bed that night, thinking that she now lived in a city where the mightiest building facades had been decorated by a man with the mysterious name of Picasso. It was a Thursday afternoon, just before 6 p.m., outside the Regjeringskvartalet. They needed to think about going home. They hurried over to Stortorget where they caught the Ullevål Hageby tram at the stop outside the shopping mall of Glasmagasinet. The tram arrived, it was very crowded, but Singer and Isabella pushed their way on, and Singer held on to a strap with one hand, while with the other he held on to Isabella. Right next to him stood a man also holding on to a strap, and Singer recognised him. Singer gave Isabella a poke so that she'd notice the man. They got off at Bislet. Then Singer said:

'Did you see who that was?'

Isabella shook her head and looked down.

'That was the weatherman,' said Singer solemnly.

They walked up Pilestredet, heading towards Suhms gate. When they were back home in their apartment, Isabella was tired and pale, and she disappeared into her room where she played with her doll's house, quietly and sombrely. Singer sat down in the living room to think.

About how his life would proceed in the future. About whether he was capable of going through with it. At seven thirty he turned on the TV to watch the daily news programme. At the very end the weatherman showed up, and it was the same weatherman they'd seen holding on to a strap in the tram about two hours earlier. Singer called to Isabella, and she came running.

'There he is,' said Singer. 'Look! The weatherman! The man we just saw on the tram. And now there he is! On TV! Isn't that strange?'

Isabella looked at the TV.

'Uh-huh,' she said. 'That's him.' Then she went back to her room to continue playing with her doll's house.

Isabella had started school, in the second year at a big Oslo school filled with children she didn't know. Every morning Singer and Isabella would leave the apartment and walk downstairs together and out to the pavement on Suhms gate, where they said goodbye to each other, and Isabella turned right and headed for the intersection on Kirkeveien while Singer turned left and headed for the Deichman Library in the centre of town. Singer usually turned round to watch her go, seeing her scurrying along Suhms gate, wearing her backpack, heading for the inter- section on Kirkeveien, where she stopped along with all the other children en route to school who were waiting to be ushered across the busy Kirkeveien by the school's own traffic patrol; then he would continue on his way, either for the tram stop near Bislet station on Pilestredet, or he'd allow himself the freedom to walk the whole long way to the Deichman, usually via Bogstadveien. As a single parent, Singer worked only during regular business hours from nine to three, which, by the way, he'd also done during the last year in Notodden. This meant that he returned home around four, and when he arrived back at the apartment, Isabella was always there. School had ended hours earlier, and she was usually in her room, either doing her homework or sitting in front of the doll's house, quietly immersed in the miniature world it offered. That's how it was, day after day. In the morning they would leave the apartment together; she walked along Suhms gate wearing her backpack, Singer turned and watched her go before he continued on his own way, and at the end of the workday, he would let himself into the apartment and there she would be, as always, in her room. Week after week.

But one day she came to him and said that she'd been invited to the birthday party of one of her classmates on Saturday. Singer felt his heart leap, he was so relieved, but he said nothing, merely asked the name of the girl, the one who was going to have the birthday party, and where she lived. But that night, after Isabella had gone to bed, he looked through her nicer clothes, wondering what she should wear to the birthday party. Finally he took out a skirt and white blouse that he remembered her wearing once when she was supposed to dress up in Notodden, and that's what he decided on, after pondering whether she might look *too* nice, but he decided she wouldn't, she wouldn't stand out in any way if she wore that particular outfit, he thought. But there was a problem. The blouse needed to be ironed. Actually, it needed to be washed as well, because it was dirty, so he immediately put it in the washing machine and washed it at forty degrees Celsius. But he didn't know how to iron. He'd never learned how, and he was reluctant to learn, because he regarded ironing as such a feminine activity that he had trouble picturing himself doing it. That's why he preferred to wear clothing that didn't need to be ironed, and if Isabella needed her clothes to be ironed, he had previously asked Isabella's grandmother to do it. But he found a solution. The next day he put the blouse in his briefcase and took it with him, and on the way to the Deichman he kept his eye out for a dry cleaner's. He found one on Pilestredet, went inside, and asked whether they could iron the blouse for him. Even though they didn't usually do that sort of thing unless they had also dry-cleaned the garment, they were willing to make an exception for him. Singer breathed a sigh of relief, and the following day Isabella was able to put on her newly-ironed blouse and go to the birthday party. When she came home from the birthday party he asked her how it went.

'Good,' said Isabella.

And life continued on as before. Their new life in Oslo. Isabella was very attached to her doll's house. The doll's house had been a Christmas present during the last year of her mother's life. And it was fully equipped with furniture in every room, electric lights, a TV that glowed the way a

TV glows in reality, lamps on the ceilings and on little tables, pictures on the walls, a fully equipped kitchen, a well-appointed bathroom, curtains and beds with coverlets. It's true that it hadn't been fully furnished from the beginning; both Singer and others had gradually bought more furnishings so that today it was fully equipped, also with dolls of an appropriate size who lived inside in a nuclear family. Isabella could sit there for hours, moving these dolls in and out of the house, moving them from room to room, as she stared inside. Occasionally she would take one of the dolls out and place it somewhere else, in another room in Singer's apartment, in the kitchen, for example, and then she'd go back to her room and sit there staring inside the doll's house again; maybe she'd stick her hands inside to straighten the corner of a miniature curtain, or she'd make the people in the doll's house move from one room to another, until, after a long time, she'd run into the living room or some other room in the apartment and get the doll she'd left there and put it back in the doll's house, in one of the rooms. It might be any of the dolls that disappeared and then returned, but it seemed as if there was some sort of set configuration, as if there were certain rules and sequences for the way events were carried out inside that little head of hers, as she sat and stared inside the doll's house, constantly sticking her hands inside for long periods of time, after she'd finished her homework.

Several months had passed since they'd moved to Oslo, and Singer was very worried. Isabella never went outside to play, she never went over to a friend's house, and even though she'd been invited to another birthday party, her daily little-girl life hadn't changed. Now and then Singer had to fight an urge to follow her along Suhms gate in the morning, at a distance, and without being seen. He would have liked to stand on this side of the street and watch what transpired on the other side of Kirkeveien after all the children were ushered across by the school's traffic patrol, to see whether she joined up with any other children for the rest of the walk to school, taking the path across the plot of land facing Marienlyst school – maybe with another schoolgirl, or at least walking with several others, a merry and carefree group – or whether she covered this last part of the route alone, and if so, constantly passing others who were walking together; because that's how it is for some who walk alone, she would pass many others, not because she walked that much faster but because those who walked to school together often stopped to do something or other, whispering a secret, for example, and she would be walking behind them for one reason or other, albeit a specific reason; this person walking alone would pass many of these merry groups of girls, or configurations of two best friends, even though she wouldn't be walking faster than they would in order to hurry to school, on the contrary. Often those walking alone – and Isabella might be one of them – walked slower than the others, more thoughtful, less carefree, but Singer never saw what transpired on the other side of Kirkeveien because he didn't want to spy on his little, and possibly very lonely, stepdaughter.

What could Singer do? Nothing. He could try to cheer up the little schoolgirl who had been brought here to the big city without having expressed any desire to come, or for that matter any *lack* of desire to come. But it didn't seem as if she particularly appreciated Singer's attempts to cheer her up. When Singer asked whether they should go to the cinema, she always said yes, but when he asked what film she'd like to see, she never managed to say whether she preferred one over another; so Singer ended up choosing what film they would see based on sheer guesswork as to which film he *thought* Isabella would most like to see, though at no point did she ever say, when he asked, whether she was looking forward to seeing it. But she would put on her coat, and then she and Singer would walk down to the Bislet tram stop and go to one of the cinemas in the centre of town, or they'd walk the rather long way over to the Colosseum to see one of the magnificent, epic kids' films that everyone was talking about, and which everyone in Isabella's class had seen. And in the dark of the cinema she would sit and stare at the promising images on the screen, at the epic story being told, which everyone had to see for themselves; she ate her sweets but never screamed in fright or laughed with joy; actually she sat there quite calmly, focused on her bag of sweets, which she even tried to eat as quietly as possible so as not to disturb anyone or draw the attention of others. Well, maybe it wasn't the attention of others she was trying to avoid with her quiet manner, but rather the person sitting closest to her, the one who had brought her here, meaning Singer. In that case, it meant that Singer was sitting next to a little nine-year-old girl who was eating sweets so quietly because she didn't want her stepfather to notice her presence more than was absolutely necessary as she sat there, at his side, looking at this epic film rolling across the screen, a film she was watching because all the children, sooner or later, would see it, and that was why Singer had brought her here, to the Colosseum, and she stared at the screen and absorbed these images and this story without disturbing anyone with her fear or joy. And when the film was over, they strolled out of the cinema and straight out to the lit-up streets in the evening, both of them walking along lost in their own thoughts; they strolled along Kirkeveien, a forty-year-old librarian and his nine-year-old stepdaughter, through the bustling and lit-up life of the big city, more intense at this time, still early in the evening, which was dark and neon-lit, although rather chilly, and Singer asked whether she liked the film, and Isabella always answered yes. But when she was back in the apartment, she was worn out and relieved to be back home at last and usually she would immediately go to her own room and most often sit down in front of the doll's house and stick both hands inside and act out some event that had meaning only for her.

After they moved to Oslo and in this way became immersed, all on their own, in the noise and anonymity of the big city, Singer had to admit that he didn't understand Isabella. It was as if he lacked a key to her heart, and this both worried him and made him cautious. He was terribly afraid of influencing her, because he knew what consequences this might have for both of them. Isabella was an introverted child, yet she did the usual child things, almost without hesitation, as if they were the most natural things in the world. She liked to jump up and down on the mattress of the bed in Singer's room, she did this now and then, and each time she would keep at it for quite a while, all alone. Otherwise she liked hiding in cupboards, and being found, plus balancing on the pavement kerbs whenever she quietly set off on her route to school. But even when she did these things, which come so naturally to children, she did them in a serious manner, which was in sharp contrast to the impression the games actually should convey. When she jumped up and down on the mattress of the bed in Singer's room, it was something she'd discovered all on her own, and when children jump up and down on a mattress it's usually accompanied by delighted squeals. But Isabella jumped up and down in silence, and with a pensive look on her face. She lacked the childlike expression even though she was a child like anyone else. She carried out all these children's games with a seriousness that was striking. Wasn't she having any fun? Even though she was doing it of her own free will, on her own initiative? In fact, she was doing it for her own sake; she jumped up and down on the mattress without first asking for permission or calling to

Singer to come and watch her. She was obviously interested in being a child and in doing all the childlike things that were at her disposal, but she didn't laugh merrily, or shriek with fright, or with horror or dread, when she did them. She displayed no childlike enthusiasm for these childlike games, but instead a pensive seriousness.

Sometimes she sang children's songs. She might do it suddenly, all on her own, or she might be sitting in front of the TV and be exhorted to sing. Sitting all alone in front of the TV, doing what the song demands a person should do, but without the joy that a child is intended to display at these songs. Isabella sang with a very serious expression, as if she were bored, thought Singer. But she had voluntarily put on the TV for the children's show, or she'd started to sing of her own accord, and why would she do that if she thought it was boring? Singer couldn't figure her out. She was a child, after all, so why couldn't she surrender fully and completely to the childishness that was her natural state? Her reality – and there's no getting around it – was to be a child, after all, a nine-year-old girl. Look, there's Isabella, nine years old; show us what is natural for you, Isabella! And in a sense she did show it to Singer and all the others. She did, there's no getting around it. By immersing herself in games, she did show them (not only by virtue of her size and her childish face and the backpack she wore) who she was. She moved around the apartment, alone, eagerly immersed in playing by herself, jumping and dancing, sitting for hours in front of her doll's house, singing her children's songs. So far so good, except for the fact that she spends so much time alone, thought Singer. But why did she behave with such intent seriousness within this childhood she'd been given, which many would say was a gift? As if the whole time she were mimicking something that she realised should have brought her delight? Singer didn't know, but now and then he would be seized by anxiety when he saw her involved in such withdrawn activity. Sometimes Singer thought it was almost eerie to see her jumping up and down on the mattress of his bed in his room with that pensive look on her face. Was she doing that because she'd heard, or seen, other children do it? Had she even heard or noticed the joy of other children as they did it, and that was why she wanted to try it herself, to see if that was how it really felt? Again and again?

Singer didn't know. But quite frankly, we expect from children a dewy anticipation about life, and an innocent surrender to the fact that they are children. When this is lacking and is instead replaced by a deliberate seriousness, then what? It causes concern.

Singer was concerned. He tried, as mentioned, to cheer her up, for example by taking her to the cinema. But he also became more and more worried about her as time passed, because she spent so much time alone. It would be better if she'd spend more time with other children, but at least she did that in school, and then she no doubt laughed, he thought, though without conviction. But there was so little he could do. He couldn't intervene and offer her guidance because he had no idea how to guide her. And so he was left perplexed and concerned. Perhaps others would have tried inviting over other children for Isabella to play with; Singer had colleagues at the Deichman who had children the same age as Isabella, and he could have tried to make arrangements so that Isabella could spend time with them, since she wasn't finding any playmates on her own. Or he could have suggested, even insisted, that she invite her school friends home, in fact he could have suggested that Isabella have a party of her own, even though it wasn't her birthday; he could have said that the most fun parties weren't birthday parties but parties that are given simply because you wanted to have one, but he couldn't bring himself to suggest this. Or he could have enrolled Isabella as a member in some sort of club, a sports team, choir, music group, or something along those lines. But he couldn't bring himself to suggest that either. He couldn't do it, he found it impossible. He couldn't interfere in that way. He couldn't get himself to arrange friendships between Isabella and other children. He just couldn't. So he remained puzzled, watching his stepdaughter playing her solitary, introverted games in the apartment on Suhms gate.

It's true that he tried to offer her a number of temptations. He tried to describe certain things as greatly tempting, things that he'd personally thought would be tempting for a child, and a girl. Going to the cinema was one of these things. Taking ballet classes was another.

'Lots of children dream of becoming dancers when they grow up,' said Singer. 'So they start going to classes at the ballet school when they're about your age.'

But Isabella refused to be tempted. She had no dreams of becoming a ballerina when she grew up, Isabella had no idea what she wanted to be when she grew up. It looked as if Isabella thought it was enough to be a child.

'What do you do at the library?' she suddenly asked him one day.

'It's called the Deichman Library,' he said. 'You need to remember that if anyone asks because there are lots of different libraries.'

'But what do you do there?'

'I'm a librarian.'

'But what does a librarian do?'

'Oh, they do lots of things, it all depends on what kind of librarian you are.'

'But what do you do?'

'Me? Oh, I, well you won't see me. I'm downstairs in the basement. That's where the exciting books are, the ones that nobody cares about anymore, or the ones that are so important that nobody is allowed to see them except for a few librarians. That's where I am, down there. All day long, I never see the sun.'

'But what do you do there?'

'I take care of the books,' said Singer. 'I do that all day, and when I go home in the evening, another trusted librarian arrives to take care of them.'

'Do you just sit there staring at the old books?'

'That too. To be honest, that's mostly what I do. But I also go around and see to it that they're okay.'

'Are they okay?'

'Yes, but they tend to have trouble breathing, so I have to take them out, one by one, and give them an airing. This is what I do.'

Singer went over to the bookcase and pulled out one of the oldest books he owned. He held the book by the spine and let the pages slowly fan out. He stood there like that for a long moment, solemnly. Then he cautiously ran his fingers over the spine, searching for a specific spot, looking as if he were concentrating all his attention on finding it. When he'd found the right place to grip, he paused for effect and then: Bang! he closed up the book with a smack.

'That's what I do,' he said. 'It's awfully complicated, because each book requires its own technique. But when I'm done, the book has had a proper airing and will stay clean for a long time. Once I get going, the dust really flies, let me tell you,' said Singer.

'I don't believe you,' said Isabella.

'What don't you believe?'

'That that's what you do at the library.'

'But it's true,' said Singer, 'truer than reality.'

'No,' said Isabella and ran off to her room.

Singer was rather bewildered. It's certainly not easy to amuse her, he thought. And then he repeated the trick, just for himself. When the bang came, and the fanned out white pages closed up into a compact book package, he couldn't help smiling. But she didn't find it amusing, she didn't even believe me. It's certainly not easy being me. There aren't many temptations she'll fall for. Open a book, hold it along the spine in a special way, and then close it up with a bang, that's my life. Down in the basement of the Deichman. Truer than reality.

And so the days passed, the weeks and months passed, and Singer's concern about Isabella's solitude grew. And behind it all was the spectre of her quiet being, and the possible ordeals she encountered in her games. The serious child. The one that Singer, puzzled and concerned, pictured before him. The one who was always alone, and for whom he could do nothing except what he was already doing, such as providing both her and himself with what they needed in terms of food, clothing and sources of entertainment in order to live a modest life, largely unnoticed but more or less accepted by those around them. The latter was especially true of Isabella. His concern about how she was doing at school had made him speculate about whether she was being subjected to scorn from the other children. And so he tried to ease this potential scorn and dismissiveness by dressing her so that she would stand out as little as possible from the group, in terms of appearance. This applied to everything relating to her appearance, even including the lunch she took with her. For example, how many open sandwiches should she have in her lunchbox? Two or three? And what kind of sandwiches? Could she have three with brown goat's cheese? Wasn't that asking for trouble, wasn't it even ridiculous to have three open sandwiches, all exactly the same, especially with slices of dense goat's cheese? On that point Isabella was able to offer a certain degree of help. At long last he'd been able to drag out of her the fact that she should not have more than two open sandwiches, and only one should have brown goat's cheese, though she didn't know what should be on the other one. When it came to clothes, however, Isabella had little to contribute, she paid scant attention to clothes, and her taste was too childish, with a penchant for pink, which was impossible because it was this childish taste that can so easily provoke dismissiveness among nine-year-old girls in the same class. Unfortunately, Singer didn't have much to contribute either when it came to clothes. But he was definitely worried. So worried that he often left the Deichman during his lunch break and went over to a chain store that sold clothes for children and teenagers. It was called Hennes & Mauritz. There he walked among the racks as he listened to what the mothers and their daughters talked about when they tried on clothes and he looked to see what sort of clothing they preferred, and in this way he wrangled out of them some useful tricks, which would hopefully prevent Isabella from being dismissed. At least not because of her clothes. Or so he hoped.

Sometimes he would be paralysed with anxiety as he came home from his job at the Deichman Library and stepped inside the silent apartment where the serious child was moving about, almost without a sound. What had he done? But there was no going back.

At the library, his life proceeded as normal, Singer was immersed in his own work, and the hours flew by in all their tediousness, almost without his noticing. The same as always, without leaving the slightest trace of anxiety inside him. It was only when he came home and saw his stepdaughter that the anxiety returned. Now and then he had an urge to stop, to hold his hands in front of his own face, as if to hide, and scream: 'No, no!' But only now and then. Mostly he was simply worried; he went around in the bewilderment of his own worry.

But one day when he let himself into the apartment – and by the way it was still winter because there was snow on his coat – he heard voices coming from Isabella's room, and he immediately went over to her room, pausing on the threshold. There he saw two quiet girls sitting next to each other, peering inside the doll's house as they stuck their hands in to change the configurations inside.

From that winter day forward, Singer's life changed, at any rate in terms of the leaden weight in his heart. Now when he let himself into the apartment, he would occasionally find two quiet best friends, who often had their heads together and were giggling in Isabella's room, or they'd be running around the apartment, where they both seemed to feel at home even though they, and particularly the friend, would be slightly more discreet whenever Singer showed up, in the sense that the friend would stop abruptly, in mid-jump, as soon as she caught sight of him, before once again running through the rooms of the apartment. After a while there were occasionally three quiet girls in the apartment when he came home from his monotonous library job at the Deichman. Three classmates who filled the apartment with their quiet games. New activities, but little noise from them, and when there were three girls, the apartment was used more fully, in all its width and breadth, than when there were only two and the doll's house was the focus of their attention. When there were three or four, they would crawl and run and stand everywhere, he found them standing on the sofa, hiding in cupboards, behind doors; once when he came home one of them was even standing on the dining table and holding on to the chandelier as if she were lifting it up so as to show it off. When she noticed Singer, she hurried to get down from the table, but she moved too fast and she tumbled to the floor and hurt herself, so Singer had to console her before she got up and curtsied, like the well-brought-up child she was.

Such incidents made Singer guess that they played with a wild abandon whenever he was away and Isabella was home alone after school, though he saw scant signs of this. When he came home, they transformed into the well-brought-up and quiet little girls that they were. But as for what they did when he wasn't there, he could only guess, based on little things that he found moved around. Once, for example, he noticed that the photograph of Isabella's deceased mother, which stood in a prominent place on a table in the living room, had been moved a bit. He assumed that Isabella had taken it down and temporarily put it somewhere else, for example on the floor in front of her, as she told her friends about her mother. Although Singer had no clue what she might have said.

Occasionally Isabella would now have overnight guests, from Saturday to Sunday, usually the first friend who had made an appearance, and sometimes Isabella would also stay overnight at her house, and then Singer would have a totally free weekend, though he didn't quite know what to do with it. He went out to eat, but the restaurant scene had changed since he was a young man in Oslo, most of the places he'd known were long gone, and the ones that were left had a different clientele, or rather the same clientele, but the people had changed, they'd grown older and looked a little the worse for wear. Singer didn't feel comfortable among them, even though he knew some of them from the past, and he might sit down at their table because there was something he wanted to talk to them about, but the names they'd each mention didn't mean much to the other anymore. For that reason he didn't really appreciate his free weekends as he probably should have – he wasn't more than forty-two years old after all, and he should have been having adventures, and time passes quickly, it runs away, and before you can even take a breath another year is over, and Singer would be forty-three. No, he appreciated the times when Isabella had overnight guests more than when she spent the night elsewhere. Then Singer would let the money flow, as they say. One of the things that the serious child Isabella truly perceived as a great temptation, one that she couldn't refuse and clearly found fascinating, was being allowed to get sweets, *purchasing* it herself. When she held the little scoop in her hand, standing in front of all the sweetie bins in Storkiosken, Singer would notice a slight trembling in her otherwise purposeful introvertedness. He would send Isabella and her friends down to Storkiosken, with a fifty-krone note to share, and he saw how her eyes practically sparkled as they put on their coats and ran off. And half an hour later he'd hear their footsteps on the stairs, and they'd come bursting into the apartment, each carrying a bag of carefully selected sweets from the bins in Storkiosken.

In such situations Singer sometimes had an urge to repeat the trick with the book that he'd held by the spine and slammed closed, but something told him that Isabella wouldn't exactly appreciate that. Instead he told the, in this instance, two serious, sweet-eating girls that he'd make sure they got library cards to the adult section of the Deichman Library before they were actually allowed to have them. He couldn't promise them access to the adult section when they turned twelve, but when they were fourteen he'd be able to ensure that they got library cards to the adult section, which was the real book collection of the Deichman Library. Then a whole new world would open up for them, he said, but the two sweet-eating girls merely gave him enquiring looks, their expressions disinterested. It was and would continue to be difficult for Singer to figure out Isabella and her best friends. Now he no longer needed to cheer up Isabella for her own sake or for his, and yet he was left with a peculiar feeling of irremediable loss every time he failed to impress her and her friends and get them to stare at him, wide-eyed.

Yet Ingemann did manage to do this. By now Ingemann had given up his acting career, which had never been as successful as he'd hoped. He'd started working for commercial TV, first in front of the camera, but now behind it, not as a cameraman but as an ideas man. He lived in a fairly miserable two-room apartment in Majorstua, but he was brimming with energy and a zest for life, even though he too was well over forty. But he was now earning good money, as manifested by the fact that he'd bought himself a very expensive car, which stood parked at the kerb on the street where he lived, right outside the dilapidated building where he had a two-room apartment. Often when Singer went to visit him, taking Isabella along, Ingemann would stand at the window looking down at his car with a self-satisfied expression, which did not seem at all repellent because it was the expression of a man who, after all, lived in a fairly miserable two-room apartment, fairly devoid of any comforts and lacking in orderly living arrangements. It was also quite dark inside, and in the summer it was unbearably hot and not much brighter; the apartment was on the first floor and dark even on bright summer days, projecting a strong sense of being closed up in a cramped and stifling existence, from which there was no possibility of escape. But Ingemann would stand at the window, looking down at his fancy car, new and shiny, and after they'd stood there for a while, he'd say:

'It's so nice of you to come over. Let's go out to a restaurant, it's my treat.'

And off they'd go, for example to the Theatre Cafe, where Ingemann would treat Singer and Isabella to dinner, with red wine and cognac for Singer, and one fizzy drink after another, as much as she wanted, for Isabella. Singer noticed that Ingemann was also generous with the tips he left, something that he happened to remember as typical of his friend in the past, although now his generosity seemed to know no bounds.

Sometimes Singer might also hear a honking outside his own window on Suhms gate, and then both he and Isabella would run to the window and, sure enough, there was Ingemann's car; he was honking because he wanted them to come down and go for a drive. This man, with his fairly phoney charm, was the one who could manage the feat of making Isabella laugh.

Singer had not expected this. Singer himself thought Ingemann could be rather tiresome in his attempts to be a so-called entertainer who amused those around him in his spare time. It's true that he was capable of witty remarks, but all the notions that followed the witty remarks could seem fairly annoying to Singer, even though Ingemann was his friend, and he'd known him almost as long as he could remember. This was not always the case, of course; as a rule Singer both had fun and thrived in Ingemann's company, but that was mostly because he was Ingemann, and Singer felt connected to him, even when Ingemann could seem a little phoney. These were merely aspects of his friend, aspects that Singer couldn't imagine Ingemann without, but the fact that these aspects were able to entice laughter from his serious stepdaughter, that was something he'd never thought possible. Yet it *was* possible.

Ingemann made great efforts to amuse Singer's step-daughter, who seemed to have little appreciation for these efforts. He tried tickling her, but she pulled away, in a polite manner, and responded only with a socially acceptable, and for the occasion, fairly restrained, titter, which did not encourage Ingemann to try again. Instead he tried other tricks. He opened a fizzy drink bottle for her using his teeth. That impressed her, but provoked no merriment. He continued to try to impress her with a series of tricks from his boyhood that had once proved successful. And they were still successful, Isabella was more or less impressed by all these ancient tricks, but they didn't cause any frivolous laughter. Usually she would give him a serious look, but with an approving expression. She was not dismissive of his tricks, but she never asked him to perform any others, nor did she ask him to repeat those she had clearly approved of or even appreciated. Until one day when he tugged at her nose. Ingemann tugged at the nose of Isabella who was then eleven years old. She looked utterly astonished, she stared at him open-mouthed, but she didn't laugh. Not at that instant. But a moment later she burst out laughing, bright childish laughter, prompted by something else entirely.

And that did it. Ingemann had made her laugh. Singer felt an inexpressible relief at seeing her finally start to laugh, even though he wasn't the one who'd been able to entice her to do it. He felt as if his problem had been solved, even though he wasn't the one who had solved it. Isabella was still a serious child, but now and then she might burst out laughing, prompted by the strangest notion on Ingemann's part. When Singer and Isabella were alone, she never laughed, she didn't care to laugh. But when Ingemann was present, she might laugh now and then. Ingemann's presence made her laugh. His phoney charm and old tricks summoned a merriment in her that she otherwise tried to hide from Singer. Singer hadn't managed to entice laughter from her, even though he'd tried. That's a fact. Now he no longer needed to worry about that fact. He had Ingemann, after all, and Singer could withdraw into himself. Live his own life.

And so it was that when Isabella entered puberty and joined the 'ranks of teenagers,' as that term was used in Singer and Ingemann's youth, it was Ingemann and not Singer who offered her guidance. She felt attached to Ingemann and not to Singer, even though it was Singer she lived with and who also provided for the young teenage girl. But he had lost her, whatever that meant.

Whatever that meant. Singer had known Ingemann all his life, they'd been inseparable throughout their childhood, and later in life each had regarded the other as his friend, no matter where each of them had lived. Now they both lived in Oslo, in separate milieus, and they were interested in different things, that has to be assumed. But now and then Ingemann would show up at Singer's apartment on Suhms gate and invite Singer and his stepdaughter out for one reason or another. For example to take a drive on a Sunday. Isabella nodded, her expression serious and deliberate, when Singer told her they were going for a drive with Ingemann. They went downstairs and out to the street where Ingemann's fancy car was parked. In front, in the passenger seat next to the driver's seat, sat a beautiful woman, her hair fluttering. She shook hands with Singer through the open car window, as Isabella stood behind him, and the woman gave the teenage girl a friendly nod. Ingemann jingled his car keys and got in behind the elegant wheel, in the driver's seat, while Singer and Isabella got into the spacious back seat. Then they set off. The car accelerated dramatically, and they raced through Oslo's quiet, Sunday-afternoon streets.

It was beyond the scope of Singer's imagination to wonder why Ingemann had come to get him, Singer, or why he was suddenly sitting in the back seat of his friend's car together with his stepdaughter, while Ingemann sat in front with a beautiful woman; yet up to now Singer had imagined this configuration to be natural for both of them.

The car raced along the E-6, heading for the small market town and former industrial centre of Moss, where, on the green and quite flat island of Jeløya there was a well-known gallery called f15. At great speed, and resting comfortably on the soft seats, were all four passengers. Ingemann and the beautiful woman conversed a bit, apparently talking shop since both of them, as Singer understood it, shared the same perception of reality and had jobs in the same field, although working for different companies. Sunday in Norway, in Østlandet, the south-eastern part of the country, at the head of Oslo Fjord, on its eastern side. An outing to a well-known art gallery housed in an old manor house on the island of Jeløya near Moss.

Yet Singer was feeling anxious as he sat there. An impossible configuration had developed, he saw that now. Ingemann behind the wheel, jovial and merry, sharp and phoney at the same time, driving confidently, at great speed, along the E-6 as he alternated between talking companionably with the beautiful woman with the fluttering hair, and partially turning his head to offer cheerful comments to the anxious Singer and his thirteen-year-old stepdaughter sitting together quietly in the back seat. Ingemann behind the wheel, in a companionable unit with the beautiful woman, most likely his new lover. Singer and Isabella, together, as the other unit, in the back seat. You'd have to be blind not to see it. The two friends, Singer and Ingemann, in a car, each in his own unit, driving along the E-6 on a Sunday afternoon. If that wasn't blatant enough, it became even more so after driving through the green island of Jeløya, parking in the car park outside the Alby manor, and then walking from the car park to the manor itself, where Gallery f15 was housed; they stayed in the same configuration even then, in what seemed a completely natural way: Ingemann and the beautiful woman walking companionably ahead, with Singer and his thirteen-year-old stepdaughter right behind, with Ingemann now and then turning his head to offer some cheerful remark to Singer, and Singer smiling wanly in response, a remark that was, however, caught by Isabella, in all the ungainly alertness of her body. Singer became more and more withdrawn, and anxious. He also felt anxious as he sat again in the back seat on the way home after their visit to Gallery f15 and lunch, which was Ingemann's treat, at the Refsnes estate, and he felt linked to Isabella – which either he'd never had the opportunity to feel before, or he'd squandered these opportunities to draw close, whatever that might mean – and Isabella was linked to him, Singer, like an unavoidable fate which she accepted without complaint, the two of them in a merciless unit that made him feel dizzy as he sat there in the back seat, meaning together with his little teenage stepdaughter, and he understood that his friendship with Ingemann had ceased to be a reality.

Isabella was now stretching out, slowly, through several years, towards her own womanhood, as she continued to live with Singer on Suhms gate and made herself inconspicuous. For his part, Singer also continued to live his quiet life, in the metaphorical basement of the Deichman Library, as he went back and forth to work through Oslo's streets, back (and forth) to his own apartment, where he'd let himself in (and out) with a little click of the Yale lock. When he came home, the young lady would be looking at her face in her own mirror in her own room, with the door closed. He knew that she was sitting there, looking at herself in the mirror, because he had gone in once unannounced and seen her; he had immediately muttered an apology and averted his eyes because he'd neglected to knock on the door, and ever since he'd made a point not to burst into her newly developed life in that manner. She would come out and walk through the rooms with her astonishing, newly stretched-out form, to find things, discard things, for example a magazine that she'd drop onto a table; or she'd sit down in an armchair with her legs carelessly, and unconsciously, draped over the armrest as she watched TV, and then disappear into her room again, where she sometimes played music, just like other teenagers, but not nearly as loudly as he'd heard, or read, that other teenagers did, and again with the door closed.

Singer didn't like the situation. Isabella moved without constraint through the rooms and grew up; she stretched up in height and reached towards her own forms, all the while continuing to be herself – Isabella *an sich* – and completely unconstrained by him. Singer found himself hovering at a respectful, and anxious, distance. What was this? He felt superfluous, yet here he was, after all, in the same apartment as a fifteen-year-old girl, who was in his care. She was still an obedient girl who did what he asked her to do. And if she occasionally did not do what he asked her to, she didn't make a scene or fuss but simply neglected to do it in a discreet manner, as if she had accidentally forgotten. Exhibiting the greatest self-confidence, she moved around in the apartment and grew up, stretching towards life and her own future as a young woman; it was in that direction she grew and conformed. Singer could see that. She walked around in the presence of a stranger, a man who also lived here and who provided for her. She was completely unconstrained by the fact that he provided for her. It was as if she didn't even notice he was there. She had nothing against him per se, but he was of no importance to her, that was what Singer came to realise, now that Isabella was stretching towards her womanhood. And he found this even more painful now than when she was a child. Because now it kept pointing back at himself: at Singer, the forty-six-year-old librarian who lived such an insular life.

Occasionally he would ask her how things were going at school; she was now in secondary school, still at the Marienlyst school building close to where they lived. Then she would answer pleasantly, telling him about any difficulties at school, or which subjects she liked best, and sometimes she would also ask him, Singer, about things that had to do with her schoolwork, factual matters regarding English grammar, historical conditions, political figures, geographical places, and many other things. And Singer was happy to reply, trying to be as factual as possible. It could be that she found his response a bit dry, but there was nothing to be done about that. Otherwise he knew very little about her. Her friends came and went, a couple from her childhood, but also several new ones, classmates from secondary school. Once the phone rang and a young voice, a boy's voice, asked to speak to her. She hesitantly began talking on the phone, and Singer went out to the kitchen. When he came back to the living room, the phone was hung up and Isabella was back in her room. She didn't say a word about who had called, and Singer didn't ask, but later on he couldn't see that this phone call had had any effect on how she lived her life.

He didn't know what sort of music she played, even though he could hear it clearly, though faintly, through the closed door, and he didn't recognise the music, he made no connections to it, which isn't especially strange since it was music for teenagers. A couple of times he did ask, in an attempt to be friendly, about the tune she was playing, and she always told him, both the name of the singer, whether it was a specific solo act or a group, and the name of the song, and she spoke this solo act or the band's name, and the title of the song with obvious respect. But Singer had a bad habit of forgetting quite quickly both who was singing and what the title was, so that the next time he happened to ask her about the music he heard playing, it occurred to him as he asked, that this tune sounded exactly like what he'd heard the last time he had asked, not even a week ago, and he would abruptly stop and begin talking about something completely different, a topic pulled out of the blue, such as: oh, now it's about to rain, and there'll be thunder because it's so sultry, pointing to the open balcony door where some heavy, threatening clouds had appeared in the sky, almost black in colour, about to splinter the sunlight on that all-too-sultry May day. Because he did not really want to demonstrate in this way, so clearly and directly, his lack of interest in what she, and her friends, found so immeasurably fascinating. When it came right down to it, he didn't want to have that sort of attitude towards what she found so fascinating, even if, as was now apparent, it was actually true that he felt completely indifferent to what sort of music she and her peers listened to. He couldn't very well start taking an interest in that type of music just because his fifteen-year-old stepdaughter was so fascinated by it, could he? Even though this might have been opportune, he felt such a strong resistance to the very idea of pretending to take an interest, for her sake, that it upset him greatly, and it continued to upset him for weeks afterwards, every time he thought about it, for example as he sat in his metaphorical circumstances in the basement of the Deichman Library.

Now and then he felt a desperate urge to make her notice that he existed on his own terms, that he was visible, connected to what bound him, to his own stamp, or to existence. But he couldn't do it. He tried, but the only result was that he stood there, bewildered and anxious, in the background of her journey towards life, afraid to influence her or touch her with his presence, even though he wished to be seen. The few attempts he made were merely pathetic. Like the time she had two school friends visiting, and he heard them playing music in her room, and he heard it was the exact same music, most likely even the exact same record, or CD, that she'd been playing when he asked her a few days ago what she was playing. Afterwards the door to her room opened, and Isabella and her friends came out and settled in front of the TV to watch the music channel. But before they got too immersed in this new activity, Singer casually asked, turning to Isabella, what they had just been playing, there was something familiar about the music he even said, and that caused Isabella, in the presence of her friends, to sigh with resignation and tell him: you asked me the same thing the last time I played it, two days ago. It was so-and-so, singing such-and-such, she stated firmly, placing emphasis on each syllable of the solo act's name and the title of the so-called song, while each of her two well-brought-up friends raised a small hand to her mouth, to hide a slightly exasperated sneer that Isabella's stepfather should be so out of it that he hadn't even tried to remember the names of what interested them and what made their very young lives move forward and go round. Isabella cast a resigned, and triumphant, glance at her two well-brought-up friends, and at that instant Singer experienced one of his brightest moments as Isabella's substitute parent and provider. Finally he had a function. Finally he was able to be of service. At that moment Singer was able to smile to himself as he found himself the focus of Isabella's triumphant resignation as she glanced at her two friends and their well-brought-up gestures, as they raised the palms of their small hands to their mouths.

Only later did it occur to him how pathetic the situation and his behaviour had been. He felt a strong distrust towards himself; were there no limits to what roles and what situations he could see himself taking on, in a deliberate fashion, simply in order to appear to himself, and only to himself, as someone who would go to any lengths to please her? He might obliterate his own being, or distort it, simply so that she would be able to live out her youth in a normal manner, and with him involved; that was what Singer concluded when he later thought about the matter.

And so this scene became an example of Singer's convoluted relationship to existence and to himself. Trapped in his own self he stood there permeated with existence, in a bright moment in his life with regard to his fifteen-year-old stepdaughter, who in the presence of her friends, could sigh at how old-fashioned and out of it he was.

That summer Singer took Isabella on a long road trip through Europe during his brief, and Isabella's lengthy, summer holiday. The trip took them to Lisbon. First by car-ferry to Hirtshals, and from there all through the flat, lush and green landscape of Denmark, stopping at country inns for meals – unfortunately without indulging in a little drink, since he was driving – and overnight lodgings, where in the evening he did have a little drink while he brooded over the day's drive. Onward through northern Germany and along the Rhine until they entered France at Strasbourg, and then across France, south of Paris, heading for Bordeaux and the Bay of Biscay. From there they entered Spain, where they stopped at Santiago de Compostela, which is a pilgrimage site because Jesus's beloved disciple Jacob is buried there, according to the truthful account that Singer didn't even blink at when he heard it, merely taking note of it, before they drove along the weather-beaten Gallic coast, with its tempting shellfish dishes in the little cafes in the fishing villages, not nearly as expensive as Singer had thought, until they drove into Portugal and reached Lisbon. They stayed a week in Lisbon, and Singer walked around, breathing in the city's atmosphere along with his stepdaughter. He showed her everything that was worth seeing, cathedrals and cloisters, lighthouses and modern bridges across the Tagus River, and he showed her exactly where the Tagus ended and the Atlantic Ocean began. He explained about world empires that rose and fell. He even showed her little cafes where fado was played, for the tourists. And they travelled on the trams. Isabella took in everything with an impassive expression, even when he told her about the earthquake in Lisbon and took her to see the cathedral that still stood as it was left after the earthquake struck, a naked ruin, a sunken cathedral, as Singer, rather imprecisely, in a metaphorical sense, expressed it. One day they drove down to the Algarve coast, to satisfy the fifteen-year-old girl's urge to see the Atlantic Ocean. Truth be told, they'd spent almost every day north of Lisbon in the venerable and fairly quiet resort town of Estoril so Isabella could go swimming, but she still insisted on going down to the Algarve coast, where all the people were, as she said. And there were definitely people, even Norwegians, and Isabella met a girl her own age out in the ocean, and when she came out of the water she looked perplexed.

'Planes fly here,' she exclaimed to Singer. 'It only takes two hours. And here we spent days sitting in the hot car. And they're all staying *here*, not in Lisbon.'

We could describe the drive home as well, but we won't. Singer drove home with great, suppressed energy, taking a slightly different route, while Isabella mostly stared up at the sky to see if there were any planes. But once they were back home, when they happened to see Ingemann, Singer noticed that Isabella, with that deliberate expression of hers, had absorbed a lot of impressions after all, because she began telling Ingemann about Portugal and the Portuguese, and she didn't put any particular emphasis on the delights of the Algarve coast but instead talked about the earthquake in Lisbon.

It was early in the autumn, it must have been on a Sunday morning, when Ingemann suddenly showed up. Singer hadn't seen Ingemann in a long time, he hadn't seen him since spring. While Ingemann and Singer were chatting, mostly about Ingemann's new plans, which Singer listened to with great sufferance because they had nothing to do with him, Isabella suddenly appeared and came over to stand between them. She must have heard from her own room and through the music of her CDs that he'd arrived, and she immediately came in, although moving languidly. Now she stood there, quietly, holding in her hands the wide-brimmed straw hat that she'd bought in Portugal, on the Algarve coast. A few minutes later, when the conversation Singer and Ingemann were having touched on the summer and Singer's summer holiday and the road trip to Portugal, Isabella interjected a few remarks. About Lisbon. About the earthquake in Lisbon. She tried to describe the cathedral which still stood just as it had after the earthquake, like a sunken cathedral, she told Ingemann. Ingemann nodded knowingly and then spoke directly to the precocious teenage girl.

'So you found it interesting, I see,' said Ingemann, and Singer noticed that Ingemann used the word interesting and that Isabella looked as if she liked the fact he'd used that particular word. Strange how he manages to do that, thought Singer, quite impressed. But Ingemann went on:

'We do too.' (Meaning find the sunken cathedral in Lisbon interesting; this is the author's, or for that matter Singer's, remark.) 'We filmed there last year, and we're thinking of going back to Lisbon this year. Lisbon, you see, is an exciting city for us. The city has atmosphere, both for material things like clothing, and for living things, like people. Start filming in the yellow Lisbon tram up the steep streets to the Alfama heights, and you'll get the whole thing for free, let me tell you. Oh yes, there's a future in Lisbon. For us.'

'Oh,' said Isabella. 'Oh, I took that tram. Lots of times.'

'But look here,' said Ingemann, pleased, holding out his hand, which, during the entire conversation he'd kept discreetly hidden behind his back, and now he brought into the light a big bottle of whisky. 'This is for you, Singer, a belated birthday present!' he exclaimed heartily, and Singer, flustered, accepted the whisky bottle that Ingemann, in an almost miraculous way, had managed to hide in the hand he'd held behind his back during their entire conversation. His birthday! Of course he'd had a birthday, it was during the trip to Portugal, in the middle of their holiday, as always. It had been a long time since Singer had cared to mark his birthday, even to himself. This year it had come and gone without his even once recalling that it was his birthday. Not even a random newspaper left on a coffee table had reminded him of the date. And Isabella had forgotten it long ago. Before, when she was younger, he used to dutifully remind her of the occasion a few days in advance so that she, like other children her age, would have time to mark a birthday that was not her own but someone else's, someone who was close to her. But by now three or four years had passed since he'd reminded her of his birthday, and Isabella herself had forgotten all about it. The only people who ever remembered it, consistently and without fail, were Isabella's grandparents in Notodden, and so when they arrived home from Portugal, there was a postcard for Singer in the mailbox, sending him the very best wishes for his birthday on the __th of 19__. Singer had swiftly stuck the card in his pocket without mentioning to Isabella that he'd received a birthday card from her grandparents, because she'd forgotten about the whole thing, much to Singer's own satisfaction. Because Singer thought it was a relief not to have to celebrate his birthday. He thought himself lucky that his birthday fell when most people were on holiday, and even better, it was always in the middle of his own holiday, so that he didn't have to sit in the Deichman Library, in the presence of his colleagues, with a big, disgusting piece of cake in front of him and pretend to appreciate the fact that they were making a fuss over him in that way. When you've reached the age of forty-seven, it's no longer amusing. He had personally sat there, playing the role of a cheerful colleague, and watched especially his middle-aged colleagues in their fifties, lonely, thin-haired men who with a sheepish smile sat there looking down, then away, at their piece of cake as their colleagues, with Singer among them, began singing, almost maliciously, the happy birthday song, and he was glad that wasn't him, thinking that he would have preferred to skip it. He wanted his birthday to disappear, dissolve in water and sink to the bottom. A day like all the others. That's how he felt about it, wanting to manoeuvre that day into silence, and outside of time, time lived and gone for good, so that eventually not even a scratch on his skin would remind him of the day when it occurred, or of that time; that's what gave Singer a great sense of satisfaction. Then he felt that he was once again in sync with himself and could breathe a sigh of relief while, without thinking about it, he endured yet another day in his life without noting that forty-seven years had now passed since his birth. Such is Singer's life, it proceeded without any need to mark its passage, thought Singer, moving with his own unique rhythm, yet not totally without self-awareness, in spite of everything. To be yanked out of the automechanism of life in order to celebrate his birthday as a boisterous reminder was something that broke with what Singer regarded as his essential nature.

Yet he was genuinely pleased when Ingemann handed him a big bottle of whisky as a belated birthday present. Because it was from Ingemann and not someone else. His connections to Ingemann ran deep, back to their child-hood; 16 April was Ingemann's birthday, 12 March was Gunnar's, and 17 July was Arne's. So Ingemann beamed happily when he handed Singer a big bottle of whisky as a belated birthday present, seeing that Singer was visibly moved by the gesture. He couldn't hide anything from Ingemann. Singer was so flustered at being handed the whisky bottle, as a present, that he didn't know what to do with himself.

'Well, I suppose we should open it,' he said in confu-sion as he began unscrewing the cap, looking around for two glasses and wondering where on earth to find them. 'You need to go out and buy us some soda,' he said to Isabella.

'Hey, don't do that,' laughed Ingemann. 'Don't open it now, in the middle of a bright Sunday morning; no, you need to save it for a day when you really need a stiff drink, because let me tell you, there's nothing like a good whisky when you really need one, when you're dead tired and at the same time pleased with yourself. But to think that you, Singer, you of all people, would even consider having a party at ten-thirty on a Sunday morning, I didn't expect that of you,' said Ingemann, and again he laughed heartily. Isabella laughed too, because Singer had thought of drinking whisky at ten-thirty on a Sunday morning.

'All right, all right, I suppose I'll have to wait,' said Singer, and he laughed a bit too. 'Thanks,' he said. 'It was nice of you, Ingemann, to remember what I'd personally forgotten,' he added. 'It's been years since I remembered the day. But I remember yours, even if I haven't given you a present, because you no longer host birthday parties, at least none that I've been invited to.'

'No, I've given that up,' said Ingemann. 'But I do remember the day, and I go around internally celebrating myself. And I get into such a festive mood that everyone notices and they come rushing with flowers and cake and wine, and frequent pats on the head, kisses, and hugs all day long,' said Ingemann, beaming.

Isabella stood there, twisting the straw hat in her hands and laughing at what Ingemann had said. Ingemann noticed her standing there laughing, and he turned to her.

'So, how's it going, sweetheart?' he said. 'What year are you in now?'

'Last year of lower secondary school,' replied Isabella (sweetheart).

'Are you kidding me? I can't believe it. You're sure growing up fast,' he said. A moment later he said, 'I have a present for you, too.' And he got out three tickets, which he held out in a fascinating little fan formation, clearly showing that there were three.

'Tickets to a new TV show on the TV-Norge channel, the first in the series. Hottest show of the year. Three tickets. Here, you can take two of your friends with you.'

Isabella was thrilled. She took the tickets and clutched them to her chest. This wasn't the first time that Ingemann had shown up with tickets that entitled the ticket holder to be part of the TV audience for an evening, but previously the tickets had been just for Singer and Isabella. This was the first time Ingemann gave the tickets solely to Isabella, and three of them, so she could take along two girls her own age. The fact that Ingemann had offered the tickets in this way came as a relief to Singer. He was now freed from accompanying his stepdaughter when she took her place as an invited, and specially chosen, guest in the TV audience for various TV shows, which had meant that he too was part of the TV audience, occasionally seen by hundreds of thousands of viewers sitting at home in their living rooms, and perhaps they caught sight of a middle-aged man and a little girl seated in the studio with expectant looks on their faces. But for Isabella, the shows had been momentous occasions. Receiving tickets from Ingemann had meant that she could sit in TV studios, whether it was NRK, TV-2, TV-3 or TV-Norge, as a member of the audience for various shows, which for Isabella marked rare golden moments in her childhood; and so it had been only natural that Singer should accompany her and sit there playing an audience member for these shows, which he never, in his wildest imagination, would ever have chosen to watch if he'd been sitting at home in his own living room. The fact that Isabella, even as a teenager and young lady, should be offered these kinds of tickets by Ingemann, was no doubt something she appreciated, especially because she was also visible on the TV screen, as an audience member, seen by others, her classmates, who made a point of remarking on this at school, which had increased her status among her friends, and there had been times when Singer had sensed that this was the very thing that might benefit his little stepdaughter. To be a member of a TV audience had doubled, and extended, the enjoyment for her, because these shows were seldom broadcast live. Isabella (and Singer as her companion) were present at the filming, and then the shows were broadcast at a later date, so Isabella was able to sit in front of the TV and watch, excited about catching sight of herself, and Singer, in the studio. Singer himself did not sit in front of the TV on these occasions but he would be nearby, in the same room, sitting in a comfortable chair and reading a book, for example, and now and then he would cheerfully call out: 'Are you there?' or 'Did you see us?' and Isabella would answer: 'I'm watching the show, not trying to see if I'm there.' But when Isabella, or Singer, or even both of them happened to appear in a big close-up, she couldn't contain herself and shouted: 'There we are, there we are!' And then Singer had to rush over, but he was always too late, because audience members appear on the screen only in very brief clips.

Isabella could continue to be a TV-audience member, though now as a young lady. Ingemann had come over and given her three tickets, so she could generously invite whomever she liked from her group of friends. Oh, those three tickets meant a spotlight would shine on Isabella in the school playground among the other young girls, it was a gilded moment, the tickets glowed. And for Singer they signified a release.

This doesn't mean that being a member of the TV audience had been directly irksome for him, it was much too absurd for that. Here was the middle-aged librarian showing up in a TV studio to be in the audience for something that all the other audience members regarded as no less than a big event, while he felt he had to grin and bear it. He was there to gild his stepdaughter's childhood, and he had little trouble pretending to be an expectant audience member, both before the broadcast and during the broadcast, when he risked having the spotlight turn on him for a close-up. He wasn't thrilled about having a close-up (at least not at first, until he found out that he could turn it to good purpose, or to his own benefit); otherwise he had few problems with being a TV audience member. Gradually he'd even started to like the idea that people he knew might see him as an audience member – not in a close-up, he couldn't bear the thought of that, but in a sudden glimpse when the TV cameras scanned the audience. There he sat (with Isabella), in the middle of the studio, anonymously present amid the crowd, and maybe someone who saw it would suddenly give a start as they sat in a chair at home in front of the TV and exclaim: 'But, but, goodness, that was Singer, it was! What on earth is he doing there!!?' The same surprise would be evoked, of course, from seeing him in a close-up, yet that seemed to Singer a little much, almost obtrusive in its absurdity, but that small glimpse of him as an audience member amid all the others, he liked the thought of that. Yes, he enjoyed the thought of that, and the minor commotion it would cause. Truth be told, he looked forward to going to work at the Deichman Library the day after Isabella told him that he'd been visible as an audience member briefly during the evening's popular TV show. Because maybe someone would be waiting for him, for example a colleague, who would say as he, or she, saw Singer arrive, quiet and modest, as always: 'Hey Singer, I couldn't believe my eyes, but I thought I saw you on TV yesterday. In the audience during *Casino*. Can that be true?'

And then Singer could say: 'Oh, right, it's true enough, I didn't see the show myself, but I was in the studio when it was filmed three weeks ago, we know someone who occasionally gives us tickets to TV shows, it's fun for my stepdaughter.' And then he would go downstairs to his metaphorical basement to count book spines, catalogue titles, air out the ancient volumes, etc., etc., along with other colleagues, and both his co-workers at the counter and his discussion partners down in the basement, who had of course heard the rumours from upstairs about Singer being on TV as an audience member for *Casino*, would give him wondering looks, as if he were a mystery.

Was it important for Singer to appear as a mystery to those around him? At this point in his life? Aside from his stepdaughter Isabella, for whom he was responsible, and Ingemann, who was his old, although unfortunately no longer good friend, Singer hadn't developed close ties to anyone during the seven years that had passed since he'd moved back to Oslo. He didn't socialise with his colleagues in his spare time, for example; he never invited any colleagues to his home, and he was never invited to any of their homes either. Nor did he ever go out with them, to a cafe after work, or make arrangements to go to a football match with anyone. Nothing of that nature had occurred. He participated in gatherings under the auspices of the library – public lectures in the evenings, author readings, etc. – and he went to the Christmas party and other social events in connection with his job, including seminars, which did have a certain social and festive quality. Otherwise, seized by restlessness or boredom, or a feeling of nothingness, he might seek out the old cafes of his youth, to see if anyone was there, and they usually were, but when he saw them, he felt merely depressed, as previously described in the scene recounting Singer's return to the capital seven years earlier. Mostly he wandered about alone on this earth, if you exclude his two relationships: with Isabella, who was his responsibility, and with Ingemann, who was his inescapable friend. It didn't bother him. The days passed, one after the other, and were gone without him really missing them, but now and then he would be taken aback and think: Where did they go? He didn't know whether he was happy or unhappy; but I can't be unhappy, he thought, it would be meaningless to make such a claim. Although, I might be, but my unhappiness is the kind that it would be meaningless to point out. Even to myself.

Yet there was something mysterious about his existence, and that was something he wanted to emphasise. He was a mystery to himself, no one could deny him the right to make that claim. His life proceeded in a metaphorical state in the basement of the Deichman Library where he guarded the books. There he sat, taking part in serious, slightly morose discussions with like-minded colleagues about archive techniques and alternative cataloguing systems – labyrinthine diagrams of the stacks, improvements to determining a book's whereabouts – and to what extent these could be inserted in a meaningful way into the computer systems. Discussions on a high, even sublime level, but unfortunately of no interest whatsoever and completely incomprehensible to anyone other than the initiated librarians in the Deichman's deep vault. For them, the initiates, Singer could finally perform his little trick of holding a book spine forward and down, in this way opening the pages and airing them as he closed the book with a dry little bang, the trick that had been so unsuccessful when he performed it for a quiet, vital child some years ago, but now: the others, the initiates, his colleagues, chuckled with admiration. Singer was in his element. Singer the mystery. Singer who had nothing against appearing to be mysterious to others, because in this way he was regarded by them in the same way that he, often with bewilderment, regarded himself; except that the others didn't regard him with bewilderment, but instead with more of a respectful amazement, a slow whistle, like when he showed up on the screen as an audience member for the popular but completely idiotic TV show *Casino*. They hadn't expected that. By nature he was sort of an intellectual, after all; in fact, they probably regarded him as some sort of failed intellectual since he possessed no particular external brilliance. They hadn't expected that, seeing Singer as an audience member for the popular TV show.

Now they're wondering, because now they realise they haven't figured him out. They haven't captured Singer in their self-composed concepts of who he is. They can't say – as they had thought and at no time doubted – that Singer,

he's such-and-such, that's who he is. No, Singer is a festive
audience member in the studio, he was one of them, during
the show *Casino*, appearing clearly on the TV screen,
delightedly immersed in whether the main player, a
contestant, is going to win a car in the lottery of life, this
man who goes around here contentedly in his worn-out
clothes. Ha ha, thought Singer. Look at that festive and
delightedly excited audience member on TV! That's Singer,
that's him. The slightly reserved Singer, who keeps so
modestly and deliberately in the background, with his mild
sense of humour and his self-effacing manner. Strange.
There must be some incomprehensible crack in Singer's
personality, they might have said, almost respectfully. And
what sort of connections must he have? Someone who plies
him with special tickets to those kinds of shows? Strange,
Singer thought they would say, among themselves, and to
themselves. That's how he thought he appeared, as Singer
the mystery in the eyes of others. He liked thinking that.
Singer the mystery. His own bewilderment at not being
able to come to grips with himself – merely continuing
on while he stood outside and watched the whole thing
– became transformed into a respectful wondering in the
eyes of others. That was certainly something. That's something, by God, thought Singer when he analysed his own
life as he sat in the apartment on Suhms gate and stared
at the wall with his forty-seven-year-old stare. At least it
makes me stand up straight, he thought. For a moment,
he added. Because I'm going to die, after all. And what

good does it do me that I've been a mystery both to myself and to others?

Now he was standing in his own apartment on Suhms gate and looking on with a sense of relief as Ingemann handed the three fanned-out tickets to Isabella so she could take two of her friends along to the newest show on TV-Norge. His days as an audience member were finally over, he'd achieved his goal. But Ingemann had something more to offer on this Sunday morning. He wanted to extend an invitation. And it was for Singer. Ingemann invited Singer to a party he was hosting up in Nydalen, a promotional party, or whatever it was, in the fancy offices up in Nydalen. This was not the first time Ingemann had invited him to a party in the offices of his company up in Nydalen, but previously Singer had always declined, for various reasons, saying, for instance, that he didn't have clothes that would be suitable in such a modern setting, or that he personally wouldn't fit in, that it wasn't his milieu, that he'd be an outsider, etc., etc., there were any number of reasons, and he would tell Ingemann some of them. But this time he said yes. When was it? On Friday in about two weeks.

'Well, that's kind of short notice. But I'll come.'

When he said it was short notice, Singer meant that there wasn't much time for him to obtain the necessary outfit so he could attend Ingemann's big party. He had to get a new suit, and a suit that was modern, which he didn't have. First he'd have to find out what modern suits looked like, it wasn't enough to take a look at Ingemann right now, since he wasn't dressed the way he'd dress for the party, instead he was wearing casual attire and not a suit, or whatever was considered modern these days for attending a promotional party. Then Singer would have to get the money for this type of suit, or modern outfit, if, contrary to expectations, it should turn out that it was not considered modern to wear a suit at all. And he didn't have the money. In his forty-eighth year he was still living hand to mouth, as the provider for himself and a teenage girl, on his fairly lousy librarian's salary. He was used to pinching and scraping, as they say, or at least used to say. Frugality was in his blood, and he had no regrets about that. But now it would have been good if he'd had enough financial wiggle-room so he could afford to buy a fashionable suit, or a fashionable set of clothes.

Well, there was a solution, and he'd have to make use of it, even though it had been years since he'd last done so. He got out the envelope that contained Adam Eyde's betting systems and took out the little system. He sat down at the dining table in the dining room and soon covered the whole table with betting slips he'd filled out according to Adam Eyde's little system. He took them over to the nearest betting office, paid his money, and got his slips stamped in the required manner. Then all he had to do was wait until Saturday when the betting results were announced. But it didn't work. It took a while after the results were announced before he had gone through all his slips, but when he'd done so, it turned out that the system hadn't worked. He'd lost everything he'd bet, money that he really couldn't afford to spend. The days until his next pay cheque were going to be fairly meagre, and he wouldn't be able to buy himself a trendy suit or trendy set of clothes. He'd bet everything, and lost. Luck had deserted him, as frequently happens for someone who bets everything on one card and has no opportunity to try again. Because he didn't have an opportunity, the party was on Friday, and the next chance he'd have to make use of Adam Eyde's little system was on Saturday, meaning the day after the party. As things now stood, he couldn't go to Ingemann's big promotional party in the offices up in Nydalen.

He considered other solutions with some desperation; for example, he got out the two old suits he owned and hung them up on the balcony to air out, in the faint hope that an airing-out would help. It didn't. He saw that at once when he brought them back inside. He couldn't attend a promotional party in modern offices up in Nydalen wearing either of these suits, one more impossible than the other; the light-coloured one, which in spite of everything he regarded as slightly more modern and *comme il faut* than the dark one, was actually worse. He thought about asking Ingemann for help, maybe he could borrow a suit from him, though that was impossible right from the start, since Ingemann had an entirely different body type, but maybe Ingemann knew someone in his social circle who had the same body type, someone whom Ingemann – by offering some excuse, which Singer couldn't think up but no doubt Ingemann could – might persuade to lend a nice suit which he wouldn't personally be wearing on Friday, even though he was going to the same party. But it was the last part of this statement that extinguished Singer's dream of being able to attend the party, because it meant that Singer would arrive wearing a suit that was undoubtedly modern and *comme il faut* enough, but would be recognised with a broad grin by another of the party's guests, and this wasn't some-thing that the forty-seven-year-old librarian from the Deichman Library's metaphorical basement wished to endure. He stayed home, without telling Ingemann that he wouldn't be attending.

But Isabella and two of her friends went to the new TV show at TV-Norge and sat there, young-lady-like and lovely, as part of the audience. Later Ingemann again appeared at the apartment on Suhms gate. He didn't say a word about the fact that Singer hadn't shown up for his party, but he did invite him out to a restaurant. Isabella showed up as soon as she heard his voice in the apartment and stood nearby, listening to what they were talking about. Ingemann joked with her, saying something about the bird-like appear-ance of girls her age, girls who seemed so light and fluttery and amusing, and Isabella laughed her 'bubbling young-lady' laugh. After that he took from his pocket three more tickets for the next episode of TV-Norge's new TV show, and held them out to her in the same fanned-out form as last time. Isabella beamed, glancing triumphantly at Singer who had failed to attend Ingemann's party, even though she'd heard Ingemann invite him and Singer say yes without hesitation; on the contrary, he'd said yes with a hint of anticipation in his voice. Then Ingemann and Singer left the fifteen-year-old teenager at home and went to the Theatre Cafe to have dinner. During dinner a beautiful woman in her mid-thirties showed up and sat down at their table; she was Ingemann's new flame, as Singer understood. This disappointed him slightly, since he'd wanted to have a talk with Ingemann about Isabella, about how difficult it was to be responsible for her, especially now, as her roots to her childhood were beginning to lose their hold. Last summer, as usual, she'd spent two weeks with her grandparents in Notodden. She'd left, as usual, with happy anticipation, but she'd come home in an indifferent mood. She no longer derived any benefit from visiting her grandparents in Notodden. That part of her life was over. But if that was true, then what did she have left?

He still thought that he could talk to Ingemann about such matters, and in complete confidence, or at least as far as it went. This in spite of the fact that little to nothing of what Ingemann said continued to hold any great interest for him, and also, in spite of the fact that what he actually felt like telling Ingemann, which was no longer very much, he was having trouble putting into words, and the words he did try, in his own mind, to say, as a means of practice or a test, while he sat in an armchair in the living room at home, came out in such a way that he honestly doubted

Ingemann would understand, or even attempt to fully comprehend; instead the words would probably seem like nonsense to Ingemann, even though he still considered him to be his best friend, actually his only friend, and the one in whom he could picture himself confiding. Now and then it seemed to Singer that Ingemann actually felt sorry for him, and that he'd invited him out to the Theatre Cafe mostly to cheer him up, to breathe some life into him, infuse a little fun into the dreariness of his daily life. This did not please Singer, and he hoped he was wrong.

But when the beautiful woman in her thirties showed up, and he realised this was Ingemann's new flame – she was not the first, new flames were constantly showing up at Ingemann's side, and at his table – Singer felt a pang. They were both close to fifty by now, and with the same background, from the same town, and yet how different they had turned out, and just the thought that Ingemann actually felt sorry for him seemed to Singer completely unbearable. What had he done with his life? This was the thought of a man who, not for a single moment, harboured any conviction that his life could have been any different.

But he was still in the middle of it. Isabella was now stretching out more directly, more purposefully, towards her coming womanhood, and she was more Isabella *an sich* than ever. She turned sixteen, she turned seventeen, and she was in upper secondary school. She was still a quiet girl, with a serious look to her face, but she'd developed a sense of independence that made her more amenable than obedient. For example, she filled her days with her own rhythm, which meant they no longer ate dinner together in the dining room. Singer's assertion that a dining room was meant for dining, and a kitchen was meant for preparing the food that should be eaten in the thus-designated *dining* room, no longer made any impression on the young lady, who usually sat with one or two of her friends in the kitchen eating noodle soup, while Singer steadfastly clung to his old habits and ate his dinner in the *dining* room. He was fast approaching fifty and was fully aware that if his daily life weren't marked by some solemnity and by constantly repeated, though simple, ceremonies, it would be difficult to seize hold of and endure it, at least for a man so marked by irreparable loneliness, or distance, as he was. Isabella had also found herself a part-time job so she was able to earn her own spending money, something that had made Singer tell her, a bit clumsily, that he would give her money for anything she needed, she just had to tell him, and provided she really needed it, or wanted it, because things weren't that bad for him financially, he assured her, almost mumbling, even though, he had to admit, he might have given her a different impression occasionally, but she shouldn't take what he'd said so seriously, because that wasn't what he'd meant. But Isabella simply brushed him aside and said that she liked having a part-time job, and that all her friends had jobs too.

The apartment on Suhms gate was now filled, as before, with music from the TV, and from the CD player in her room, the door of which was usually closed, and now the scent of perfume also hovered over the rooms, from Isabella herself and from her friends, who sashayed about the apartment. They would stand at the balcony door, which could be opened if the weather permitted, and stare outside, while the room behind them resounded with music, often from a TV that was on although no one was watching it. They would stand next to the curtain hanging in front of the window of the balcony door and stare outside at the future, the way it appeared from a window or a half-open balcony door, on Suhms gate. Singer might let himself into the apartment at the end of his workday at the Deichman and find the place filled with young ladies like that. He would sit down in his armchair with his newspaper, ready to read. Around him sashayed the young ladies, very quietly, with their silver-toned voices.

So Singer sits in his armchair, in his regular place, with his newspaper, or he lets the newspaper fall onto his lap or next to the chair, like a leaf, and he merely sits there, his eyes closed as he stares straight ahead while listening to the young ladies sashaying around, with their perfume scent and their mascara-lined glances, and now and then he hears one of them say: 'Shh, I think he's asleep,' while they sashay around him; but Singer isn't asleep, or at least he's awake enough that he can hear them as he sits there, with his eyes closed, with a newspaper that falls, like a leaf from the trees, in a peaceful moment of his life.

Now and then Ingemann showed up at this apartment where Singer resided, surrounded by sashaying young ladies who sometimes walked to and fro but mostly sat and whispered in Isabella's room. Ingemann parked his fancy car outside the building where Singer lived, and he honked the horn. When the doorbell rang a few minutes later, Singer knew it was Ingemann. Ingemann came into the apartment and wanted to take him, Singer, along on some outing, or he had simply dropped by with no other purpose than to say hello, as he said. Ingemann, who talked about himself and his interests over and over again. About what he was doing, about what the consequences were, about what plans he'd made, and about all the cunning and all the tricks he had to employ in order to see these plans come to fruition, and about the world as a whole, Ingemann's world, of which he was a prisoner, as he expressed it to Singer. It was as if Ingemann, by talking this way about himself and the life he was now living, was trying to breathe life into Singer, trying to get him to stare with anticipation towards something other than the wall, which he usually had in front of him, when he was in fact peering straight ahead, with his eyes open. He was imprisoned by his own time, Ingemann said about himself, and with the hope that he might cheer up Singer. But Singer remained uninterested in what Ingemann said. It went in one ear and out the other. In any case, he remembered little afterwards, even though it was news from a man who had shaken off the disaster and dreariness of his life as a third-rate actor and become an ideas man and a sharp-sighted observer in the wings of the stage where the deeply felt peculiarities of our time are created. For that he reaped his reward, his well-deserved reward, in the form of tons of money, thought Singer as Ingemann's news went in one ear and out the other. Sometimes Ingemann might seem downright despondent because he noticed that Singer didn't show any particular interest when he tried to entice him with everything that life had to offer – what it at least had to offer to Ingemann, and as a consequence, in keeping with Ingemann's magnanimous spirit, also to Singer, if only he would open his eyes and see it; and he plied Singer with temptations, using mimicry, exaggerated glances, enthusiastic turns of phrase, phoney charm, in short everything inherent in his own personality. He might even resort to old tricks, which he again performed before Singer. He would turn to his acting repertoire, choose some comical props from Singer's apartment – an ashtray, a candleholder, a big broom, an old hat – and act out the classic roles, which he'd never actually been qualified to shoulder during his acting career, though he still knew the lines by heart ten years after he'd left the stage; major dramatic roles from the world theatre, Chekhov, Ibsen, Shakespeare, and finally Singer would allow himself to be enticed by his friend's attempts and he couldn't help smiling. Good old Ingemann, thought Singer then. My good friend, my loyal friend, he will never betray me. He has not lost his soul; on the contrary, he comes here to visit me, trying, if possible, to save my soul. Thank you, Ingemann, he thought, deeply moved, as he somewhat reluctantly had to smile at Ingemann's acting skills. And so they sat there, the two friends, the librarian and the former actor, in the librarian's living room, while the young ladies, without the two friends noticing, approached; there were three or four of them, with Isabella behind the others, and they now gathered around the two friends, laughing with admiration, bubbling at Ingemann's attempts to cheer up his old friend by employing old tricks. Isabella's friends were well aware of who Ingemann was, he was the one who had given Isabella the precious gem that they often watched on the video player. It was a secret tape of a promotional film that would never be shown, mostly because it was way too ahead of its time.

Isabella and her friends had gathered around them, forming a young-lady circle of loveliness and laughing admiration. The three or four friends in blissful and everlasting *naïveté*, but Isabella kept slightly to the background, with a somewhat pensive look on her face because she was doubly present in this scene, as she occasionally glanced at one or the other of her friends to find out, or ascertain, something about their blissful and everlasting *naïveté*. Because she was regarding Ingemann in a different way. Singer could clearly see Isabella *an sich* as she glanced towards her blissfully and everlastingly naive friends. He could see the Isabella-ness radiating out of her, as she stood there, introverted, yet vibrating towards Ingemann, who was standing a metre and a half away from her, and who, it cannot be denied, approved of this Isabella-ness that radiated from her young-lady body, leaning towards him; in fact, he celebrated it.

It was more than five years ago that Singer realised his friendship with Ingemann had ended, in terms of reality, and yet they had continued to spend time with each other, as if nothing had happened; in fact, Ingemann hadn't even realised that the friendship had ended, in terms of reality. By the way, in every novel there is a big black hole, which is universal in its blackness, and now this novel has reached that point. Surrounded by spirited young ladies, with all their sweetness, we find ourselves together with Singer in a novel that is like a big black hole. Why is Singer the main character in this novel? And not only the main character but the one around whom everything revolves? Fortunately, the other characters in this novel are completely unaffected by the fact that they are characters, or ideas, that exist only in that they revolve around this main character. I wish I could have said something that Singer wouldn't be able to ponder. There's something I would have said about precisely this point, but I have no words for it. My language ceases when Singer's pondering ceases. Yet that does not make us identical.

So the friendship with Ingemann had ended more than five years ago, something that Ingemann wasn't personally aware of, because it had continued to function, albeit as a former friendship, it has to be said. But the friendship ceased to exist as a reality, because Singer was 'out'. He was gone. He understood that. And to understand precisely those kinds of things, at the same time as you are here, with your alive body, almost fifty years old and vulnerable, that can give you the feeling that you've been hurled out into space, like a satellite sent out there, as in a hurled movement, an outcast capsule. Singer noticed a ringing in his ears as he saw Ingemann surrounded by a circle of delightful young ladies who admired him, and behind the others stood Isabella, who was enjoying the fact that the others admired Ingemann, and she was leaning towards him, shut inside her now finished form, so to speak. Ingemann approved. Singer had no reason to blame Ingemann for that. On the contrary, Singer had much to thank him for. But he was no longer his friend, he hadn't been his friend for more than five years. It was now time to speak up so that Ingemann would finally realise this. And so, Singer told Ingemann he had to leave and he should not come back, because there was no point in him coming back. At least not for my sake, he said.

'You don't have to come here for my sake,' said Singer, 'because it's years since there has been any sort of friendship between the two of us. It's undoubtedly my fault that things have turned out this way, but that's how they've turned out, and for my part it has become a nuisance to see you here in my apartment. Why don't you leave, there's nothing for you here,' Singer told Ingemann, with the circle of delightful young ladies, so pure and present, standing around him. And so Ingemann left. A bit astonished, open-mouthed, you might say, but he left.

The delightful young ladies fell silent after Ingemann had gone, and soon they disappeared into Isabella's room, closing the door after them, and not a sound could be heard from inside. Stunned, Singer remained in the living room. After an hour or so, the door to Isabella's room suddenly opened and one of the young ladies came rushing through the living room, while one of the others still inside closed the door behind her. After a while this was repeated, as many times as there were young ladies, not counting Isabella, inside Isabella's room.

Isabella never mentioned this confrontation between Singer and Ingemann, and it wasn't really a confrontation, because Ingemann had simply left. Isabella continued living her own life, although possibly even more apart from Singer than previously; she didn't directly avoid him, yet if Singer thought that was what she was doing, he could have pointed to a sufficient number of indications to confirm this in his own mind, if that was in fact what he wanted to confirm. But that was not what he wanted to confirm. And most likely Isabella was not avoiding him; he hadn't done anything to her, after all. On the contrary, Isabella seemed the same as usual, even behaving in a friendly manner whenever she addressed him. And yet, in spite of every-thing, he had robbed her of Ingemann, who never showed up at their apartment on Suhms gate again. Yet that didn't seem to affect her, which greatly astonished Singer. On the other hand, she was now eighteen years old and no longer needed to meet Ingemann in Singer's apartment if she wished to meet with him, so that he might breathe some of his own imprisoned time into her, so that she might appear as a delightful young lady. This was not a thought that pleased Singer, but if that was the situation, then there was little he could do about it. In a way it had seemed like an ending, but an ending that once again made him feel like a capsule hurled out into space. For that reason he was greatly relieved when he happened to witness a little incident inside Isabella's room. Isabella had a friend visiting, and suddenly Singer heard a big commotion coming from inside her room, the sound of furniture being shoved aside, and a clattering, and he went to her room and from the doorway he witnessed how Isabella's friend had found a photo in Isabella's room, and she was now laughing over it, a photo of a young boy, and Isabella flung herself forward to wrest the photo away from her friend, partly embarrassed, partly laughing. Singer had been drawn to the scene because he'd heard a big commotion through the half-open door to her room, and he'd stood up, almost inadvertently, and without thinking he'd gone to her room, and now he stood in the doorway and watched as Isabella, with a disconcerted look, tried to wrest a photo of a young boy out of the hands of her amused friend, and he couldn't help but conclude that Isabella was, in some way, involved with the young boy in this photo. He had no idea how that might be, and he would never find out, but the incident had such an encouraging effect on him that he laughed, a brief and dry laugh, as he stood there in the doorway and looked at the two eighteen-year-old young ladies in Isabella's room engaged in what he perceived as a wild tussle over a photograph of a boy. Yet his brief outburst of laughter made Isabella furious, because she, we have to assume, felt that she'd been found out in some way by Singer, who without being invited was standing in her doorway and catching a stolen glimpse of her private young-lady life. As she calmly took the photo out of the hands of her now frozen-looking friend and put it away in her chest of drawers, with the young boy's face down, she asked in a caustic tone of voice whether there was some specific reason why he was standing there and watching what they were doing. Her voice was ice-cold, her whole being utterly deliberate and tense. Singer was shamefaced and assured her that it was not his intention to intrude, but he'd heard a bang, a really loud bang, he said, and he tried to laugh that little dry laugh again, though this did not particularly mollify Isabella, and her friend stood there like a frozen image, staring at him with astonishment. And so he continued to apologise for behaving as he had, it wasn't something he usually did; you have to agree, Isabella, I don't think it has ever happened before, I don't think so, he said, and the friend again gave him an astonished look, while Isabella seemed disconcerted. He then realised that it would be best if he left, and after he'd left, he felt even more shamefaced, especially because of the astonished look on her friend's face when he'd tried to explain.

Singer didn't like subjecting himself to Isabella's suspicion that he was snooping into her private life, and particularly not in the presence of one of her friends, who had looked at him with such astonishment because he'd tried to explain away such an accusation. He took great care not to snoop into her life; actually, he should have been upset that she behaved as she had towards him, because there was no reason for her to react in that way. In the eleven years he'd lived, all alone, with Isabella, he'd been extremely careful not to influence her, so as not to intrude on her life. He'd tried to influence her, but then immediately withdrawn when he realised that he hadn't succeeded, nor would succeed. He'd never wanted to intrude on her life, in order to possess it and in that way shape her, because he had no right to do so, because who was he, Singer, when it came right down to it? He had no idea; but what he did know was that when he asked himself what right he had to intrude on her life, shape it, mark it, he always ended up ascertaining that he had no right to do so, and always with a reference to that unanswered question about who was he, Singer, when it came right down to it.

And so, shamefaced, he had withdrawn on this occasion as well, because he had inadvertently stood in her doorway and caught a stolen glimpse into her highly private young-lady life. He didn't know her. He wanted to know her, but he couldn't do that without intruding on her life, stealing a glimpse, in this way. When Isabella reprimanded him for the intolerable nature of his action, which he hadn't even intended to take, he was annihilated by her ice-cold voice and subjected to the astonished look of her friend, and he had also seen that Isabella was disconcerted by the fact that he was so clearly annihilated by the fact that she'd expressed her annoyance that he, Singer, had seen her in a situation that she didn't want him to see. Consequently, he had to realise that he'd been caught in such a manner that was possibly awful and in any case irreparable, that he felt exposed, plain and simple, and directly connected to the facts of the situation as his eighteen-year-old step-daughter became annoyed, and then admonished him, in the presence of a witness, when he stood in her doorway and caught a stolen glimpse of her personal life, which had always seemed so alluring, which he'd always wanted to understand. And so the only thing he could do was to look forward to the day when Isabella finished secondary school and could move into her own place, beyond his reach.

Singer began preparing himself for the life that awaited him after Isabella graduated from secondary school and moved out on her own. He had a clear idea that when Isabella moved out, he wouldn't see much of her anymore, he could only imagine that he would disappear from her life for good. For her he would then become part of the past she'd lived through, a past with which she was now finished. At any rate she wouldn't see any reason to visit him again. He hoped that she would occasionally think back on those years, and without feeling any sort of discomfort, regard those years merely as the past, a time that no longer had anything to do with her present life. He had no opinion as to what would become of her. He had no idea what she would become or where she would live or whether she would get married and have children, and if so, how soon that might happen. Maybe she would get married at some point and have a child, and maybe she would then visit Singer with the child, wanting to show him the child. And of course he would like that, and he'd tell her as much when she arrived, but actually she could just as well refrain from visiting, because he couldn't manage, at least right now, in his imagination, to take any particular interest in Isabella's future child and husband, or to get involved at all in an internal discussion with himself about whether he would then want her to visit him with the child, possibly also with her husband, in order to show him the child, or possibly the child and the husband, because, in spite of everything, he had taken care of her when *she* was a child and unable to take care of herself, and for that reason she had lived with him while she was growing up until she could move into her own place after graduating from secondary school.

But for the time being she was still living here, walking around in Singer's apartment and being Isabella *an sich*, stretched out towards her own forms, her own future, unconstrained by the fact that she was living here with

Singer, while Singer sat in his armchair in the living room, his eyes half-closed, as he thought about what the future might look like. He couldn't deny that he was looking forward to being all alone, having no one else living in the apartment. It was a fact that he was looking forward to this and there was nothing to do about it, except maybe feel slightly taken aback that the situation had turned out this way, and Singer *was* a little taken aback that the situation had turned out this way. Now that Isabella was living her young-lady life and no longer had need of him, in any way whatsoever, Singer found himself strolling through the streets in the evening. He often went down to the city centre with its crowds of people and a trace of the big-city rhythm in the air. He liked to walk along Industrigata to Bogstadveien in Majorstua, and then continue on to where it crossed Hegdehaugsveien, and all the way to the end where the Lorry restaurant was located. There he'd cross the street, go past the Lorry, usually without going in, and walk round the corner to Wergelandsveien, continuing past the art gallery called Kunstnernes Hus, where he could see the silhouettes of the restaurant guests and the light from the cafe, and then head for the centre of town. He might go over to a cinema and stand there watching life unfolding before a show started, first people coming out of the cinema, and then those going in for the next show. Often he would go into the foyer and stand there with the film-goers who were waiting for the doors of the auditorium to open. Occasionally, but not often, he would buy himself a ticket and go in with the others and watch the film. Now and then, but not too often, as he passed the brightly lit restaurants where he saw people sitting close together around the tables, drinking and toasting each other and smiling, he might also have an urge to go inside and sit down at a restaurant table, and sometimes he did precisely that, although very rarely, and he never went into a restaurant he had just passed; instead he would choose another one, an out-of-the-way place where he thought he might be left more alone. And sometimes, as he stood outside one of the brightly lit and glittery cinemas, or even inside the foyer, watching the frenzied and anticipatory hustle and bustle, he might run into one of his colleagues, or some other person he happened to know. As a rule it was a colleague, and usually someone younger than himself. She was there with her partner, or some of her friends, and often she didn't make do with giving Singer a friendly greeting, no, she would come over and ask him which film he was going to see, because in the big cinemas a number of films were shown at the same time, which makes the rhythm outside these buildings, and inside the shared foyer, even more frenzied and restless, and all the more fascinating to watch. Since he always stood outside and studied the posters for every film before going into the foyer, he would answer the much younger female librarian's question by mentioning the title of the film he thought best suited him. Often it turned out that his female colleague was also going to that particular film, along with her partner or her friends.

If so, this led to a minor dilemma for Singer, since he didn't have a ticket for the film he'd just said he was going to see, and the next morning, during lunch at the Deichman Library, it was highly possible that she, his female colleague, would ask him what he'd thought of the film from the day before. Of course he could have offered some random remarks, but he didn't want to do that, because if he was going to comment on a film, he wanted to say something specific about it, especially since he knew he was quite good at expressing himself when it came to both books and films. So he would wait until the doors opened to the auditorium where the film in question was going to be shown, and he'd wait for the female colleague and her companion, or companions, to disappear inside, and then he'd go over to the ticket booth and ask if there were any tickets left for the show. Sometimes there were, and hence the minor dilemma was solved, but most often the show would be sold out. On such occasions he felt a bit worried because he thought he might find himself in an awkward situation at lunch the next day. But fortunately he found a solution for tackling this sort of problem as well. He could simply say – and it was the truth, or rather it ended up being the truth – that he hadn't had a ticket to the show when he spoke to her, meaning the female librarian, last night, but he hadn't seen any reason to mention this to her, because he'd been hoping there might be tickets left that had not been picked up before the film started; and it was that sort of ticket that he, Singer, was expecting to get, intending to go over to the ticket booth and inquire, when she, his colleague, had shown up, along with her partner, or her female companions, and asked him which film he was going to see, and he had of course replied that he was going to see this particular film, that is, if there were tickets left; but unfortunately, when he got to the booth right before the show started, most likely at the very moment the lights in the auditorium went out and the doors were cautiously closed, at the last second, so to speak, it turned out that there were no tickets left that hadn't been picked up for that particular showing, so he hadn't been able to see the film after all, even though he'd gone out in the evening specifically to see it – that's what Singer thought he would say if his female colleague, the next day at lunch, and in the presence of all the other librarians, happened to ask.